BLOOD ON THE CAT

NANCY RUTLEDGE

Introduction by
OTTO PENZLER

AMERICAN MYSTERY CLASSICS

Penzler Publishers
New York

This is a work of fiction. Names, characters, places, and incidents either are the product of the author's imagination or are used fictitiously. Any resemblance to actual persons, living or dead, businesses, companies, events, or locales is entirely coincidental.

Published in 2025 by Penzler Publishers
58 Warren Street, New York, NY 10007
penzlerpublishers.com

Distributed by W. W. Norton

Copyright © 1945 by Nancy Rutledge
Introduction copyright © 2025 by Otto Penzler.
All rights reserved

Cover image: Andy Ross
Cover design: Mauricio Diaz

Paperback ISBN 978-1-61316-666-6
Hardcover ISBN 978-1-61316-665-9
eBook ISBN 978-1-61316-667-3

Library of Congress Control Number: 2024949913

Printed in the United States of America

9 8 7 6 5 4 3 2 1

INTRODUCTION

Just so you don't get nervous: no cats have been injured or bloodied in this book. While the prospect of a cat, or a dog, or any furry critter, being physically abused in a detective story is more than enough for a reader to avoid the book, there would be a great sense of disappointment if at least one human wasn't murdered.

Rest assured, your bloodthirsty desire will be satisfied in *Blood on the Cat*. Not only will you encounter a corpse in the first few pages, but you will be pleased to know that the victim fully deserved the worst.

The case comes directly to the door of newspaperman Killian McBean via the curious explorations of Smoky, his cat. The police and, inevitably, McBean, confront a murder investigation with a major challenge: almost everyone in the little town of Cognac has a reason to want Old Gluts Farr to be dead. As the richest man in town (not itself a reason to hate someone but certainly justifiable when the millionaire is also corrupt and so fond of his power that he uses it whimsically), he is convinced that his position and wealth give him justification for hurting people. He spends no time considering its ramifications and has no fear of retribution. That is, until he gets a large bread knife jammed deeply into his back.

The town's corrupt chief of police has been in Farr's pocket so he suddenly must sort through an arm's-length cast of suspects in order to keep his job.

At the top of the list is Killian McBean. Farr held the mortgage on McBean's newspaper office, the top floor of which served as his home. Relentlessly exposed for his crude power plays and vindictive behavior, Farr vowed to close down the weekly paper. Although McBean wore a brave face about the impending closure, he remained frightened and angry about it.

His printer Ethan Droom carried a grudge against Farr for decades, blaming him for the loss of his leg in the tycoon's lumber mill. Whenever he got drunk—no rare occasion—he would yell and curse his nemesis with the usual threats of killing him. People sometimes say that sort of thing when they get mad; many do not mean it literally.

It would not be unreasonable to skip past the new teacher, Theodora Meredith, because she appears to be quietly timid, her hair tied up in a braid coiled atop her head. But when one of her students commits the trivial crime of stealing an apple, Farr forces the town to send him to a reform school, breaking her heart as her motherly instincts send her into weeping spells for the poor boy.

Another newcomer to the town, the librarian Irene Hubbard, had just found her dream job only to learn that Farr was intent on closing the library to save expenses, motivated by cutting his tax bill.

Even Farr's own son, Dennis, a nasty bit of work in his own right, hated his father for forcing him to break up his marriage to a woman he decided was unsuitable. Dennis' attitude toward his father was not improved when he was disinherited. Coincidentally, he learned the news just a few hours before the murder was committed.

It is probably reasonable to add one more person to the suspect list, though apparently without motive. A glamorous blonde drove into Cognac on the day that Farr was killed and had a serious accident. Her hard bump on the head was severe enough to result in amnesia, even causing her to forget her own name and identity.

Blood on the Cat is a pure detective story and a good one. Lots of suspects, lots of motives, lots of clues, and written by an author who evidently learned at least some of her craft by having read Arthur Conan Doyle.

When Ethan Droom's daughter Jean rings Killian's doorbell very early in the morning to say her father is missing, she tells him that she came to him first for help but that he appeared to be drunk so she went to the police. When they refused to pay attention to her, she came back to tell him of the situation. On her first visit, she saw a man on his porch and he asks if there had been a car nearby.

"No," she says, then amends her response to say, "At least I didn't see any. I didn't notice particularly."

"If you're ever going to be a reporter," he replies, "you'll have to learn to observe. Not just *see* but observe, know what you're seeing." In the first Sherlock Holmes story, "A Scandal in Bohemia," Holmes famously admonishes Watson by saying, "You see but you do not observe." Holmes had just made numerous accurate remarks about his friend's new life, prompting Watson's astonishment.

Nancy Rutledge (1901-1976) was the author of ten works of crime fiction between 1944 and 1960 under her own name, two of which were published only in England, and she also had a mystery novel published as by Leigh Bryson, a Handi-Book paperback original, in 1947.

Although largely neglected today, Rutledge was popular enough in the 1940s and 1950s to have eight of her mystery novels serialized in *The Saturday Evening Post*, the best-paying periodical of its day, and one that appeared complete in one 1960 issue of *Redbook* (which, incidentally, had also published the first appearance of Dashiell Hammett's last novel, *The Thin Man*).

Born in Chicago in 1915, Rutledge described herself as a native Midwesterner. She received a degree in chemistry and an M.A. in English literature from Northwestern University. She later moved to Burbank, California, where she resided until her death in 1995. In a brief autobiographical sketch that accompanied the first edition of *Blood on the Cat*, she wrote, "I have always wanted to be a writer and intend to keep at it all my life. Eventually I hope to be a good one."

The first two detective novels produced by Rutledge, *Beware the Hoot Owl* (1944) and *Blood on the Cat* (1945), were published by Farrar & Rinehart. She then had a mixed career with two books published only in the U.K. (*Murder on the Mountain*, 1957, and *Escape into Danger*, 1960) and several mystery novels seeing only magazine publication.

One of the novels published as a *Post* serial and never published in book form was *Death Stalks the Bride* (1958), which was the basis for an episode of the television anthology series *Climax!* that aired on May 15, 1958. Titled "The Disappearance of Daphne," it is the suspenseful story of a young heiress who falls in love and impulsively marries a dancer after a brief courtship but quickly fears that he was responsible for the disappearance of his former dance partner. It was nominated for thirteen Prime Time Emmy awards.

OTTO PENZLER
November 2024

CHAPTER ONE

Smoky's eyes shone yellow and green in the rainy darkness, but her body was only a black shadow punctuated by a dot of white at the tip of her tail. She slid around the corner of the building noiselessly and ran up the railing to the porch. Here she stopped abruptly, her ears back, her wet fur beginning to ruffle. A large object lay on the porch floor, dark and unmoving. Smoky spat at it warningly, received no answer, sat down and regarded it patiently. She circled it, sniffing. Finally satisfied as to its harmlessness and lack of interest to her, she walked over it to get to the window sill. She saw no signs within of what she was seeking, so she walked over it again, descended from the porch, and ran up the large maple tree in front of the building. Halfway up she transferred herself to the roof above the porch, crossed it and landed with a quiet plop on the upstairs window sill.

"Mraw!" wailed Smoky. "Mraw! MRAW!"

A sleepy groan from within. "Go away, cat. Scat!"

"MRAWWW!"

"All right, all right. Pipe down. I'm coming."

"Mraw," came mildly from Smoky.

Inside the room, somebody stumbled against a hard object,

swore, stumbled against a chair and turned it over. Finally the light went on and a sleepy man in a long red flannel nightshirt opened the window. Smoky accepted the service graciously and slid in.

"A fine time for a lady to be getting in," grumbled the man, shivering in the cold. "It's four o'clock in the morning!"

Smoky purred agreeably.

The man shut the window, turned off the light and stumbled back to bed, jerking the covers up.

Smoky jumped up on the bed and began to sharpen her claws on the mahogany baseboard.

"*Scat!*" The man pulled the bedcovers up over his head.

Smoky purred on, sailed out into space and landed on the dresser. She began to investigate the objects on its upper surface. In a minute an assortment of keys was flying off in all directions as she carefully pawed one after another into space.

"Go ahead," moaned the man bitterly. "It won't take me more than an hour or two to find them." He pulled the pillow over his head, too. Smoky went on batting the keys.

The man had another thought. He sat abruptly up in bed. "My watch!" In one jump he landed on his feet by the dresser. Smoky regarded him with mild surprise.

The watch, a large yellow gold one of old-fashioned design, lay unharmed where he had left it. He grabbed Smoky by the back of the neck.

"If you aren't sleepy, I am," he said firmly. "I can't sit under the stove all day like you. Today's Wednesday. Copy day. Scat!" He put the black cat out in the hall and shut the door firmly. As he picked up the watch again, it snapped open, revealing a colored picture of a smiling young woman with blue eyes and long dark hair. Briefly, he stood looking at it. His eyes softened, then became hard and cold. He snapped the watch shut with an angry gesture.

"Damn that cat!" He turned out the light and got into bed.

Smoky made several tentative passes at the door to be sure it was tightly shut, decided it was, and resignedly went off to investigate the contents of her milk bowl.

The man was asleep almost as soon as he put his head down. Sound asleep, too, because when he was awakened by a sound on the porch below, he got up and stumbled to the window before he remembered: Smoky was in. He opened the window, anyway, and yelled out into the rain.

"Who's there? Somebody want something?"

Below, under the porch roof, all sound ceased instantly. For a moment he heard only the hard cold rain. Then there was a quickening, a dull bumping sound, as if something heavy were being dragged across the wooden porch floor.

The man leaned out the window, listening. He was instantly wide awake. Hurrying across the room in the chill darkness, this time he did not stumble. His clothes were piled neatly on a chair by his bed; he yanked off the red flannel nightshirt and thrust on the shirt and trousers, slid his cold bare feet into his shoes and soon had the bedroom door open. He did not turn the lights on. In the doorway, he stopped to take a flashlight, hesitated, then in the darkness slid his hand into the second bureau drawer and took out a gun. Noiselessly he went out into the hall and down the stairs.

Quick as he was, however, there was no one in sight when he got to the front door. He stood behind the door, careful not to show himself as he opened it. He moved abruptly on to the open porch, listening.

The night was dark and raw; the rain came down in hard wet

sheets. Otherwise he heard nothing except the hollow sound of his footsteps when he walked. The porch had no basement under it, but was raised on posts with loose lattice work camouflaging the bare ground underneath; screened in summer, now in November it was open except for the roof and its supports and the wooden railing enclosing it.

The man called out. There was no answer. He flashed his light into some wet bushes on either side and down the driveway, but saw no one. Shivering, he turned off the flashlight and came in and relocked the door.

Smoky's eyes shone from where she was sitting on the post at the bottom of the stairs.

The man went up the stairs in the dark, but turned on the light in the bedroom, smiling a little grimly as he returned the gun to its drawer. Old habits were strong. Too strong. He scowled at the watch.

It was then that he saw the blood.

It seemed to be everywhere, not much of it, but undoubtedly blood—the dried brownish stains that no one who had seen much blood could mistake, even diluted with rain water. It was on the bedspread, in scattered marks, on the dresser, on the window sill. The trail was not hard to follow. Wherever Smoky had been, there was blood.

Probably she had cut her paw. Or maybe killed a bird.

Still, in November there were few birds. A feathered connoisseur like Smoky did not descend to mere sparrows. And if she had cut her paw, it must be bleeding pretty freely.

He gave a resigned glace at the clock: four thirty. He went in search of the wounded Smoky.

Presently his upstairs apartment was ablaze with light. No Smoky. Calls, offered bribes, threats—all produced no results.

No Smoky. He lighted the stairs and went down into the front newspaper office.

The office was a large room, high ceilinged and drafty, with dark oak woodwork and blue wallpaper of small faded flowers. The room had been made by throwing together the front and back parlors of the old house, with the resultant ridge about a third of the way along the room where the connecting doors had formerly been. There were four windows, one opening on the porch, three together forming a bay at the northwestern corner of the house. To their left was a flat table and straight chair; to their right, partially occupying the bay window, a huge roller-top desk of ancient vintage and hard wear. Beside it was the room's only easy chair, a worn red leather with deeply sunken springs. A tall and stately, if unreliable, grandfather's clock occupied, with rows of files, the rest of the north wall.

Along the back wall, to the east, with its flue feeding into the old chimney, was a huge black stove, round and ugly, with web-like legs holding up its short fat body, and a bucket of coal and a basket of wood beside it. There was also a small gas burner, on which reposed a great blue metal coffee pot.

The unvarnished pine floor was covered with a thin patterned rug of considerable wear. Next to the door leading to the press-room was a sink, with its towel, soap and a shelf of thick white china mugs above it. Three chairs, antique but straight, a knee-hole desk and several brass cuspidors completed the room's furnishings. On the walls hung several framed copies of old newspapers, including the first issue of the *Cognac Courier*, and about a dozen calendars, gifts of local merchants.

The rest of the lower floor of the house, except for the long straight hall at the south running from the front door to the back and containing the stairs, had formerly been dining room, kitchen and sunparlor. These had been thrown into the huge but crowded pressroom.

The man looked for Smoky under the desks, in the wastepaper basket, in an open drawer, behind the stove. She was not to be found.

The door to the press room was not open, but he looked in there anyway. The big Mergenthaler linotype, the job presses, folder, the large old newspaper press, the three stones, the type, ink and paper cabinets and power punch and stitchers were apparently untouched.

He looked for open windows. There were none. Finally he descended to the basement. Crawling into corners and under boxes, he called repeatedly. He looked in the coal bin. No Smoky. Finally he saw her, sitting placidly high on the pipes, her paws tucked under her, her eyes half-shut as she watched him indifferently.

"Cats!" he muttered, and put her gently under one arm. Her paws were thick with coal dust, of course, so he carried her up to the sink and washed them with soap and water.

Smoky plainly thought this was going too far. She kicked and bit and scratched and spat and in general made her opposition plain.

"Germs," he explained to her, nursing his battered hands.

When her paws emerged clean and absolutely uninjured, without a cut of any kind, he dropped her in mutual disgust and went around turning the lights off.

In his search for Smoky he had seen nothing else, but he saw them now. In the hall by the front door there were big brown stains. One was in the shape of a footprint, large and mansized. It was drying blood. The stains came in the front door and gradually faded out about halfway up the stairs. There were no signs of any going out the door.

Smoky sniffed at them daintily. She shook her paws in open distaste and kept her black back to the man in haughty silence.

"A little soap and water won't hurt you," he said, absently, staring at the stains. Finally he opened the drafts and stirred the stove, lit the burner under the huge blue coffee-pot in one corner of the room and sat down at his desk. He put his feet up to think.

He had just finished searching the house from top to bottom. No windows were unlocked, and there was nobody else here. The doors had been locked all evening, except when he went out on the porch. No one could have come in then—but someone had. No one could have gotten out, but no one else was here. That noise he had heard on the porch—but if the footprints had been there at that time he would have seen them. No, he hadn't turned on the hall light while investigating. And where had Smoky gotten the blood on her paws?

Thinking, he stared absently at his shoes, and finally he saw them, and knew who had trailed the blood in the front door. For above the sole of his shoes, between the sole and the uppers, was a brown streak of drying blood.

Getting up, he put his shoe over the footprint. It was exactly the same size. He opened the front door and turned on the porch lights. After a moment he shut it and went over and cranked the phone.

"Hello, Betsy." His voice was quiet and friendly. "This is Killian McBean. Give me Amos Colvin, please. Yes, the chief of police. No, I haven't been drinking again. Get him! Fast!" His voice was no longer quiet and friendly. It became sharp and authoritative.

Betsy got him Amos Colvin.

"Hello, Amos. McBean speaking. You'd better get over here. There's probably been a murder. There's a regular puddle of blood on my front porch. And I heard a noise—"

Amos Colvin's voice came over the phone, querulous and hostile. "Is there any body?"

"Not that I can see, but—"

"Then how can there be a murder? Go back to bed and sleep it off."

"I haven't had a drop."

"All right, all right. But don't think you can wake me up in the middle of the night with any of your press day stunts to sell *Couriers*. To hell with you."

"Listen, you fat fool," Killian McBean's voice grew colder and colder. "This has nothing to do with press day. Today's Wednesday anyway. Copy day. I'm calling as a citizen reporting to the chief of police. If you want to make it a newspaper issue, though, it won't look very good if a corpse is found and it comes out that the chief of police wouldn't even hump his fat carcass out of bed to investigate it."

Silence. Then the fretful, sleepy voice of Amos Colvin. "I'll be over. And if you're tight, so help me, I'll run you in!"

Killian grinned. "It's a deal, fat stuff." He hung up.

He ran up the stairs to his apartment, which was three upper rooms of the old house remodelled into kitchen, living room, bedroom and bath. The water in which he shaved and took a shower was icy cold.

Killian McBean was a man of perhaps forty, whose lean tough body made him seem younger, and whose tired eyes and face made him seem older. There was grey at the temples of his black hair and it was thinning at the sides. His nose was rather prominent, as was a front gold tooth. Even for his five feet ten his arms were disproportionately long, and his hands exceptionally large and powerful.

But it was his eyes that were his most outstanding feature: cold grey eyes, aloof and disbelieving. Occasionally a twinkle came into them, or a momentary softness, but it soon faded into a granite hardness. His smile, too, was sceptical, almost mocking.

Dressing carefully in a blue shirt and heavy grey suit, he selected a somewhat loud striped tie. The matter was carried out without haste and with meticulous neatness. He threw back the covers and opened a window to air the bed; he folded the red flannel nightshirt carefully over a coat hanger and hung it in the closet. Then he straightened the bathroom, hung the wet towels over the shower rack to dry, and carefully put the top back on the toothpaste tube.

Finally he turned out the lights and went downstairs again. Someone was knocking quietly on the back door.

"Who is it?"

"It's me. Jean. Open the door, Uncle Killian."

Killian swore under his breath. "What are you doing up at this hour?"

"I'm looking for Father."

"He isn't here. Go home and go to bed."

"Don't be a zombie, Uncle Killian. It's important!"

He swore again and opened the door. A young girl of about sixteen came in quickly, shaking off the rain. Without being heavy, her figure was well rounded in her brown skirt and red sweater, and her cheeks were plump and rosy. She had a crop of windblown very short hair, a skin that was as smooth as an apple's, straight white teeth and sparkling blue eyes. Jean was not pretty, but interesting, merry and friendly.

The words poured from her now at a mile a minute. "Uncle Killian, Father has made like a bird and I can't find him anywhere. It's my fault. I'm a Dracula's daughter, and he's such a good Joe and right out of this world but somebody's always rocking his dream boat and that Bennet Farr is such a Sad Sam I don't really care if somebody kills him anyway only not Father—"

"Whoa!" said Killian. "Is that English?"

"Uncle Killian, this isn't any place for off-time jive!"

"You don't say."

"You've got to listen to me!"

"I'll listen to you," said Killian gently. "Only try to remember I'm among the uninitiated. I'm a generation too old to understand jive. Have consideration for an old man—and stick to English."

"All right, Uncle Killian. Of course you're not really—old, I mean—you just try to pretend you are and you may fool some people but not me because I know at heart you're strictly solid—"

"*What happened to your father?*"

"That's what I've been trying and trying to tell you. He was drinking again and brooding about losing his leg and all—you know how he does and talking about killing Old Gluts Farr—and I went out to make him some coffee and when I came back he was gone and so was his gun and I've looked and looked and I can't find him anywhere."

"Get your breath," advised Killian callously. "Even as a little girl they say you could get out more words without taking in breath than anybody alive. Did you try the pool hall?"

"Yes, of course. Bill hadn't seen him all evening."

"How about the Metropole?"

"I tried that and the police station—"

Killian made an impatient gesture. "Sometimes I think Ethan

made a mistake in not drowning you before your eyes were open. Do you mean to tell me you went to the police station and told them—"

"But, Uncle Killian, I was so worried! Anyhow, nobody was there."

"Why didn't you come here?"

"I did. Right away. But I saw you sitting on the porch—"

"You saw me where?"

"Sitting on the front porch. Leaning, really, and I knew you weren't—quite yourself."

"I haven't been out of bed all night."

"It's all right, Uncle Killian. I'm a woman now and I understand life. I know you drink sometimes. I'm sure you must have a secret sorrow or something that makes you—I guess it's something to do with that woman you have in your watch—"

Killian McBean's tone cut like a whip. "When I want your analysis of my character and motives, Jean, I'll ask for it."

"But, Uncle Killian, I only meant—"

"I'm not interested. Now I'm telling you, if you saw a man on my front porch, it wasn't I. What made you think it was?"

"I couldn't see anything but his figure, it was so dark. But I just thought it was you because he was here and he looked about your size—and he was sitting down and leaning as if he had been—well, drinking—"

"Could it have been your father?"

"No."

"How do you know?"

"I saw both his shoes—they were sticking out in front of him."

"Was there a car there?"

"No. At least I didn't see any. I didn't notice particularly."

"If you're ever going to be a reporter," Killian stated coldly, "you'll have to learn to observe. Not just *see* but observe, know what you're seeing. Something that's right in front of your eyes may mean the difference between a good and bad story, or even a true and false one."

"Uncle Killian, we've got to find Father!"

Killian heard a car turn in the driveway. He crossed the hall in two long strides, took his cloth raincoat from the hall rack and came back to put it over Jean's shoulders. It was a victory model, not rubberized but merely water-repellent cotton material.

"Put this on before you catch pneumonia or drown. Go home now and stay there. Whistle. Walk down the middle of the street and when you get there call me up. Get going." He opened the back door and steered her out it.

"But, Uncle Killian—"

"Get going."

"All right," said Jean. "There's something awfully mysterious about you, though." She looked up at him. "Do you know lots of people here in Cognac think you were a gangster in Chicago while you were away those ten years?"

Killian shoved her out into the wet darkness, giving her a fatherly swat as she passed. He watched her disappear and stood listening after her. Someone pounded on the front door, but he did not pay any attention until he heard Jean's whistle going along the road. Then he shut and locked the back door and proceeded in a leisurely manner toward the front one. When he opened it, it admitted a shivering, sputtering fat man.

CHAPTER TWO

"Hello, Amos." Killian grinned at the sight of him.

The short fat man waddled in, huddled untidily in his wet sheepskin coat. His close-set eyes peered nearsightedly out of horn-rimmed glasses. He snarled at Killian.

"So help me, McBean, if you got me up on some wild-goose chase—"

"Did you look at the front porch?"

"It looks like blood," admitted Amos Colvin grudgingly. "But knowing you, it might be red ink."

"You can have it analyzed. That should not only tell you whether it's blood or not, but whether it's human or animal."

"What d'ya mean, animal?"

"There's an awful lot of it," Killian advanced cautiously, "but I suppose there is at least an outside possibility it might be a dog or a cat—"

Amos Colvin exploded loudly. "If you got me over here to see the aftereffects of a catfight—"

Killian McBean shrugged. "I'm simply a citizen reporting a suspicious set of circumstances to the chief of police. My responsibility is ended. Do what you like. But you should have an analysis made."

"I don't hold with none of them newfangled chemical cops," said Amos. "If somebody's dead, they'll turn up and we'll know whose blood it is. Otherwise the hell with it; it don't matter none. Is there coffee in that pot?"

"There's always coffee in that pot." Killian McBean went over and took down two thick white china mugs and filled them from the blue metal coffee pot on the burner. "The *Cognac Courier* dispenses hospitality with an impartial hand—even to the corruptest chief of police in four counties."

"Thanks," said Amos Colvin dourly. He poured some of the coffee into the saucer, blew on it and drank it with loud gasping gulps.

Killian sat down and drank his from the mug. He recounted the events of the past hour in some detail, leaving out Jean's visit and any mention of her father's absence. Of necessity, since he omitted Jean, he also had to omit the fact she had seen a man on the porch. The phone rang. He spoke into it briefly. "All right. Lock the door and stay there," and hung up. Before Amos had time to voice his question, the phone rang again.

"Now listen," Killian said abruptly into it, "when you're told to do something, do it and don't ask questions—oh, I'm sorry, Betsy. I thought it was somebody else. Sure, he's here. Just a minute. For you, Amos."

Amos took the phone in one hand, still clutching his coffee saucer in the other. "What d'ya want, Betsy? The hell there is. The hell you say. I'll be right over. Tell Mr. Farr I'll be right over."

"The magic name," said Killian McBean. "What hoop does Bennet Farr want you to jump through now, Amos?"

"You shut your mouth," said Amos. "Bennet Farr is going to foreclose that mortgage on your paper when it's due in a couple of months and after that we'll run you out of Cognac so fast you'll never know what hit you."

"It isn't due yet. And I'm still in Cognac." Only Killian's eyes showed that the chief of police's barb had penetrated. "I ain't got time to be wasting on you and your catfights. The hell with you. I got important business. Mr. Farr just saw a bad accident out at Indian Mound on the road."

"Anybody hurt?"

"Some girl, Betsy said. Farr called her and said he saw the car piled up against a telephone pole and the girl in it, unconscious."

"What," asked Killian coldly, "was Bennet Farr doing out at Indian Mound at five in the morning? Everybody in town knows he never gets up till noon."

"You mind your business," said Amos Colvin.

"That's the beauty of being a newspaper editor, Amos. Everybody's business is my business. You'd like it fine."

"Go to hell," growled the chief of police.

"I think I'll just come along with you, Amos. I wouldn't choose you as a traveling companion, because I'd hate to be caught dead with you, but a story is a story. Indian Mound is only half a mile away, but it's raining and my car is at the garage getting its battery recharged. I just got in from the convention last night about seven."

"You're not coming anywhere with me."

Killian McBean settled back in his chair. "O.K., Amos. I just thought it might look good in the *Courier*: 'The accident was promptly reported to Cognac's chief of police, Amos Colvin, who was on the scene in three minutes.' That's about how long it'll take us to get there."

"Get going, if you're coming with me," said Amos ungraciously. "And don't tell Farr I brought you!"

"I wouldn't breathe a word," said Killian with an elaborate wink.

Three minutes later they were at Indian Mound, the right-angle turn on the road which branched off from the main highway to Chicago for the town of Cognac. A considerable crowd had preceded them there, the lights of the cars illuminating the scene dimly. By now the rain had slackened; it was getting colder and the precipitation was turning to snow. Several dozen people stood around, wet and shivering.

"The beauties," grinned Killian McBean, "of a party line." He jumped down and ran over to the wreck. The car was a small green coupé, about five years old, with California license plates. The entire engine and front part were crumpled into an indistinguishable hunk of metal, flat against the telephone pole. The cab of the car was a mass of blood. The back tires and storage compartment were untouched.

Killian shook his head. "Some wreck. What happened, Terry? Anybody see it?"

A tall, very thin young man was standing there looking extremely worried. He spoke apologetically, as if it were somehow his fault. "Apparently not. I can't find any witnesses. Bennet Farr saw the car and somebody in it, but he didn't stop to take any closer look. He was afraid it might be a fake, like robbers or something, and anyway he said if it wasn't they ought to have a doctor as soon as possible. So he just went on to the town and called. He was pretty upset, didn't even come back. Betsy scouted around for Amos and me after calling Old Doc. I guess about everybody heard about it, one way or another."

"Looks like it, Terry," said Killian. "Kind of tough break for you, in your first week as state's attorney."

Terrence Gillespie looked more worried and apologetic than ever. "I suppose it's all right," he said. "But there doesn't seem to be any reason for the accident—of course it was raining, but the turn is well lighted and there wasn't any fog or anything. And there's all that blood."

"Just the girl in the car?" asked Killian.

"Yes. Apparently."

"What do you mean, apparently?"

Terrence Gillespie twisted his lank body uncomfortably. "She's still unconscious. Knocked out. But Old Doc says she doesn't seem to be hurt except for the bump on her head and a couple of minor cuts. No apparent cause for all that blood. It's all over the car and her clothes. And if it isn't hers, whose is it and where are they?"

"Better organize a search through the woods around the Mound," said Killian matter-of-factly. "I suppose another person could have been hurt and crawled off to get help."

Terry brightened. "I'll see about it right away."

"And don't worry so much," said Killian. "No wonder you've got ulcers. What's this I hear about you and the new assistant in the library, Irene Hubbard?"

Terry's face became a brick red by the light of the car headlights. His thin, underdeveloped body stooped more than ever and his tone became more meek. "She—she's fine, I guess. I—haven't seen her in two days."

"Anybody can always make an excuse to see the assistant to the librarian," said Killian. "Start reading, boy, start reading."

"Thanks," gulped Terrence Gillespie. "I guess I will—read more."

Killian grinned at him and moved back through the crowd. "Where's the girl?" he asked.

"Back there." The crowd opened to let him through. "Celia's helping Old Doc."

Celia Austen's long auburn hair flamed from her shoulders; it had slipped from the loose knot in which she generally wore it. Her face was shining from her exertions, and her nose was plainly freckled. She was very small, only a little over five feet and with a slight build. Her nose turned up above a surprisingly firm mouth and a heart-shaped chin. She knelt now on the frozen ground beside the figure of an unconscious girl, her fingers moving deftly as she followed the doctor's directions.

Old Doc was Cognac's only doctor now that Young Doc was in the south Pacific. He stood shivering and growling and stamping his feet. "Noseyest damn town I ever saw," he complained. "Five o'clock in the morning and everybody within five miles beats the doctor here. Get back, damn you, give us room. Hello, Killian."

"Hello, Old Doc," said Killian. He grinned in friendly fashion at the white-haired old man. "Hello, kid."

Celia flashed him a smile. "I was wondering where you were. After all, I'm only the *Courier's* unofficial social reporter, and I'm afraid I'm not up to covering accidents for you yet."

"She badly hurt?"

"How the hell do I know?" growled Old Doc. "She may have internal injuries. She certainly got a terrific wallop on the head. I never saw a worse one."

"Good thing you had that nurse's aide training in the city, Celia," said Killian. "So you think she'll come around O.K., Old Doc?"

"Looks like it," the old man advanced cautiously. "Don't see why she shouldn't. But you never can tell about a bad knock on the head. May make her simple-minded."

"Who is she?"

"We don't know," said Celia. "There isn't any identification in her purse and Terry went through the bags, in the back of the car and he says there isn't anything there, either. They're tracing the car by license numbers now, of course."

"Probably stolen," said Old Doc glumly.

Celia looked up at Killian and laughed. "He isn't half as tough as he sounds, really."

"He brought me into the world," said Killian. "You too, kid. And Bennet Farr was his first baby case. That's the only two good things I can say for Bennet Farr—Old Doc delivered him and he has got his son engaged to you."

The girl's smile clouded. "Don't let's talk politics, Killian. We're friends—but everybody knows I've always been crazy about Dennis—and Bennet Farr is his father—"

"Sure, kid," said Killian grimly. He bent over and looked at the unconscious girl who lay on a blanket on the ground, shielded by umbrellas. She was a very thin blonde, probably still in her twenties. Her cheekbones were high and prominent, her chin strong and determined. There was considerable blood on her clothes. Under her moderately priced fur coat her legs showed long and slim; she was rather tall.

Killian McBean whistled. Celia looked up at him and laughed. "Not you too," she said. "I thought you were supposed to be woman-proof. Every other man in town has been making excuses to come over and see if there was anything he could do—just helpful, you know—but Killian McBean!"

Killian laughed too, but he was not amused.

"How long has she been out?" he asked.

"Not over half an hour. Old Doc doesn't want to move her until she comes to, if he can help it. Father Farr saw the wreck—" she hesitated, looking at Killian.

"It's all right, kid," said Killian. "God knows what you see in that Dennis Farr—nobody ever could see it, especially after—but you've always felt that way and if you do, more power to you. The guy must have something for you to stick to him. You can't help it if his old man's the corruptest crook in the state. Barring Chicago, of course. And maybe Springfield."

Celia frowned at him, unsuccessfully. Finally she laughed. "No hard feelings, Killian?"

"Hell, no," said Killian McBean. "There's no sentiment in the newspaper business. I run a newspaper; I'm a reporter. I'd sell my mother's soul for a good story. Don't ever forget that, kid. She's coming to."

"Old Doc!" said Celia.

The unconscious girl fluttered her eyelashes and opened eyes that were golden-brown. There was a blank, bewildered look in them.

"Take it easy," said Killian McBean.

Old Doc, grumbling, knelt stiffly on the wet ground beside her and took her pulse. "Not bad," he muttered finally. Celia kept her small hand soothingly on the girl's.

The girl spoke in a trembling voice. "What happened?"

"There was an accident," said Celia. "You hit your head."

"Where am I?"

"Cognac," supplied Killian McBean, as if there could be only one. "Population, 1439. Pardon me. I forgot the new Bacon twins. 1441. Chief industry, farming. Chief vices, hard drink and chewing tobacco."

The girl smiled at him uncertainly. Under her strained stunned expression, she seemed to be trying very hard to think.

"We're going to take you up to my house," said Celia, "just as soon as you feel able to move. Try not to worry. You've had a bad blow."

The girl attempted to focus on her. Her eyes managed it; her mind did not. "But," she said finally, "what am I doing here? Who am I?"

"My God," said Old Doc. "I should have expected this, but I didn't. She's lost her memory."

"Ordinary medical occurrence?"

"After that wallop? My God, yes. Of course it'll only be temporary. A few days at most, probably."

The girl looked at Old Doc in alarm. She looked at Celia, then at Killian. "Don't you know me?" she appealed to them. "I can't seem—to remember anything—my head aches so—"

Old Doc cursed fervently. "Anybody's would, with that bump."

"Never mind that now," said Celia. "There's lots of time. We'll take you up to my house and you can stay there and rest as long as you like—it may take several days—and you're not to worry about anything."

"Aunty Pliny is going to like that!" said Killian low-voiced to Celia.

She flushed under her freckles. "There's no hospital," she said. "There's plenty of room—the girl is hurt and has amnesia—"

Killian shrugged. "She might be anybody. There's still a lot of blood to be explained."

CHAPTER THREE

Several hours later Killian McBean sat at his desk in the outer office, pounding at a typewriter, with Smoky on the chair next to him. Several times he tore the sheet of paper from the machine, crumpled it in disgust and threw it on the floor. There was quite a pile of papers. Outside day had come; it was nearly eight o'clock. And it had stopped raining and snowing.

The door swung back so that the lettering on its face showed, "THE COGNAC COURIER," it read, "Come In and Take the Weight off Your Feet."

"'Morning, Ethan," said Killian, without turning. "Coffee's heating. Better have some."

"T'hell with the coffee," said Ethan. "T'hell with everything. Gnats! I'd show those Japs and Jerries if it wasn't for my leg." His voice was thick and slurred. He spat tobacco juice long and artistically at one of the cuspidors.

"Sure you would, Ethan." Killian still did not turn. "You showed them in the last war, anyhow. They don't give out the Croix de Guerre for nothing, you know."

"But that was the last war!" Ethan's voice rose to a shrill sob.

"I could show 'em now—I would too if Old Gluts Farr hadn't got my leg—"

"Sure you would, Ethan." Killian got up and sauntered casually over to the stove. "I think I'll have some coffee anyhow. Have some with me?"

"T'hell with the coffee." Ethan stumped into the back room and patted the large newspaper press affectionately. "'Morning, Gwen." He stumped back into the front office.

Killian poured two mugs, took one over to Ethan. Ethan Droom was around sixty-five or seventy, a slight, stooped man with piercing brown eyes. His hands shook as he took the coffee. Killian went back to the stove and fussed around adding more coffee and water to the pot.

"You think I'm drunk!" accused Ethan shrilly.

"I know you are."

Ethan laughed merrily. "Gnats! Best damn printer in the country," he said.

Killian laughed, too. "My father always said you were. What's good enough for my father's good enough for me. The copy is pretty nearly ready for the first run—two, three, six, and seven. I've got to polish one editorial a little and check a couple of country correspondents. I got some job printing from Paul Huston yesterday. I put it on your desk. Take a look at it when you've got time. It's nine by twelve handbills."

Ethan brightened. "I always got time," he said. "Guess I'll have some more coffee." He got up and walked more steadily. The coffee spilled when he poured it, but he got a second mug.

"Some sandwiches on the counter," said Killian. "I didn't have time to stop for breakfast. Sloppy Pete's sent 'em over."

"Gnats," said Ethan, taking one. "I want to see about those

handbills." He went back into the pressroom. Killian typed a little longer, then got up and went over casually and shut the door between the rooms. Ethan was asleep, his head on his arms. Killian came back and cranked the phone and spoke into it in a low voice. "Two, ring five. Hello, Jean. It's O.K. about that matter we were looking into. Sure, perfectly O.K. Asleep in the back room at the moment. How about those high school notes? Well, get them in this morning. I'm putting out a paper, not running a kindergarten. Never mind the alibis. Get them in!"

He hung up, grinning a little. After a moment he went back to his typing.

Small auburn-haired Celia Austen and a tall husky young man came in. They were an incongruous pair—she so tiny and he so big. There was an adoring look in her eyes, moreover, that was not in his. His manner was slightly condescending to her and short to the point of rudeness with Killian.

"Father wants to see you," he announced, "right away."

Killian tilted his chair back and surveyed him coldly. "You don't say!"

"Killian!" said Celia.

"You'll come, McBean," said Dennis Farr, "if you know what's good for you."

Killian grinned, turned his back and went on typing.

Dennis Farr grew angry. "The nerve of a two-bit country editor with a mortgaged paper putting on airs with Bennet Farr!"

"Denny, dear, please!" said Celia rather helplessly. The air of efficiency which had surrounded her as a nurse's aide at the scene of the accident was now gone. She looked harried and unhappy.

"Tell Bennet Farr," said Killian distinctly, "to go to hell." He added pleasantly, "And you go with him. Not you, Celia."

"I ought to knock you down!" roared Dennis Farr.

Killian tilted his chair a little further back, dusting his hands casually. He looked Dennis Farr up and down and down and up, coldly.

"Please, Killian," said Celia. "I think it's a story, really I do. Father—Mr. Farr said it was the biggest story this town had had in years."

"So he gives it to me. I'll bet!"

"He—Mr. Farr was very upset. He said it would be a sensation."

"Get thee behind me," Killian could not completely conceal his interest, "but don't shove!"

"He's down at the Metropole."

"The hotel? What's he doing down there? What's the matter with his own house?"

"That's none of your damn business," snapped Dennis Farr.

Celia put a soft hand on his arm. "We—don't know, Killian. Honestly. He—seemed to be afraid of something."

"My father is not afraid of anything!" roared Dennis.

"Darling, I didn't mean—"

"You ought to watch what you say. You're very inclined to be tactless, Celia."

"I'm sorry, Denny."

Dennis accepted this in grudging silence, glowering at Killian. "He wants you to go in the back way. The door's open."

Killian raised an eyebrow.

"Please, Killian," said Celia.

Killian regarded her coldly, then shrugged. "I may drop in a little later. The front way. I'm busy now."

"Why, you—" growled Dennis Farr.

"Come on, Denny," pleaded Celia, her hand on his arm. Dennis allowed himself to be led away, protesting arrogantly.

"What happened to the amnesia girl?" asked Killian of Celia as she was halfway out of the door.

"She said she felt better. I left her lying down. She's still pretty dazed and weak, and her head aches terribly. Old Doc left her a sedative but she hadn't taken it. She's worrying so about not knowing who she is. I should have stayed with her, but Denny needed me, and—"

"If Denny needed you," said Killian critically, "You'd abandon a newborn baby in a blizzard."

Killian went on typing for perhaps five minutes, crumbling sheets of paper and throwing them away. Finally he appeared satisfied. He cranked the phone and telephoned a brief account of the accident to a Chicago newspaper. Then he picked up the crumpled papers carefully and mopped the coffee Ethan had spilled. After putting on his coat and hat, he hesitated and at last went back to the pressroom for a final look at Ethan. He came out looking both worried and bewildered.

Ethan was not there.

Killian hesitated by the telephone, thought better of it, and went out the back door. Smoky brushed against his ankles. She sat down on the top step, dozing casually.

The one street of Cognac was without subterfuge, straight and to the point. It was nameless and referred to simply as The Road. The Road branched from the main highway at a distance of about three miles. After the one right angle turn at Indian Mound about half a mile north of Cognac proper, it ran straight through the town from north to south, a dead end street going nowhere else.

Houses faced each other on both sides of it, with farms reaching out behind them, and the stores were clustered opposite each other at the middle. The houses were mostly frame, usually white with green shutters. Only a few were newly painted, but all were clean and attractive. Service stars hung in many of the windows, some of them gold. Back on the hill to the south and set apart from the rest of the village, were two brick houses, much larger and more expensive than the rest, but not as homey. The newspaper office was at the extreme north end, the first house on entering Cognac by The Road. The hotel was in the middle, facing east, opposite the school and the post office.

Killian had a brisk stride, but it took him some time to walk the three blocks from his newspaper office to the hotel. He stopped to talk to everyone about everything. His interest was friendly, but quietly persistent. Questions formed themselves naturally.

"Hello, Eb. What's this I hear about you selling a carload of hogs in Chicago? How much did you get a hundredweight? You don't say. Not bad. Not bad at all. Say, I was talking to Dud Pounds the other day and he said you had your mother-in-law visiting you. That'd be Mrs.—let's see, Sally was a Worth, wasn't she?—Mrs. Worth. From—sure, Moline. How long's she going to stay? Well, that'll make a good visit. I'll run a little notice about it; all your friends will be interested. And young Eb's home on furlough? You don't say. We'll certainly have to get that in. Tell him to stop in the office before he goes back. Fine boy, young Eb. Did he tell you I looked him up at the camp when I went up to the city to the convention last week? Just got back last night, you know."

He came to two young women. "Morning. Are the new schoolteacher and the new assistant to the librarian out to see the sights before work? What do you know?"

The shorter of the two girls, who was also somewhat the other's junior, answered. There was a twinkle in her eye. "Hello, news hound."

"City girl," said Killian.

The shorter girl laughed good-naturedly. "How long do you have to be in Cognac before people stop saying that about you?"

"Well," said Killian, "of course it makes a difference. If you marry a local boy and have—say, six children—maybe in twenty years—"

The taller girl spoke. She wore glasses, and had long dark hair braided around her head. There was an inconspicuous attachment in her ear and her voice had the slightly flat tone often common to the hard of hearing. Her black dress and coat were neat to the point of primness. "Good morning, Mr. McBean."

"Until you came to town, Theodora," Killian grinned at her, "nobody had called me Mr. McBean in years."

Theodora Meredith frowned at him. "A schoolteacher has to keep up certain standards, you know. It wouldn't look well for me to be calling strange men by their first names."

"An assistant to the librarian doesn't have to be so careful," the shorter girl laughed. She wore no hat, and her hair was short and straight. She held herself very erect and made an attractive appearance in a heavy blue suit and coat. "All I have to worry about is whether Old Gluts Farr will succeed in getting the library closed as an unnecessary frivolity. He's certainly trying hard enough."

"Cheer up, Irene," said Killian. "You've got me."

Irene Hubbard laughed again. "He doesn't like you, either."

"Mr. Farr," stated Theodora Meredith coldly, "should be exterminated."

Killian and Irene stared at her.

"You know, Theodora," said Killian finally, "I think you have hidden depths. I'm beginning to think you and I could have a beautiful friendship. What did Old Gluts do to you?"

"He's just sent Tommy Briggs to the reform school for taking a few of his apples," said Theodora flatly. "Tommy didn't mean any harm—there were apples and apples just going to waste—and he spoiled a boy's whole life just to gratify his sense of power. And that's just one thing. He's always snooping around, trying to cut expenses so he won't have to pay such high taxes. He doesn't care if the children get any advantages at all, or if the teachers starve, just so he can save a little more money!"

"When was all this about Tommy Briggs? How'd it happen I didn't hear about it? I saw Tommy last week." Killian was shocked.

"It was just Monday. While you were at that newspaper editors convention," said Irene. "Old Gluts did it so fast we hardly realized what had happened. Went into court the next morning, and with that yes-man judge of his it was all over in a few minutes."

Killian swore. "We'll have to see about that. Reform school's no place for Tommy. A little wild, maybe, but nothing a good licking wouldn't cure."

There were sudden tears in Theodora Meredith's eyes. "Oh, Mr. McBean, if you only could!" She gulped, shocked at the possibility she might be seen crying in public. She scurried hastily toward the Hotel Metropole.

Killian looked after her in surprise. "I always thought she was an icicle."

"Oh, no!" Irene Hubbard protested dutifully. "She feels things terribly. She cried and cried when they sent Tommy away. She—

you know he has no mother and she felt sort of—as if she had failed him. Can you really get him out?"

Killian frowned. "I can try, certainly. I'll try the official channels first and if that doesn't work I'll give it an editorial workout."

"I don't see," said Irene, smiling at him, "why anybody says you're cold-blooded."

"City girl," said Killian. They walked on to the Hotel Metropole together. The Metropole was a rambling white frame edifice, three stories high and perfectly square. Considered as a palace when it was built some fifty years before, it had borne the years sturdily. Now it barely struggled along, with a few permanent guests, some transients, a cook who did dinners "on order," and one part-time hostess.

In the lobby Killian stopped to talk to her. She was a slight elderly woman with thin white hair and a long sharp nose. She wore a bright red dress and rhinestone ear clips, and teetered on very high heels. Irene Hubbard took her key and went on up the stairs; she and Theodora lived at the hotel.

"'Morning, Aunty Pliny."

"Trash! Don't you Aunty Pliny me," said the old lady sharply. "I know you and your buttering ways. You needn't try to rub me smooth. You're just trying to find out the news, that's all."

Killian grinned. "Well, you can hardly blame me, Aunty. If there's any news in town, you'll have it."

The old lady in the red dress made a sharp clicking noise with her tongue. "What I know is my own mind, not yours. You stole my husband's newspaper!"

Killian shrugged wearily. "I wish we didn't have to go over and over that every week. When your husband bought the *Courier* from my father, it was solvent and well equipped. Your husband ran it down and mortgaged it to Bennet Farr—ran it nearly into bankruptcy. If I hadn't taken it over from him he would have lost it completely. I made him the fairest deal I could. Jim was the first to say that, himself, before he died."

"Trash!" said the old lady. "You stole it. Jim put all his cash in it, and you didn't fetch him hardly any."

"He got the cash from Farr when he put the mortgages on. I took over the mortgages."

"Trash! No good wastrel, that's what you are."

Killian grinned. "Let's see the register."

Aunty Pliny made the sharp clicking noise with her tongue again, but shoved a worn brown leather book at him. Killian ran his eye down the page and with a stubby red pencil wrote a couple of names on an envelope in his pocket.

"I didn't know Ladd had checked out," he said. "And who's this Eberts?"

"Traveling farm-equipment service man, he said," snapped Aunty Pliny. "Looked worthless to me. He's been gone three days, anyhow."

"Driving?"

"No, train."

"I don't see Bennet Farr here," said Killian casually. Aunty Pliny's eyes popped. "*How did you know that?*"

Killian shrugged. His eyes twinkled. "A newspaper man does not divulge the sources of his information."

"Trash," said Aunty Pliny. "Trash! Room 210, he is."

Killian chucked her under the chin, grinned at her outraged cackle, and mounted the carpeted stairs three at a time.

The geography of the Metropole was rather peculiar, due to the somewhat eccentric tastes of its founder, Jeremiah Danzig. The second floor had only four rooms for guests, while the third had eight. The entire south side of the second floor was a long since abandoned auditorium. Jeremiah Danzig had fancied his own powers as a public speaker, and had built the auditorium with the hotel to exhibit them. Even free refreshments had not been enough to cause Jeremiah's speeches to be well patronized, however, and since his death the auditorium had been padlocked and abandoned; Cognac's gatherings took place in the high school auditorium.

The main stairs, running directly up to the second and third floors, were straight mahogany with thick flowered carpet. They went up by Aunty Pliny's desk, near the front of the lobby. The guests' rooms on the second floor faced north; room 209 was opposite the top step, room 210 to the east of it facing also on the street, and rooms 208 and 207 to its west, the latter facing on the gardens. The corridor was carpeted, but the back stairs, opposite 207 and leading to the kitchen, were bare.

At the top of the stairs, Killian turned to the left and knocked loudly at the second door, marked 210.

There was no answer.

Killian frowned, knocked again. No sound came from within the room. He tried the door. It was unlocked. He opened it.

A large well-dressed man lay face downward on the floor, facing the front window. There was a fresh red stain on the carpet under him.

Killian shut the door behind him and crossed the room in two quick strides. He knelt beside the man, but did not touch him. One look was enough to tell him it was no use. Bennet Farr was dead. There was a long-handled bread knife driven deep into his back.

CHAPTER FOUR

The room was not the Metropole's best, though Bennet Farr was Cognac's most affluent citizen. Being the northeast corner room, it fronted on the street instead of the snowy gardens to the west of the hotel, and was moreover small, dark, and dingy. It contained a single metal bed, a dresser, a straight chair and a desk with a Gideon Bible on it. Using his handkerchief, Killian pulled out the drawers of the desk and dresser in rapid order; they were empty except for a few sheets of blank hotel stationery in the desk. On top of the desk was a door key with a tag marked 210. He opened the closet—only Bennet Farr's overcoat and hat. A search of the pockets revealed a handkerchief, a handful of loose change, and a cigar case with several of the strong imported cigars which Bennet Farr was never without.

Killian McBean stood back and surveyed the scene. Without the corpse, the room was as bare and impersonal as a room could be. Remove the body, clean the carpet, and it would be just like thousands of other rooms in thousands of other small hotels. Yet Bennet Farr lay dead on its floor.

Killian stooped and picked something off the carpet. It was small and metallic. He frowned at it, studying it, then put it in his pocket. It was seven point printer's type. He hunted carefully for more, but found only the one piece.

Finally he knelt beside Bennet Farr's body and gingerly went through his pockets, turning him as little as possible. He found only a set of keys and a wallet. The wallet contained five tens and a twenty dollar bill, several ones and a fifty cent piece. Mounted on either side were pictures of Mrs. Bennet Farr and their son, Dennis Farr, taken in cap and gown on the occasion of his graduation from an eastern university some four years before. There was also a clipping from an old newspaper. Killian's eyes flickered as he read it. It was dated in October five years before, when Dennis Farr had been a senior in college.

"DENNIS FARR WEDS CHORINE
ELOPEMENT TO WALDO, CONN.
IMMEDIATE DIVORCE SAYS BENNET FARR

There followed a brief but somewhat malicious account of what was very evidently a gin wedding. Papa Farr had arrived by chartered plane and snatched his erring son from a local hotel early the next morning. He was in no condition to move, but had to be carried. The abandoned bride, an attractive miss from a stage show playing locally, had no comment to make, in fact could not be reached. She was known professionally as Rosa Kincaid. Bennet Farr had issued a statement to the press, saying the whole thing was a mistake, and there would be an immediate divorce, etc. A blurred indistinct picture of a girl accompanied the article. Her eyes were half shut, her face largely in shadow. Recognition from such a picture was impossible; she might have been anyone.

Killian carefully replaced the clipping, wiped the wallet to remove his fingerprints, and replaced it in the dead man's pocket.

He stood up to take one last look around, shook his head, and moved toward the door. After listening for sound of movement in the hall, he went out into it, closing the door behind him. No one was in sight.

He had been in the room for perhaps three minutes.

Sauntering casually down the hall, he looked at the five other doors on the corridor. The name on the one next to Bennet Farr's, 209, read Theodora Meredith—the new teacher. 208's card said Irene Hubbard—the new assistant librarian. He opened the door of 207; the room was empty. So was its closet.

Going out into the corridor again, he passed the door to the old auditorium without stopping; its rusted padlock had plainly not been opened in years. Also opposite 207 there was a broom closet. Killian opened its door. There was no one in it now, but there had been. A man's cloth raincoat, still damp, hung on a hook.

It was Killian's own raincoat, the one he had put on Jean that morning when he sent her home. Down the side of it was a long smear of blood.

Killian McBean looked at his raincoat for a space of perhaps thirty seconds. His eyes were hard and calculating. His mouth became a grim forbidding line. He started to go out, shrugged, and took off his overcoat. Putting a handkerchief around the fresh bloodstain, he donned the raincoat and pulled his overcoat over it. Fortunately the overcoat was amply large; he buttoned it, and except for giving a somewhat stuffed appearance, the inner coat could not be detected. More than five minutes had passed since he left Aunty Pliny; he could not waste further time. He walked quickly down the front stairs and spoke loudly and angrily to the elderly woman at the desk.

"You tell Old Gluts Farr the next time he sends for me, to be home, Aunty Pliny," he said. "I'm a busy man. When I make an appointment, I keep it."

"Didn't he let you in?"

"He isn't there."

"He hasn't gone out. He must be there."

"Well, if he is, he isn't answering the door. I knocked and knocked. He didn't pay any attention. I thought maybe he was dressing or something, so I gave him plenty of time, but he never answered. As Amos would say, the hell with him."

Killian walked out the hotel front door and strode down the street to the *Courier* office. He waved a cheery greeting to several people, but without seeming to hurry, he did not stop to chat.

Inside the newspaper office, he went at once to the pressroom at the back. Old Ethan was apparently asleep at his desk. Killian looked at him closely, but did not touch him. He went out and shut the door. Mounting the stairs three at a time, he locked the door of his apartment behind him. Then he took off his overcoat and the bloody raincoat beneath it. Fortunately the handkerchief had kept the raincoat from staining either the overcoat or his suit coat. But the bloodstain was still very much in evidence on the raincoat.

Killian knew too much about bloodstains to think it could be washed out. Long after all signs of it were apparently gone, a competent chemist could not only prove that it had been there, but its type and classifications. There was no way Killian could explain having Bennet Farr's blood on his raincoat. He took no chances on having to.

Fortunately his scissors were handy, and he put them to use now. With swift impatient gestures he cut off the buttons. Then he sawed and tore the raincoat and handkerchief into narrow strips of cloth. Putting the buttons into a box in a drawer that was filled with other buttons, he took the strips of cloth downstairs and put them in the stove. After opening the drafts and putting in some papers, he poked the roaring fire until all traces of the cloth were gone. It did not catch easily, but when its kindling point was reached, the chemically treated cotton flared suddenly and burned quickly with a hot blue flame. When it was burnt, he doused the fire with ashes and got the ash bucket. He emptied the stove of ashes, carrying them out and scattering them the length and breadth of the garden. The wind was blowing rather strongly and the finer ash was carried away immediately. The rest did not stay long.

Killian came in and rebuilt the fire in the stove. Five minutes later he was working calmly at his typewriter, smoking a long and foul-smelling pipe with every indication of perfect enjoyment.

The door opened behind him and a woman sneezed. He turned, smiling, and saw the girl who had been hurt in the auto accident. The dazed, stunned effect of shock had worn off only slightly. Her face was grey and she looked as if she were going to be sick. She had borrowed a fur coat from Celia; it was much too short for her.

"Here," said Killian. "You'd better have some coffee. Sit down." He got up and went over and filled two of the white mugs. One he took over to her. She did not take it, but just sat looking at it, her brown eyes blank and shocked.

"Damn." Killian put the coffee down and took her cold hands, chafing them roughly between his. After a minute he reached back for the coffee, holding the mug himself and forcing some of it through her lips. "Why in hell did Celia let you run around loose?"

The girl choked a little over the coffee, but it began to warm her. She smiled at him, and even though her face was very thin, she had dimples. Killian glared at her. "Damn," he said again. "I thought you were supposed to be in bed."

"I couldn't stay there alone in that house. I felt so lost and—frightened, somehow. As if something—unpleasant—or—dangerous was hanging over me. I got up and tried to walk around the town a little to see if anything meant anything to me. I'm pretty weak—but everybody has helped me."

"Does anything mean anything to you?"

"No."

"It will," said Killian, "in time. After all, you were on the road to Cognac. It doesn't go anywhere else. You must have had some reason for coming here."

"I've—got to—find out who I am," said the girl wistfully, "I thought maybe when you thought about it—they said you know everybody—don't you know me?"

"No," said Killian shortly.

The girl covered her face with her hands and began to cry softly. "Stop that!" snapped Killian.

She did stop, looking up at him in shocked surprise and bewilderment. She seemed to be attempting to get up. "I'm sorry," she said pitifully. "I didn't mean to bother you."

"Drink your coffee," said Killian. He refilled the coffee mug. This time she was able to hold it herself. He brought her a sandwich, and she ate it. A little color began to come back into her face.

Suddenly she screamed.

Killian whirled abruptly, but saw only Smoky, who was settling down on his green desk blotter for a nap.

"I can't bear cats!" wailed the girl. "I never could bear cats!"

Killian pulled his eyebrows down. "How do you know?"

The girl turned her brown eyes full upon him in a strong and effective appeal. "I don't know," she said slowly. "How did I know?" She wrinkled her forehead and put her hand up, as if to hold the weight of her aching head.

"Forget it," advised Killian. "Cats won't hurt you."

"But I don't like them!"

"Look," said Killian, "I don't like Brussels sprouts or women with strong perfume or spot radio announcements or lots of things. But they're part of life and I accept them as such. You'd better start doing that about cats."

"But I don't like them!"

"So you said." Killian McBean went back to his typewriter. He took an assortment of envelopes from his pockets and began to decipher his scrawled, illegible notes on them. As fast as he got one deciphered, he typed up the short news item. When he had finished with the envelope, he tore it up and went on to the next.

"Please," said the girl almost frantically. "Please talk to me. Maybe that way something will come back to me. It's awful, not remembering. Why doesn't someone know me? *Someone* must know me." She seemed to be trying to convince herself of the fact.

"My paper goes to press tomorrow. The first run is this afternoon. It isn't even set up. I've got to finish the copy."

"You don't suppose," said the girl, "that I could have some connection with your paper?"

Killian whirled and gave her his closest attention. "What makes you say that?"

"This," the girl reached inside Celia's coat and brought out a legal looking paper. "I found it—inside my own coat. It seems to be the only paper I have."

Killian took the document and read it through without a word. He looked up and stared long and thoughtfully at the girl. Momentarily his eyes blazed. Then he read it through again.

"You—I don't like it when you look at me like that," said the girl. "It makes me feel—funny. It isn't anything wrong, is it?"

"It's a mortgage on my paper," said Killian. "A man named Gluts—Bennet Farr did hold it, but apparently he assigned his interest in it to a Leslie Landis. I didn't know anything about the assignment of interest, but that's what it says."

"Do you know who they are? Could they have any connection with me?"

Killian ran his tongue over his gold tooth. "Bennet Farr lives here in town. The biggest red brick house up on the hill is his."

"Can't we ask him if he knows who I am?"

Killian did not change his expression. He agreed coldly, "We'll do that."

"What about this—this Leslie Landis?"

"Does the name sound familiar to you?"

"I don't think so. I don't know. I can't remember!"

His eyes narrowed, watching her. "Maybe," he said, "you're Leslie Landis."

"You mean that's my name?"

"Maybe."

"Anyhow," she appealed hopefully, "we can find out by asking Mr.—what was it?—Farr, can't we?"

"Sure," Killian actually grinned at her.

Terrence Gillespie, the long lean young state's attorney, opened the door. He took off his hat and leaned against the wall watching them glumly.

"Somebody stuck a knife in Bennet Farr," he announced. "We just found him down at the hotel. He's dead."

"No!" said Killian McBean in pious surprise. His eyes lit up with undisguised pleasure. "Whatta story!"

"But—he can't be dead," stammered the girl. "I need him to tell me who I am!"

Terry looked unhappily at the ceiling, the floor, the opposite wall, anywhere but at Killian. "I—I'm sorry, Killian," he said apologetically. "But I'm afraid Amos is going to arrest either you or Ethan Droom. Aunty Pliny says you were both there this morning—and there was printer's type all over the room."

CHAPTER FIVE

"So you think Ethan or I killed Bennet Farr and scattered type all over the room to make sure you'd know who did it?" asked Killian. "It's insulting. I don't mind being accused of murder, but I'm damned if anybody as dumb as Amos is going to call me stupid."

"You—might have been in a hurry," said Terrence Gillespie inadequately.

Killian winked at the girl. "I was in a hurry."

"We—it really looks more like Ethan, anyway," said Terry apologetically. "There'd be no reason for you to have type in your pockets. Everybody knows Ethan always carries a pocketful. He loves the feel of it, I guess."

Killian reached into his right hand pocket. Wordlessly he scattered a handful of type out on the desk.

"I wish you hadn't done that, Killian," said the youthful state's attorney.

"Quit apologizing, Terry," said Killian coldly. "If you have enough evidence, arrest me. If you haven't and have enough on Ethan, arrest him. Otherwise get the hell out of here and stop taking up my time. I've got a paper to put out. It's never been late yet and it's not going to be now."

"I was hoping you'd take a more cooperative attitude," said Terry. "It's my job to uphold the law in this matter, Killian, and I've got to do it, in fairness to the public."

"Sure. The People's Friend. Wasn't that your election slogan? But it's my job to put out a paper and I'm going to do it too." Killian turned his back and went on deciphering the notes on the envelopes and typing up items from them.

The girl smiled wanly at Terrence Gillespie. "You look so young to be so official. I suppose you are official, aren't you?"

"I'm the state's attorney, Terrence Gillespie."

"Oh!" she sounded impressed. "Do—do you know me?"

"I'm afraid not."

Smoky jumped down from the desk and ran up the arm of Terry's chair and got into his lap. He held her without noticing, stroking her under the chin. Smoky put her head back and purred loudly. Whenever he stopped stroking, she bit him gently on the thumb. The girl shuddered delicately and turned her head away.

"I hate cats," she said.

"They are nice," said Terry absently. He stared at Killian McBean's back.

"Look, Killian," he said apologetically. "If I persuade Amos not to arrest you or Ethan—technically, that is—until after you put out this week's *Courier*—"

"It would help," admitted Killian over his shoulder.

Terrence Gillespie got up, stumbling over his own feet and carefully depositing Smoky back on the green blotter. "I'll see what I can do," he promised. "I have to go slowly; you realize my professional reputation is at stake. But after all, I suppose somebody could have framed you—with the type, I mean. Your office is always wide open and anybody could get some type. Certainly lots of people had motives for killing Bennet Farr—his wife and son and Celia for the money, I suppose; Ethan because he's so bitter about his leg; you because he was trying to take over your paper; Theodora because of Tommy Briggs; even—even Irene because of her job at the library—"

"Aunty Pliny because he got her husband's last cent and left her penniless," supplemented Killian. "You yourself—everybody knows he would have stopped at nothing to get you out as state's attorney. And Amos would make a likely suspect. If they had a fight, and Amos was going out on his ear—. There isn't anybody in town who wouldn't make a likely suspect, as far as that goes. Bennet Farr has had a mortgage or a loan or something he's gypped nearly everyone on."

"Yes," admitted Terrence Gillespie. "Probably a lot of people would have wanted to kill him—but how many of them would know he was at the Hotel Metropole?"

Killian wound his long arms in back of his head and nodded thoughtfully. "A good point."

"Celia and Dennis say they told you," said Terry, "and if Ethan was here, I suppose he could have heard. Aunty Pliny knew, of course, and Theodora or Irene might have seen him in the hall of the hotel. But otherwise—"

"I knew it," said the blonde girl suddenly. "I heard that red-haired girl tell that fat man out by the car."

"So Amos knew too."

"She said he was to go in the back door, it was open," said the girl. "I didn't know who he was then, of course, but I remember the name. She called him—Father Farr."

"Was she talking very loudly? Could anyone else have heard?"

"I don't know," replied the girl. "I don't think so. I don't think she meant even me to hear."

Killian shrugged. "That seems to limit the suspects, but it may not, Terry. You've always got to remember X, the unknown factor. One of us may have done it, or a total stranger may have seen him going into the hotel and followed him. A robber surprised in his room might have killed him."

"Cognac hasn't had a robbery in fifteen years. Besides, he wasn't robbed."

Killian's grin was grim. "If you aren't going to arrest me, Terry," he said coldly, "I might as well be getting down to the scene of the crime for my story. I'm a newspaper man as well as a suspect, you know. This ought to hit page one all over the country. I may be able to pay off that mortgage yet!"

"I don't know how Amos will feel about—" began Terry.

"To hell with Amos," said Killian McBean coldly. Then abruptly to the girl, "Have you got any money?"

"There was—quite a lot in the purse they said they picked up with me."

"O.K. Come on along and we'll get you a room at the hotel."

The girl shrank back. "But isn't that where—"

"You've got to get over being so squeamish," said Killian. "Cats, murders, everything bothers you. There's no reason for you to stay at Celia's. They have good beds at the Metropole. What you need is some sleep."

The girl smiled her wistful smile at him. "If you say so. You—you'll try to find out who I am, won't you?"

"Sure," said Killian. He picked up the mortgage, looking at it with longing. He hesitated. Then, "Meantime I'll put this in the office safe."

The room was still dark, drab and dingy. The only difference now was that it was also crowded. Old Doc was there, sitting at the desk scrawling laboriously at a report with a pen that scratched loudly. Amos Colvin was there, nearly filling the room with his bulk. So was his assistant, a small timid man named Jones, who was also an auxiliary fireman and as a sideline delivered milk.

"The murderer must have been very strong. That knife is in up to the hilt," Old Doc was saying.

Amos Colvin roared like a bull at the sight of Killian. "Get him out of here! He's a suspect!"

Killian put his elbow accidentally into Amos' stomach, with considerable force. "Press," he said firmly. "One side, fat stuff."

"Now, Killian," remonstrated Terrence Gillespie unhappily.

Killian circled Bennet Farr's body. "Where did the knife come from?"

"Somebody stole it from the hotel kitchen," explained Terrence Gillespie glumly. "It was empty and the back door was unlocked."

"He probably knows all about that," said Amos Colvin significantly.

Killian had gotten a battered envelope from his pocket and was making scattered notes on it, chewing his stubby red pencil. The story he was going to write absorbed him utterly. Paying no attention to Amos Colvin, he circled the corpse and the room like a bloodhound, sniffing. He demanded to see the contents of the dead man's wallet and pounced on the clipping about Dennis Farr's marriage. The questions he shot came like bullets.

"How long's he been dead, Old Doc? Not more than ten minutes when he was found? Well, I waited for him for nearly five; Terry said he was found right after I left, so the murder must have taken place in the five minutes or so before I came upstairs, unless the murderer was in his room while I was knocking. Maybe while I was talking to Aunty Pliny. Who discovered the body? Aunty Pliny, huh? She must have come right up after I left. Was there anybody in the room? No, I suppose there wouldn't be. Any fingerprints? Well, you ought to be looking for them by now. What've you been doing? Did anybody hear any sound of a struggle? Was the door locked or unlocked? Well, when are you going to start questioning people? What do you suppose that clipping in his wallet means?"

By this time Amos Colvin was sputtering with rage, Jones was regarding Killian with silent amazement, and Terrence Gillespie himself was getting more than a little annoyed. Only Old Doc's pen scratched on; he did not look up.

"Look here, Killian," Terry said with unexpected firmness. "You can't barge in here and tell us how to run this investigation! We're the officers of the law, not you."

"Sure you are," said Killian in the elaborately soothing tone one uses to a fretful child. Then he snapped suddenly. "And has it ever occurred to you—you officers of the law—that in a couple of hours at the most this story is going to be a national sensation? That reporters and photographers and sob sisters and curiosity seekers are going to pour in here from all over the country? You've got to have something prepared to tell them. You can't just say you haven't had time to look for fingerprints or question anybody or—I'll be back. Got to get this much on the wires. I ought to get a front page by-line out of this and a pretty good bonus. Maybe Farr's mortgage will get paid off yet."

"That gives you a motive!" squealed Amos Colvin.

Killian laughed. "Sure, fat stuff. I'll dicker about the best deal I can get for syndicating my confession, too." He pinched Amos' fat cheek, drawing forth a subdued roar and bolted out the door.

In the space of seconds he was cranking at the telephone in the lobby, demanding long distance. The story he reported was clear, concise and definite. The man at the other end of the line seemed well satisfied, asking only a few questions and giving a few instructions. Killian nodded his head violently and made a note or two on an envelope.

"Don't worry, George. I'll give you full coverage," he said. "I appreciate your confidence in not sending another man down. Sure. I'll let you know as soon as I can get it. Sure. Sure, OK."

He hung up and turned to go out on The Road.

"Killian!" called Irene Hubbard. She was behind the desk.

"'Morning, city girl," Killian grinned. "Given up the library for the hotel business?"

"No. But the library isn't open until noon today—you know, to save heat—and Aunty Pliny was hysterical about finding him, so I sent her home and took over the desk. There isn't anything to do, really. Mostly just answer the phone. There were only Mr. Farr and Theodora and the Pines and the Grays and me registered here, and the Pines are out of town and the Grays are in Florida, so I just give Theodora her key and take calls and sort the mail."

Killian McBean shook his head. "That's what you think now. Let me know what you think in a couple of hours. People are going to pour in here like rain through a leaky roof."

"You think so?"

"Where were you when all this was going on?" he asked abruptly.

Her eyes widened. "In my room, I guess, or else on The Road, talking to you. They—haven't decided exactly when it happened, have they?"

"You came in with me and went directly to your room?"

"Yes."

"Did you see anyone?"

"Only you and Aunty Pliny in the lobby."

"Nobody else? And nobody saw you?"

"No."

Killian grunted. "Did you hear anything? I mean, after you got to your room?"

Irene Hubbard thought carefully. "I don't think so. Only you when you were pounding on the door."

The McBean eyebrows went down. "Oh?"

"You did pound for quite a time, you know," Irene met his eyes squarely. "And I heard you calling from the hall. And then you waited in the hall a while and I heard you pounding some more. Finally I heard you going down the stairs again."

Killian thought this over for fully a minute. "I don't think you could have heard me going down the stairs," he said finally. "The carpet is pretty thick."

Irene nodded. "All right."

"You're sure it was me you heard?"

"Of course. That is—it sounded like your voice. It was you, wasn't it?"

"I got there a couple of minutes after you came up. Say three or four. I talked to Aunty Pliny about that long."

"That was when I heard you."

"What about Theodora?"

"She didn't hear anything. She's deaf, you know. Not totally, and she can get along fine in normal conversation by reading lips, but she wouldn't hear things like knocking on doors."

"Her room is next to Farr's, isn't it?"

"Yes."

"Convenient for the murderer."

Irene hesitated. "She—she told Terry she saw your printer Ethan Droom in the hall when she came up, though. He was just going around the corner to the back stairs. She only saw his back, but of course she could see his wooden leg. She said she thought there was some woman with him: she saw a flash of skirt."

"I suppose Theodora has no witnesses that she was in her room at the time of the killing?"

Irene's gasp was unconvincing. Her whole story was, for that matter. "She was alone. But, Killian, you don't think she—"

"She might have. You might have. I might have. Until the case is solved, anyone might have." Killian patted her hand. "I hope you didn't, city girl."

"Thanks," Irene smiled sweetly at him. "Do you work all the time?"

"Most of it."

"Don't you take time off to eat dinner?"

Killian laughed. "I haven't had breakfast yet."

"I mean—do you always eat alone?"

He kissed her lightly on the cheek. "I didn't know you cared, city girl."

"Killian!" she blushed. "Right here in the lobby!"

"Maybe the library would be better at that. I'll drop in some night and we'll go down to Sloppy Pete's and wrap ourselves around a couple of steaks. How's that?"

"Lovely. Do you think I'm a huzzy for asking you to take me to dinner, Killian?"

"Sure." He winked casually. "So long, city girl."

From the stairs the angry face of Terrence Gillespie watched Killian leave.

CHAPTER SIX

KILLIAN MCBEAN's predictions proved only too true. Within three hours, Cognac was crowded with strangers. The noon train disgorged them; several cars jammed with reporters and photographers arriving from Chicago; farmers and others poured in from near by farms and villages.

"Gnats! You'd think we struck gold," grumbled Ethan.

Killian looked up from his work. "Maybe we have."

The porch had now been scrubbed clean, and all was in order. The remodeled McBean home, now housing the *Cognac Courier*, was stucco below and brown shingle above, with the porch green over loose white lattice work, and the shutters white.

Since it was the first house at the north end of Cognac, everyone entering the town had to go by it. Many of the visitors from near by were subscribers of the *Courier*, and following Cognac custom, dropped in for a cup of coffee and a chat with the editor. Most of the reporters and photographers did, too, some curious, some condescending, some frankly envious. Killian received them all with enthusiasm; his greeting was warm and friendly, his handshake firm and cordial. Only his eyes remained aloof, cold, thoughtful.

The telephone jangled frequently, and Killian used it often, checking on personal items as he worked. He also made several calls to Old Doc, to Terrence Gillespie, and even to Amos Colvin, following the progress of the investigation of Bennet Farr's death.

"They seem to be getting nowhere fast," he growled at Ethan. "No fingerprints but Farr's. The door was unlocked and the key on Farr's desk. Nobody saw anybody in the kitchen at the time the knife was supposedly stolen. The only clue is the printer's type."

Ethan had sobered up with remarkable suddenness and was hobbling about his duties with an intensity that was noticeable. He did not answer Killian, or indicate any interest in the investigation, but every time the phone rang, he contrived to have some justifiable reason for being near by. He drank frequent cups of coffee, and his hands became steadier with each cup. He worked at a remarkable speed.

Between visitors, Killian also worked fast at the copy, typing hard, discussing makeup with Ethan, putting the finishing touches on the editorials, reading proof as it was set up. They talked about the Farr case only as newspaper men discussing The Story of the Week.

Finally, about two o'clock, Killian pushed back his chair. "That should take care of the first run," he said. "I've written and read copy on pages two, three, six and seven and most of the copy for the second run is ready to set up. General news, country correspondence, briefs, personals, editorials, features, farm news, legal advertising, all under control. Guess it should keep you busy for a while. Want some expert help?"

Ethan snorted and stamped his wooden leg for emphasis. His voice rose shrilly. "Gnats! I don't need any help. When I'm not capable of setting up my own paper and running Gwen—why I was setting up the *Courier* when you were in three cornered pants!"

Killian grinned. "I just thought I'd ask. I knew you'd never let anybody else touch Gwen. She'd probably bite anybody who did." He put on his overcoat and hesitated in the door. Finally he said, "Better get some lunch," and went out.

He stopped in THE ALL-NITE GRILL, known informally to all in Cognac as Sloppy Pete's, and had two rare hamburgers with onions and some more coffee, eating and drinking absently, with his eyes fixed on the picture of a large blonde Venus, and his mind nowhere in the room. Sloppy Pete's was nearly empty, because of the late hour and the fact that Pete, its proprietor, had all but run out of food feeding the visitors.

The Grill was a long thin building, with a plate glass window filled with blooming begonias. It had bright blue walls covered with some extremely modernistic art to which Pete modestly admitted giving birth. There were six or eight oilcloth covered tables and a long linoleum covered counter with built-in chairs around it. Killian, when alone, sat in one of these, chatting with Pete, an always potent news source. Today, however, he chose a table.

"Hello, Mr. McBean," said a quiet voice at his elbow.

Killian jumped. He turned to see the blonde girl who had been in the accident. She had plainly benefited by her rest. She still wore Celia's fur coat, and under it a trim plaid jumper. With makeup on, and some of the dazed weariness gone, she was very attractive.

"Well!" said Killian. "Not bad. Where did that outfit come from? Paris?"

The girl's dimples showed slightly. "There—there were some

clothes in the bags in the back of the car I was driving," she said. "At least, I suppose I was driving it—they found me behind the wheel, they said. The clothes don't seem to belong to anybody else, and they fit me."

"Sit down," said Killian. "Want a hamburger? They've run out of everything but hamburgers."

"No, thank you," she said. She sat down. "I had lunch with Celia and her aunt."

"Aunty Pliny isn't Celia's aunt," Killian was watching her closely. "Celia just took her in to live with her after her mother died. She was all alone in the big house, and Aunty Pliny had just lost her husband. Celia is away a lot anyway. Aunty prefers to maintain her independence by working a few hours a day at the Metropole, but Celia gives her a home. She isn't really her aunt, though. Everybody in Cognac calls her Aunty."

"Oh." The tall blond thought this over. "I wondered how she could be everybody's. Aunt, I mean."

"Headache better?"

"I guess so. It comes and goes. Sometimes it hardly hurts at all, and then in a few minutes it's awful."

"Any signs of your memory returning?"

"No," she said wistfully. She put her hand instinctively to her head, as if seeking its contents. "That is, I know who I am, but they told me. I still don't remember. They say my name is Leslie Landis."

"Who says so?"

"They checked the California license plates on my car. They're in the name of Leslie Landis, and so was that mortgage, and they found this out by the accident. It got tramped down somehow."

Killian took the torn piece of paper she handed him. It was a California driver's license. Although jagged along the edge, its information was clear enough: "Leslie Landis; sex, female; race, white. Color of eyes, brown; color of hair, blonde. Height, five feet six inches. Weight 110 pounds. Date of birth, May 10, 1916."

He studied her, point by point. The description was undoubtedly hers; it coincided in all particulars. He held the paper to the light, pulled it gently, turned it around and over.

There were no erasures of any sort; the form and official signatures were perfectly authentic. The license seemed undoubtedly a genuine one.

"It all adds up, doesn't it?" the girl was saying. "I must be Leslie Landis. They're still trying to check up on who I really am, though. Nobody ever seems to have heard of a woman named Leslie Landis."

Killian tossed a coin on the table and got up slowly. Leslie Landis walked beside him, only a little unsteadily. Her long legs made her stride very graceful. She had plenty of what is known as sex-appeal. Killian gave her a coldly appreciative glance. She lowered her eyes.

"I—I came in here to see you," she confided. "I was going by and I saw you and I came in. I want to ask you a favor."

Killian shrugged.

"I wondered if I could help around your newspaper office?"

The man stopped dead still and glared at her. "You wondered what?"

"If I could help around your newspaper office. You see, my coming here and nobody knowing me and all—the only thing I had was that mortgage. So—it looks as if my coming must have had something to do with your paper, doesn't it? And if it did, maybe I was connected with newspapers somehow—maybe if I got in the atmosphere again my memory would come back."

"You don't have the faintest idea how Farr came to sign that mortgage over to you?"

She shook her head. "I never saw him before. They took me in to the undertaking parlor, but—I'm sure I never saw him before."

"You can't be sure," he pointed out coldly. "There must have been some connection for him to make over the mortgage to you. That piece of paper had more than a money value to him. And he was never known to be generous with his money, either."

"Maybe if you'll let me work with you in your office, I'll remember what the connection was."

"I'm not running a convalescent home," said Killian McBean coldly. "I may not own the *Courier* long, but while I do, it'll be a newspaper. I wouldn't hire you even if you were an experienced newspaper woman, and I certainly don't want any amateurs around. I don't believe in females around a newspaper office."

She stopped uncertainly in the middle of The Road and looked as if she were going to cry. "Please help me, Mr. McBean."

"Don't wail. I'll help you all I can. But there's no philanthropy connected with running a newspaper."

"I won't get in your way, really I won't. Maybe I'll be really good. It's the only thing I can think of that might help me. I haven't anybody to turn to, or anywhere to go. It's an awful feeling, not knowing who you are."

"No doubt," said Killian with frigid patience. "But the *Cognac Courier* isn't run on a sentimental basis."

"Celia said she wouldn't be able to write the social news for you any more, now that she had Mrs. Farr to look after, and you would be needing someone—"

Killian swore. "So it was Celia's idea."

"Not her idea exactly. She just said—"

"Tell her I'll write my own social news," said Killian. "I only had her do it anyway because Bennet Farr wouldn't let me into his shindigs and everybody always wanted the guest lists and such."

"I could still get them for you. And maybe—on this murder case—there might be things I could get out of the chief of police or state's attorney that you couldn't."

"There might," he admitted grudgingly.

"And then, it looks as if I held the mortgage on your paper. And if you shouldn't be able to pay it—Mr. Colvin said it was due in about two months—the paper wouldn't be much good to me, would it? I mean, we should be able to work something out."

"Either," said Killian, "you're awfully dumb or awfully smart. I'll let you know later which it is."

She opened her golden-brown eyes wide and smiled at him. She said timidly, "Then you will let me stay?"

"Temporarily," said Killian McBean. "But it's against my better judgment. And I warn you, my interests are mercenary. I'd sell my soul for that mortgage."

She laughed outright then, a soft cooing laugh that was as attractive as the rest of her.

Killian nodded appreciatively. "Sister," he murmured, "you're good."

"I don't know what you mean!" said Leslie Landis.

"Don't you think," Leslie Landis was asking gently, "that if I'm going to be your assistant, Mr. McBean, that I ought to know a little more about the Farr case?"

"I suppose so," Killian snapped. "And stop calling me Mr. McBean. It drives me nuts. What do you want to know?"

"Well—who people are and what they might have to gain by killing Mr. Farr."

Killian answered her, but he seemed to be more sorting over his own thoughts than imparting information. "Bennet Farr was the biggest and richest man in Cognac—and the corruptest. His nickname—Old Gluts —was short for Old Glutton. He inherited some money and a small lumber business from his father, and he made more money and built up one of the most profitable lumber businesses in the state.

"Most of the timber around here was used up by the time Bennet Farr inherited his money, so he shipped in a lot of specialty woods and made expensive finished articles. He didn't employ so many men, but he made big profits. And of course he dabbled in mortgages and loans—anything with money in it. He made plenty. Then in late years he began to play politics—first local, then state, and lately national. Not as a candidate; he never ran for office. He just wanted to be the power behind the throne. He always lived in Cognac, but some pretty important people came here to see him."

"Do you think somebody from outside the town killed him?"

He shook his head. "I doubt it. Any strangers would have been reported. It had to be someone around to hear he was at the hotel. Apparently the only two places where that was discussed were my office and the scene of your accident. There were no outsiders at either place, except you—and even there, it wasn't generally announced. No, the circumstances definitely limit the number of suspects. Otherwise, the field is wide open. Practically anybody who ever knew him would have liked to kill Bennet Farr."

Leslie Landis looked bewildered. "But why? I mean, if he was such an important figure and brought all those important people to Cognac—"

"I hated him," Killian McBride stated calmly, "because he was power-mad. He wanted to grind everybody he met under his heel. He wanted to control everything; nothing was too small for his notice. My father fought him before me, and I hardly hit town again before I started in, too. Our latest battle was over the new fire engine. Cognac needs one badly; we got a priority and everything—and Bennet Farr was bucking it because it cost too much money."

"I thought you said he was rich."

"He was. But he wasn't giving up a cent to help anybody but himself. He wasn't miserly—he entertained on a grand scale, and traveled, and educated his son expensively, and put thousands into doctors for his wife—but his house was fireproof and none of his tax money was going to protect somebody else's house. He opposed the library and the schools on practically the same lines. He had all the books he needed himself; his son went to private schools. He wouldn't carry any kind of insurance or put in any safety devices for his workmen at the mill until the law made him. It was because of an unguarded machine there that Ethan lost his leg."

"Who is Ethan?"

"Ethan Droom. He's my printer. There was a time under Pliny, the man who owned the *Courier* after my father died and before I came back to Cognac, when they only got the paper out every two weeks. So Ethan went to work for Bennet Farr part time. Ethan is wonderful with his hands. He lost his leg when something on the machine went haywire—he was in the hospital for months, and he never got a cent. Farr could at least have paid his bills, but he didn't. Ethan is still paying them. And afterwards Ethan's wife died of cancer, and he always thought she could have been saved if he had had more money and fewer debts. Actually it wouldn't have made much difference, but Ethan always felt that it would. He was devoted to Penny, his wife, and he broods over it. He never mentions her, and he may say he's brooding over something else, but fundamentally that's it."

"Poor man," said Leslie Landis. "He must have hated Bennet Farr very much."

Killian shrugged. "Probably no more than the rest of us. I always felt he ran my father into his grave prematurely. Farr's own wife, Frances, openly says she owes her ill-health to his treatment of her before their son was born."

"Is she an invalid?"

"I don't know if you'd call her exactly an invalid. She has a lot of doctors and spends most of her time in bed or in a wheel chair. But as far as I know it's largely mental—I've never heard of any specific physical complaint, except from her, and she changes every week. When she wants to, she gets around town pretty well under her own power. She isn't very old. But her mind is—strange. She isn't crazy, but she's—I guess simple is the best word."

"Might she have murdered him?"

"Anybody might have murdered him. If you mean would she have had the strength to do it, sure, I think so. But if she wanted to kill him, and had the nerve, which is the moot point, why should she run the risk of being seen going into the hotel when she could do it any time at home?"

"Maybe to make it look like an outside job."

"Maybe. But personally I doubt if Frances would have the guts to kill anybody, even Bennet Farr. Besides, with him dead, she isn't a martyr any more. Frances loves being a martyr."

"I suppose she will inherit a lot of money?"

"No doubt." Killian drew his eyebrows down. "Probably she and Dennis Farr, the son, will divide it."

"He's the one who came in to see Celia at lunch?"

"That's right. They're engaged. Ever since they were children living next door to each other Bennet Farr had it predetermined that they were to marry. Celia has a good name and a small income of her own, and Bennet Farr thought he could control her and through her, Dennis. He always had a little trouble controlling Dennis."

Leslie Landis dimpled. "I'm glad he had trouble with somebody. What did Dennis do?"

"Nothing spectacular like going off to lead his own life or anything like that. He's too fond of luxury and money. But he was always wild and he drank and five years ago when he was a senior at an eastern college he eloped with some chorus girl."

"Did he marry her?"

"Yes. But Papa Farr chartered a special plane and flew down and grabbed sonny away before he came to. He jammed a divorce through the next week."

"What happened to the chorus girl?"

"Nobody ever heard. I suppose Bennet Farr bought her off. Anyhow, she never turned up again."

"And now Dennis Farr is engaged to Celia?"

"She was engaged to him at the time he married the chorus girl. It was quite a shock to her, but Bennet Farr talked her out of it. She went away for a couple of years and even after she came back, she dallied a little, but last year she took Dennis back as soon as he looked at her again. They're engaged again."

Leslie Landis shook her head. "Celia certainly seems to be crazy about him."

"She is," Killian snapped, suddenly angry. "In everything else she's spunky and independent, won't take anything from anybody. But where Dennis Farr is concerned she's always been putty, even as a little girl. Sometimes I think she's getting over it, but—"

"Do you think," asked Leslie Landis, "that she might have killed Bennet Farr?"

"I'd hate to think so," said Killian, "but the fact remains, she'd do anything for Dennis. And his father has held Dennis back for years. At least that's Dennis' story."

"Why isn't he in the army?"

"He has practically no sight in his left eye. It was struck by a piece of wood when he was a boy; one of the kids was shooting stuff around on a rubber band. He can see light and shadow out of it, but that's all."

"Do you think he might have murdered his father?"

"He would be my choice of suspects," admitted Killian. "But maybe that's just prejudice. Certainly he'll come into plenty of dough and complete independence by Bennet's death. And he never made the slightest pretense of caring anything about Bennet. Neither did anyone else, of course—even his wife."

"Maybe Dennis was mad at his father for breaking up his marriage."

"Maybe. I never heard anything about it, though. But I probably wouldn't have. Dennis Farr isn't exactly in the habit of confiding in me." Killian grinned.

"What about those two girls they said lived on the same floor at the hotel?"

"The assistant librarian, Irene Hubbard, and the schoolteacher, Theodora Meredith? I don't know them very well. They've only been in town a few weeks. Theodora came in October, and Irene about a week later. I suppose the schoolboard and library checked their references, but it's pretty hard to get anybody in a small town these days because of low wages, so they might not have been as carefully checked as they normally would be."

"Do you think either of them might have done it?"

Killian shook his head. "It's hard to say what a casual acquaintance might or might not have done under any given set of circumstances. They both knew he was at the Metropole, and of course they had the best opportunity—just wait until no one was in the hall, slip in and kill him, go back to their rooms and act as if nothing had happened. Irene has plenty of spunk to her; I think she would be perfectly capable of murder, under certain conditions. Whether the mere threatened loss of her job would be enough motive or not, I couldn't say. It would depend on how much that particular job meant to her. She might have had some other motive we don't know about. Bennet Farr was never a lady's man, but he might have done something financially to her or one of her family. Theodora was feeling pretty bitter about a pupil of hers he had sent to reform school a couple of days ago. I think she would be capable of it, all right."

"Mercy," breathed Leslie Landis. "I never saw so many people who might have killed someone. Is there anybody else?"

"There's the desk clerk, Aunty Pliny. I told you about her. She's a rather old lady, but she's pretty vigorous. She would have a pass key to his room, of course—and the same opportunity Irene and Theodora had. The motive would be one of financial revenge. It doesn't sound very probable, because she had had the same motive for at least four years—since her husband died. But as far as I know this was the first and only time Bennet Farr was ever at the hotel. She might have been biding her time. She's a pretty spiteful old lady."

"I hope that's all."

"I think so," Killian was still thinking out loud. "There's Amos Colvin, the chief of police, of course. He knew Bennet Farr was going to be at the hotel. But he says he was going to see him later in the morning, and hadn't been there. I think he's telling the truth; I don't see how anybody Amos' size could go in and out of anywhere and not be seen. And why he should want to kill Farr is beyond me. I personally know they were on the best of terms just before your accident. Unless they quarreled afterwards. Amos Colvin was Bennet Farr's man. He had everything to gain with him alive. With him dead, he'll probably be thrown out by the irate citizens. Under the lead of the *Courier*, I'm going to start the campaign next week. Unless I'm in jail."

Leslie Landis shook her blonde hair. "Don't tell me they think you did it!"

"I don't know. Maybe they don't really think so, but they're putting up quite a bluff. I don't believe Terry thinks so. I don't know. Terry has always been a sort of unknown quantity."

"The young state's attorney? Why?"

"He came here from the city about six months ago. He's a good lawyer, as far as I know, and certainly he appears to be honest, if spineless. The *Courier* backed him for the state's attorney job when the vacancy came. It was more a matter of not wanting Bennet Farr's candidate than of wanting him, I'll admit. He has ulcers so the army won't take him. But there's something very peculiar about him. He seems to have come practically out of a vacuum. There's no link with his past. Nobody ever comes to see him, nobody even writes him."

"How do you know?"

"It's part of a newspaper man's job in a small town to know who gets mail," said Killian calmly. "I'm always at the post office when the mail comes in. There are only two trains a day. I pick up a lot of personals that way. Everybody in town is always there. But there's never anything in Terry's box and he never shows up."

"Maybe he's an orphan or something."

"Maybe. But he doesn't mix much—just does his job and goes his way alone. I wouldn't say he had a close friend in town. Nobody knows any more about him than the day he came."

"I'll see what I can find out," said Leslie Landis, "now that I'm a reporter." Laughing, she put her hand through his arm and turned the not inconsiderable power of her smile on him. She looked thoughtful. "You didn't kill Bennet Farr, did you, darling?"

CHAPTER SEVEN

The massive oak door of the Farr house was covered by a large and ornate wreath, trailing purple streamers. Killian rang the bell and walked calmly in when the door opened. "Press," he said calmly to the butler. "I think Mrs. Farr will see me."

"I think Mrs. Farr will not," said Dennis Farr, appearing from the drawing room as if jerked by a string. His handsome face was lined and tired, his broad shoulders drooped. "The nerve of you, daring to come here!"

"Oh, Mr. Farr!" cooed Leslie Landis. "It's good to see you again!"

"Oh," Dennis Farr brightened and cast an admiring glance at her slim attractive figure. "Come in, Miss—they decided your name was Landis, didn't they?"

"That's right. But I couldn't possibly come in with out Mr. McBean. I work for him now. I'm a reporter!"

Dennis curled his lip indecisively. He looked at Leslie again. "All right," he said grudgingly to the butler. "See if my mother wants to see this reporter. Come in and sit down, Miss Landis."

Leslie looked doubtfully at Killian, who winked. "I'll wait

here," he said. Leslie went into the drawing room, clinging to Dennis Farr's arm.

"Why, Celia!" Killian heard her say. "How nice that you're here!"

As the door closed, Killian had only a glimpse of Celia Austen's strained face, looking at Dennis and Leslie. Her small hands were clenched tightly in her lap. "You do get around, don't you?" she said coldly to Leslie.

After a few moments, the butler reappeared, with word that Mrs. Farr would receive Mr. McBean in her upstairs sitting room.

Killian mounted the stairs behind the evidently disapproving butler and turned without directions to the right and entered an ornate sitting room, rather overstuffed with heavy antique furniture and ruffled pillows and curtains. In the middle of it stood a plumpish woman in her late forties. Her hair was bleached a violent yellow, without a trace of white to soften it around her face. The face needed softening, for while Killian could remember when it was the prettiest face in Cognac, now it was wrinkled and tired and discontented. Her voice was whining. There was no sign of any grief, however.

"Oh, Killian!" Mrs. Bennet Farr extended two flabby hands. Killian took them both in his and squeezed them. She held her face up to be kissed. She was. "I knew you'd come."

"Just a reporter getting his story, Frances," Killian grinned.

She giggled a little. "I wanted you to see the dress I'm going to wear to the funeral. This is it. Do you like it?" She paraded self-consciously before a long mirror. The dress was a shiny black material, with ruffles around the neck and down the front to the waist, and large ornate pockets in the skirt.

Killian swallowed. "Very pretty."

Frances Farr giggled again. "You always said that to me, Killian. Do you remember the first time? I had on a party dress—pink, it was, with ruffles all down the skirt—and I was going to a dance with some other boy, and you said I was the prettiest thing you'd ever seen and that some day you were going to marry me?"

"I remember." Killian did not feel it necessary to add that at the time he had been thirteen to Frances' eighteen, and that two months later Frances had married Bennet Farr.

Frances flounced around the room again.

"I'm glad to see you're able to be up and around today, Frances."

Mrs. Bennet Farr plopped suddenly into a chair. "I'm not really *able*," her whine became more pronounced. "It's just that I force myself—we must carry on, you know. But my back is killing me. All night long I had the most terrible shooting pains—and my kidneys—Killian, you just wouldn't believe the trouble I have with my kidneys!"

"Too bad," soothed Killian. "Who do you think killed Bennet, Frances?"

She giggled. "Did you?"

"No."

She looked disappointed. "I thought maybe—because you've always felt that way about me and never married—"

Killian squeezed his watch. "I didn't kill him, Frances."

"Oh," she accepted his statement and felt around. "Do you suppose Dennis did?"

"Do you think he might have?"

"I don't know," her tone was doubtful. "They had an awful row last night after dinner. But then, they've always been quarreling, ever since Dennis was a little boy. He was such a sweet little boy. Do you remember, Killian?"

"I wasn't around much then," said Killian. "I went away to school, and afterwards—he was pretty big by the time I got back."

"Celia might have killed him," said Frances Farr suddenly. "I hope it was Celia. She's such a horrid girl."

"Now, Frances!" said Killian.

"You don't know."

"What was Bennet doing out at Indian Mound at five o'clock this morning?" Killian asked indifferently.

She smiled coyly. "He was meeting some one. I don't know who."

"A woman?"

"Certainly not!" Frances flared. There was no doubting her intensity, although her accuracy was more than questionable. "It was a man. You know Bennet never looked at any other girl but me, don't you, Killian?"

"Sure. Was the man a stranger or someone from Cognac?"

She was momentarily surprised. "From Cognac, of course. At least, I suppose so." Her voice was suddenly worried. "Bennet never did look at any other girl but me, did he, Killian?"

"Of course not." His tone was soothing, as to a child. "Why did Bennet go to the hotel?"

"He called and left word that he was going to meet somebody there. I don't know whether it was the same person or not. I don't know who it was." She brightened suddenly. "It's time for my favorite radio serial. The Faddens. Do you listen to the Faddens, Killian?"

"No, I don't believe I do," said Killian.

"Stay and hear it with me now."

"I'm afraid I can't today," Killian answered. "Today's copy day."

She giggled. "You and your silly little paper!"

Killian got up. "I'll try to see you later, Frances. In a couple of days, anyway."

She put her face up again to be kissed. "How long do you think I'll have to wear mourning, Killian? Black was never my best color, you know. I'm still a young woman. I am still a young woman, aren't I, Killian?"

"Of course you are," Killian's voice was gentle, but his eyes were hard. He kissed her flabby cheek. "What were Denny and Bennet quarreling about last night, Frances?"

"I don't know exactly. I couldn't go down stairs—my heart, you know—and all I could hear was what Denny said when he came out in the hall."

"What did he say?"

"He said, 'Why don't *you* marry her, then? I tell you I won't marry Celia Austen if she has ten million dollars.'"

Killian went out into the hall and ran straight into Celia. Her tiny figure was tense and erect. She pushed back her auburn hair and glared at him furiously. For a moment he thought she had heard Frances' last remark.

But what she said was, "Killian McBean, that—that female reporter of yours is down there throwing herself at Denny in the most shameless manner, and he's holding her hand and loving it—and if you don't get her out of here, I'll—I'll kill her!"

Jean was sitting in the newspaper office when Killian came back, her usually rosy cheeks white. With great circles under her eyes, she looked more than her sixteen years. She had on the same skirt and sweater as early that morning and sat scuffing her dirty white moccasins.

"Did you get any sleep at all?" he asked her disapprovingly.

"Of course," she answered. She looked up and met his eyes defiantly. "I was asleep in bed all night."

Killian set his lips and drew his eyebrows down. He looked into the back room where her father was hard at work at his press. Ethan was very happy, stumping his wooden leg and talking to Gwen at the top of his voice, now abusive, now wheedling. Killian took a mug of coffee and sat down and lit his pipe before he answered Ethan's daughter. Then what he said was, "Did you bring the highschool notes?"

The girl brightened a little and got up and brought them to him. He looked them over coldly, criticizing the structure of a sentence here, the choice of a word there. One or two items he blue-pencilled altogether.

"What about the committees for the junior prom benefit dance?" he asked. "Where are they?"

"Are they important? They're just a lot of names."

"Certainly they're important. Names make the newspaper business—particularly the small town weekly. Everyone likes to see his name in the paper, and so do his friends and relatives. Don't forget that again. Get those committees now."

"Yes, Uncle Killian." Much of the overflowing energy had left Jean; in contrast with her visit early that morning, she appeared meek and downtrodden. "May I use your phone?"

"All right, but make it snappy. The phone in a newspaper office has to be kept open."

When Jean had called up and gotten the necessary names, she started to leave, but Killian, who had been watching her closely while ostensibly typing, stopped her.

"Wait a minute," he said.

Jean fidgeted uneasily. Talking fast, she made a valiant try at nonchalance. "Don't be goon bait, Uncle Killian," she said.

"I have a heavy date with a brush mush. I'm just drolling with schooling and I want to get in a little stardusting before that gabble gathering tonight."

Killian made an abrupt gesture dismissing her entire effort. "Are you too tired to do an errand for me?" he asked.

She brightened. "Of course not, Uncle Killian."

"I want you to go down to the garage and get my car and drive it across the county line and send a telegram for me. Don't go over thirty-five and remember I want to use the car again sometime."

"Why, Uncle Killian," she protested, "you know I passed my driver's license tests!"

"You must have bribed the inspector," he said coldly. "Or else he was blind. Remember I'm going to look at the fenders when you get home. And see that you make it well before dark. I'm very fond of having my car in one piece and uncrumpled."

"I'll be very careful," she promised. "Why don't you send the telegram from here?"

"Because it happens to be very private," he explained patiently. "And see that you don't do any talking about it, either."

Her eyes widened delightedly. "Secrets, Uncle Killian?"

"Something like that."

"I won't say a word," she promised. She regarded him wistfully. "*Were* you a gangster like they say, Uncle Killian?"

"Read it over to be sure you get the message and then get going."

She read the address of a large detective agency in Chicago.

"STEVE: PLEASE TRACE RECORD OF THEODORA MEREDITH, EMPLOYED AS SCHOOLTEACHER IN COGNAC, ILLINOIS,

SINCE OCTOBER THIS YEAR. PREVIOUS RECORD OF DEAFNESS? ALSO TRACE ONE LESLIE LANDIS, BELIEVED TO HAVE NEWSPAPER BACKGROUND. WANT NAME OF OWNER OF CALIFORNIA LICENSE A167-389. WANT DESCRIPTION ON CALIFORNIA DRIVER'S LICENSE B913482 TO CHECK IF GENUINE. ALSO RECORD OF IRENE HUBBARD, EMPLOYED COGNAC AS ASSISTANT TO LIBRARIAN. PARTICULARLY INTERESTED IN THEIR WHEREABOUTS FIVE YEARS AGO LAST OCTOBER 15TH, POSSIBILITY THEY WERE IN WALDO, CONNECTICUT. ALSO TRACE HISTORY AND PRESENT WHEREABOUTS OF ROSA KINCAID, CHORUS GIRL WHO MARRIED DENNIS FARR IN WALDO, CONNECTICUT FIVE YEARS AGO OCTOBER 15TH. WANT PICTURE. URGENT. RUSH. USE LETTERS ABCD IN ORDER NAMED. SENT TWO SAMPLES OF BLOOD THIS A.M. TO BE ANALYZED AND TYPED. SHOULD REACH YOU TOMORROW. RUSH. KILLIAN."

"Uncle Killian!" gasped Jean. "Code! Why do you want Irene and Theodora and Leslie investigated? And what does Dennis Farr's wife have to do with it?"

"I think a good deal," he said slowly. "Bennet Farr wasn't acting normally before his death. He was up and out at an hour he was always asleep; he went to the hotel instead of to his home. He was excited and sent for me promising me a story. He left the door to the back stairs at the hotel open. And he had a clipping about Dennis' marriage in his wallet."

"Yes," said Jean. "I wondered about that."

There was a moment's dead silence. Killian looked her up and down frigidly. "What did you say?"

Jean blushed and bit her lip. "I mean—did he?"

"There would be no way you could have known the clipping was in his wallet except to see it there. There has been no announcement of it."

Jean looked him straight in the eye. "I don't know what you're talking about."

"Tell the truth," he said sternly.

Ethan appeared suddenly in the doorway. "She is telling the truth, Killian McBean!" he shrilled.

Killian looked from the girl's flushed face to her father's angry one. His eyes went from one to the other several times. Finally he shrugged. "I hope you know what you're doing, Ethan."

"I know what I'm doing, all right," said the old man. He stumped back to his work, his wooden leg making a thumping sound on the wooden floor.

"As I was saying," said Killian coldly to Jean, disregarding the tears in her eyes. "There would be no reason for Bennet Farr to carry that clipping around in his wallet for five years. He must have put it there lately. Which means that something in connection with that marriage had been recently revived. The most likely supposition is that Rosa Kincaid had turned up again. She may, of course, have turned up and gone away again, without anybody being the wiser. But if she had anything to do with the story Bennet Farr was going to give me; if she murdered him, for instance, to prevent his giving it out, she must be still here in Cognac; nobody who was here at the time of the murder has left since. I checked it with the Miltons, who live at the head of The Road. They said no cars or people have left today. And of course there weren't any trains until noon. The hotel has been thoroughly searched, and there was no place else for a stranger to hide until then.

"Obviously, therefore, if Rosa Kincaid is in Cognac, she has assumed another identity; apparently one in which Bennet Farr did not at first recognize her. That shouldn't be too difficult; he probably only saw her once and no doubt she had some acting ability and experience. She may even have gone on the stage. If Bennet Farr was not thinking about her, she would probably be perfectly safe. But if Rosa Kincaid is here in Cognac, she must be one of three people—Irene, Leslie, or Theodora."

"I don't see why," Jean rubbed at her tears with a defiant fist.

Killian McBean sighed. "What do you do with your handkerchiefs, eat them? I've never seen you with one in a crisis yet." He took out his own immaculate one and got up and wiped her face with it. "Blow."

Jean did. "You t-treat me like a child!"

He patted her. "You'll be an old hag soon enough. Rosa Kincaid would have to be either Leslie or Irene or Theodora simply because there are no other young women strangers who have come to Cognac lately. She may have been a little older or younger than Dennis Farr, but probably not much. He's about twenty-eight or nine. Say she couldn't be under twenty-five, or over thirty or thirty-five. And if one of them is Rosa, it's practically certain she murdered Bennet Farr. There would be no other purpose in her coming here under a disguise."

Jean looked at him. Her lips trembled and her eyes spilled over.

"Stop wailing," said Killian crossly. He mopped her face again.

Jean looked at the pressroom. She lowered her voice to a whisper. "But, Uncle Killian," she said. "*Rosa Kincaid didn't kill him.*"

He pulled his eyebrows down. "Can you prove that?"

"*I know, Uncle Killian.*"

Killian swore. "Get going and send that telegram. Wash your

face first. I don't want girls going wailing out of my office on to The Road. It'll give the *Courier* a bad name."

"I'm not wailing!" but Jean washed her face. When she left she had even recovered sufficiently to respond in kind when a youth of high school age who happened to be passing called to her.

"What's your story, morning glory? Are you rationed, sugar?"

"Now you're flying with Doolittle," said Jean coolly. "Am I still number one on your hep parade?"

Killian shook his head in a dazed fashion, but the smile with which he watched Jean was indulgent. Then his face hardened and he went into the back room and signaled to Ethan to stop his work. Ethan refused, with gestures, over the noise of the machinery. Killian insisted. Finally Ethan complied and followed Killian to the front office, grumbling volubly, stumping loudly.

"You'll never be the newspaper man your Pa was," he shrilled. "Gnats! I'm a busy man! Never put a *Courier* out late in my life. I'm not going to start now for any whippersnapper with big city ideas."

Killian did not grin. He growled right back at Ethan. "This is still my newspaper, and I'm still deciding how it's managed. You're only making the first run. The second run isn't even made up. The *Courier* doesn't come out until tomorrow. Your reputation is in no danger. Your neck is, though. Don't you know they hang people for murder?"

Ethan grew apoplectic. "Gnats! You can't talk to me like that," he screamed. "I don't have to take no lip from anybody. I quit. I'm through. Set up your own paper. Be your own printer. Then see how smart you are, whippersnapper."

"All right," said Killian. "Go ahead and quit. Don't think I can't get another printer. And don't think I can't put it out myself. And stop that city whippersnapper business. I was born and brought up right here in Cognac. Just because I was gone a few years doesn't give me any big city ideas and you know it."

"I tell you I quit!" said Ethan. He spat a long derisive stream of tobacco juice into the furthest cuspidor.

"I heard you the first time," said Killian. "Get your things and I'll figure up your time." He turned his back, got out the books and went about an elaborate ritual of calculating. Finally he made out a check. "I think you'll find that correct," he said coldly. "I'll see about taking your name off the masthead."

"My name's been on the *Courier* masthead since your Paw founded it."

Killian shrugged. "Everything has to change sometime. You're the one who wants to quit."

"Yes," said Ethan. The fire was gone out of him now. He went about the office slowly, gathering things up, as if in a daze. Killian turned his back and went on typing.

"This is my copy of the extra the *Courier* put out the day the last war was declared," Ethan took it off the wall, handling it lovingly. "Gnats. My tobacco—my Indian relics. I suppose the first copy of the *Courier* really belongs to you, legal. But I set her up!" He eyed the framed yellow paper wistfully. Stumping into the back room, he patted the ungainly press gently. "Good-bye, Gwen. Don't take anything from anybody." To Killian, "You'll be careful of Gwen, won't you? She's pretty old now, and she's never had anybody but me run her except during the first war."

"She'll have to take her chances."

Silence, as Ethan stumped around. Presently he said, "I'm going now."

No answer.

"Good-bye, Killian."

"Good-bye." Killian McBean scowled at a word and crossed it out.

Ethan shifted his weight on to his peg leg and then back. He took a long wistful look at Gwen. "Maybe—maybe we were a little hasty."

Killian stopped typing and turned around. "You think so?"

Ethan cleared his throat. "Yes," he admitted. "Yes, I do. Gnats, Killian, you know I'm the best damn printer in the state!"

Killian ran his tongue over his gold tooth. "I never said you weren't."

A slow smile broke over Ethan's face. "Then what did you pick a fight for?"

"I didn't pick a fight. I was merely trying to point out to you that your friends can't help you if you won't trust them."

Ethan's face fell. "Oh. That." He picked up the picture frame and the Indian and pioneer relics and started for the door. "It isn't that I don't trust you, Killian. I can't help it, honest."

Killian McBean threw his eraser across the room. He tore the sheet out of his typewriter, crumpled it and threw it across the room too. "I'm not going to repeat anything you tell me, Ethan. It's just that I've got to know where you stand in this thing."

Ethan shook his white head firmly. "I can't." He opened the door.

"Oh, hell," said Killian McBean wearily. "Stop the play-acting, you old fraud. I couldn't get another printer as good as you are and I couldn't put it out myself and you know it. You've been holding that damned Gwen together for years by sheer personality. Go on back there and go to work."

Ethan's face lit up. He put his belongings down carefully. "Don't do that again," he said severely.

"I hope they don't hang you," said Killian McBean glumly.

The door opened and the chief of police and state's attorney walked in.

"We want to see you," snarled Amos at Ethan. Amos was tired and harassed, and showed it. Probably he had never moved so much and so fast in one day. The movement had not improved his disposition. He heaved his vast bulk into the room's only easy chair and sighed deeply, shutting his small eyes behind his glasses.

"Gimme some coffee," he said to Terrence Gillespie. Terry did.

"Help yourself," Killian McBean's tone was a little too polite.

Amos Colvin glared at him. "I don't want to hear nothing out of you, McBean. This here questioning ought to be done at the station, anyhow. Just acause Terry here made you some nutty deal about getting the *Courier* out, we're willing to do it here. But if you put your big mouth in, we'll arrest him and lock him up like that. The hell with it. I wanted to this morning, anyhow." It was difficult to snap fingers as fat as Amos Colvin's.

"Why him?" asked Killian. "Why not me?"

"You're not a suspect any more," admitted Amos grudgingly. "That assistant librarian's story cleared you. She said she heard you knocking and she was sure you didn't get in, and she heard you go directly downstairs. We figger the murder must've been about going on then—the murderer was probably in the room. So that clears you."

"That's her statement, not mine. I'm not bound by anything she might say," Killian pointed out. "If she's giving me an alibi, she's also giving herself one."

"The guy's nuts," Amos pointed out to Terry. "I think he wants to be suspected! Now you shut up."

"Ethan doesn't have to answer any of your questions," said Killian. "He's entitled to a lawyer, and—"

"For the last time I'm telling you, can it!" roared Amos Colvin. "I got enough trouble without taking you on too."

"I got nothing to hide," said Ethan Droom defiantly.

Terrence Gillespie, his face gravely apologetic, warned him that anything he said might be used against him.

"All right," said Amos Colvin. "What the hell were you doing in the hotel corridor outside Bennet Farr's room this morning a couple of minutes before his body was found?"

"I wasn't there."

"We know you were there, Ethan," said Terrence Gillespie patiently. "There's no use in denying it. We have witnesses. You may have been there for some perfectly innocent purpose. Or you may not. In either event, your safest course is to tell the whole truth."

"I am telling the truth," insisted old Ethan stubbornly. "Gnats! I wasn't there."

"Aunty Pliny saw you leaving the hotel."

"Meddling old bitch," said Ethan scornfully. "I reckon my word is as good as hers."

"And the schoolteacher, Theodora Meredith, saw you too. In the second floor corridor."

"Meddling young bitch," said Ethan. "Ought to be married, at her age. Gnats. I wasn't there."

They went over and over the question in a variety of ways. The answer, however, was always the same: Gnats. Ethan wasn't there.

Finally Amos Colvin threw some printer's type on the desk. "Ever see this before? It was all over the murdered man's room."

Ethan had heard of this before, but apparently it had not registered. Either that, or there was something peculiar about this particular type. He was really shaken. His hand moved waveringly toward his coat pocket. "I—" he began uncertainly.

Amos Colvin jeered at him. "Lose something, Ethan?"

Ethan turned helplessly toward Killian McBean. "Let's see that type, Amos," said Killian.

Amos carelessly knocked a few pieces of it across the desk to him.

Killian grinned. "Look at it, Ethan."

Ethan did. "Why," he said, "that's—"

"Yes," Killian put in quickly, "that's not the type we use. I suppose it's immaterial to you detectives, but we set the *Courier* up in minion, seven point type, on an eight point slug. This type happens to be ten point. There's quite a difference in size, as any printer can tell you; you don't have to take my word. Of course if you want to think that Ethan or I carry around a handful of odd type in our pockets to scatter on the scenes of our murders—"

Amos Colvin scowled. He heaved his huge body out of the chair. "The hell with it," he said. "I was all set to arrest you, Droom. But I still hold you done it. This is one of that damned Killian McBean's slick tricks, you mark my words. It may take me a little time to straighten it out, but I will. You're damned right I will. And then I'll arrest you and the hell with it. Don't try to get away." He scowled ferociously at Ethan and waddled out, followed by Terrence Gillespie, who was noticeably not talking to Killian.

"I don't see that that's going to help much," Ethan spat desperately at the nearest receptacle. "Sure, we don't set the *Courier* up in ten point now, but your paw did, and they're bound to find it out. There's plenty of it still out back. I use it for jobs. Even if we destroyed it all, they could get anybody to prove we had it from the files of the old editions. We can't destroy the files. Couldn't put out the *Courier* without the files."

"Well," said Killian McBean, "it'll give them something to chew on. Amos isn't very bright. Before he finds out, we'll have this week's *Courier* printed. And I should have an answer to my telegram."

CHAPTER EIGHT

THE FIRST run of the press had been made and most of the copy was set up and proofed for the second. Ethan was talking seriously to Gwen about it. Killian McBean sat back and stroked Smoky and pulled on his pipe. He studied the answer to his telegram.

"HASTY AND PRELIMINARY CHECK MADE ON REQUESTED MATERIAL. A HAS NO PREVIOUS RECORD IN PRESENT OCCUPATION. DIFFICULT TO TRACE PAST. REFERENCES GIVEN PRESENT EMPLOYERS NOT GENUINE, NOR IS DEGREE. NO PREVIOUS RECORD OF HANDICAP. POSTMARK ON LETTER FOUND, ADDRESSED IN HER HANDWRITING, DEFINITELY PLACES HER IN VICINITY INQUIRED ABOUT SAID DATE. NO TRACE FOUND YET OF WHAT SHE WAS DOING. NOTHING YET TO CONNECT HER WITH D. FURTHER INQUIRY BEING MADE, BUT WILL TAKE TIME."

So Theodora had no previous record as a schoolteacher, and had given the schoolboard faked references and a degree she did not have. Well, that in itself was not conclusive. She would not be the first person wanting a particular job who got it by means not strictly above board. She was a good teacher and absorbed in her work; all accounts agreed on that. More interesting was the fact that there was no previous record of her deafness. And that she was in the vicinity of Waldo, Connecticut, at the time of Dennis Farr's wedding to Rosa Kincaid. So had thousands of other people, of course. The fact in itself proved nothing—except that she might be Rosa Kincaid.

"B OWNER OF CAR IN QUESTION HAS PROVED NEWSPAPER BACKGROUND STARTING AT 17. ELEVEN YEARS ON CALIFORNIA PAPER. HAVE TRACED WHEREABOUTS ON DATE IN QUESTION. DEFINITELY IN SAN FRANCISCO, COVERING MURDER TRIAL. NO POSSIBILITY OF MISTAKE. NO KNOWN FAMILY. DO YOU WANT FURTHER CHECK? DESCRIPTION ON DRIVER'S LICENSE B91382; SEX, FEMALE; RACE, WHITE; EYES, BROWN; HAIR, BLONDE; HEIGHT, FIVE FEET SIX; WEIGHT, 110 POUNDS; BORN, MAY 10, 1916."

So the driver's license was proved to be genuine by a check of the original California state files, and Leslie Landis had been right in saying there was something familiar about the newspaper business to her. Also the mortgage deal was more or less explained. Perhaps she had bought the mortgage from Bennet Farr; many big city newspaper men and women eventually succumb to the lure of running a small town newspaper. Bennet Farr must have figured that he could not run the *Courier* himself if he took it over from Killian; he would not want Cognac to be without a paper, because he would want it to mold public opinion his way. He would figure that a woman editor would be easier to control than a man. Possibly it was just a dummy mortgage deal, with Bennet Farr still retaining control behind the scenes.

At any rate, the information proved one fact beyond all possibility of a doubt: Leslie Landis was not Rosa Kincaid.

> "C IN FIRST JOB IN PRESENT OCCUPATION. NO RECORD OF TRAINING IN SAME. NO RECORD OF PREVIOUS EMPLOYMENT DURING INTERVAL AFTER HIGH SCHOOL AND NOW, SOME EIGHT YEARS. LARGE FAMILY IN CHICAGO. THEY SAY SHE WAS NEVER EMPLOYED AT CAREER OF D, BUT ARE VAGUE ON WHAT SHE DID DO AND ADMIT SHE WAS IN EAST ON DATE IN QUESTION AND NOT IN SCHOOL. SAY SHE WAS EMPLOYED THEN BUT NOT KNOWN WHERE. SAY SHE WAS NEVER MARRIED. THINK THEY ARE TELLING THE TRUTH AS FAR AS THEY KNOW IT. FURTHER CHECK PROCEEDING."

So Irene Hubbard had been employed at various other unknown occupations before suddenly coming to Cognac as an untrained assistant librarian. Well, it was possible, of course. If she wanted to be a librarian and did not have the money to pay for an expensive course of study, experience in an actual library, even in a small town, would be invaluable. And she might have been in the east five years ago for entirely innocent purposes of her own.

Still, there was the fact that entirely of her own accord Irene had volunteered an alibi for Killian that she knew was false. If her own story of being in her room was true, she knew that Killian had gone into Bennet Farr's room, and also into other rooms on the floor. As long as the authorities, mistakenly as it happened, believed that the murderer was in Bennet Farr's room at that time, Irene was providing herself with a witness to being in her own room when the murder occurred, if Killian told the same story. He could tell no other without fatally incriminating himself. And Irene's extreme sudden friendliness in Killian's direction—was not that just the sort of thing Rosa Kincaid would do?

This of course proved nothing, except that it was still possible for either Irene or Theoroda to be Rosa Kincaid. Killian turned back to the telegram.

> "D WAS IN SECOND ROW OF CHORUS OF TRAVELLING SHOW AT TIME OF ELOPEMENT. HAD BEEN THERE ABOUT TWO WEEKS. GENERALLY BELIEVED TO BE AT OUTSET OF PROFITABLE CAREER. NO RECORD OF BRIDE AND GROOM HAVING MET PREVIOUSLY. DESCRIPTIONS OF FORMER COLLEAGUES VARY. ABOUT ALL THEY AGREE ON IS THAT SHE WAS YOUNG, NEITHER A DWARF OR A GIANT, HAD A GOOD FIGURE, TALENT AND RED HAIR. DROPPED OUT OF CHORUS IMMEDIATELY, HEARD OF ONLY SPORADICALLY. ABSOLUTE BLACKBALL WORKING, APPARENTLY SPONSORED BY EX FATHER-IN-LAW. NO RECORD OF HER CHANGING NAME. MAY BE, OF COURSE. LOOKING FOR PICTURE. SHOULD BE ABLE TO OBTAIN. ALSO FURTHER CHECKING, BUT TRAIL PRETTY COLD."

So Rosa Kincaid had a double reason for killing Bennet Farr: because his high-handedness had caused the breakup of her marriage and deprived her of the easy life she had sought, and because out of spite he had used his money and influence to blackball her subsequent theatrical career. Only Old Gluts Farr would have forced her to earn her own living and simultaneously deprived her of her only means of doing so. Killian knew how the blackball worked: Rosa, talented and full of high hopes, would get a new job, with good prospects. After a few days, when her identity was established, she would be dismissed, on some pretense. Probably it was some time, perhaps several years, before she learned the real reason for her apparently endless bad luck: Bennet Farr's unending spite and sheer meanness. Small wonder, then, that she hated the man enough to kill him!

Evidently it would be easier to prove a certain person was Rosa Kincaid than that Rosa Kincaid was a certain person. And no easy matter either way. Because, of course, the clipping in Bennet Farr's wallet might have been coincidental and she might have nothing to do with his murder.

Killian scribbled an answer to the telegram.

"GOOD WORK. PLEASE CONTINUE INQUIRIES ON A, C, D."

He called up and had the telegram sent. After hanging up, he thought a moment, and cranked the phone again. "Hello, Betsy. Isn't it early for you to be on? Oh. Too bad. Jenny's mother. What is it, flu, or just a cold?" He scribbled on an envelope with the stubby red pencil. "Tell her I hope she feels better. Say, Betsy, get me the Metropole, will you? Thanks.

"Hello. Oh, hello, Aunty. Glad to hear you're feeling better. Now, now, Aunty. That's no way to talk to the press. Give me Miss Hubbard, will you? Certainly the librarian. Do you know any other Miss Hubbards? Hello, Irene. Killian McBean. How about dinner at Sloppy Pete's tonight? Sure I mean it. And say, Irene—how about bringing Theodora Meredith? Now, now. Don't be that way. Not afraid of a little competition, are you? Sure. That's the city girl. O.K. Make it seven. Sure. Fine. Good-bye. So long, Aunty Pliny. T-t-t. That's no way for a lady to talk, Aunty."

He hung up, still grinning his wry grin.

"Gnats, Killian!" Ethan came in, a sheet of copy in his inky hands. "You didn't tell me anything about this."

"What?"

"This story about blood on your front porch."

"Didn't I?" Killian put his feet up on the desk and lit his pipe. "There's plenty going on here that hasn't been explained, Ethan. There's an awful lot of blood, for one thing."

"You mean on the porch?"

"On the porch and in that car. I'm pretty well convinced there was another death or at least a bad accident, Ethan."

Ethan brightened, then frowned. "Gnats. It wouldn't have anything to do with Bennet Farr's killing, anyway."

"It might have a good deal to do with it. In fact, it might explain it. Bennet Farr was out of bed at an hour he was never out of bed before and moving around the scene of the accident. Dimes would get you dollars that he knew more about it than he was telling. Or about something that got him pretty excited. Maybe it was whatever happened on my front porch."

"You don't really know that anything happened on your front porch," Ethan pointed out, "or at the accident either."

"Somebody made that puddle of blood on my front porch," said Killian. "And somebody bled all over that car of Leslie's. Maybe it was the same somebody, maybe not. But whoever it was hasn't turned up. It's a cinch they couldn't have gone far. Terry had a more or less hasty search of the woods made, and they didn't see anybody. That doesn't prove anything except that nobody accidentally wandered away from the scene of the accident. Whoever else was there was removed; they certainly couldn't have been in any condition to walk away.

"They haven't turned up since, so it's plain they weren't removed for any good and legitimate reason. It seems difficult to believe they could have survived without medical treatment after losing that much blood. But I made a check of all the hospitals within driving distance, and Old Doc checked the doctors, and no accident victims turned up. Therefore the most logical thing seems to be that the other victim or victims—if there was one on my front porch and another one at the accident—is dead and his or her body concealed somewhere."

"It ain't logical to me," said Ethan stubbornly. "Strikes me you're using a mighty big stick on a mighty small mule. Gnats! I don't see how you even know there's anybody else, let alone two of 'em, let alone they're dead. You got to prove it to me."

"You'll be the first to view the body, when I get it," promised Killian. "And Ethan, I'll give you a bet on the murderer's name—Bennet Farr's and whoever the other victim is."

Ethan glared at him. "Yes?"

"It's Rosa Kincaid."

"You're nuts," Ethan stated positively. "I don't know about this somebody-you-never-saw business, but I do know about Bennet Farr. No Rosa Kincaid killed him. *I know.*"

"Sorry about the steaks, girls," said Killian. "The visiting hordes got 'em. I suspect Sloppy Pete held out on them for the hometown trade or we wouldn't even be getting hamburgers."

"I like hamburgers," said Theodora Meredith.

"I like steaks," said Irene.

They all laughed. The conversation drifted pleasantly from one bit of small talk to another: the school, the library, the paper.

"Where did you say you were from, Theodora?" asked Killian carelessly.

Theodora adjusted her ear-piece nervously. "It slips," she explained apologetically. "I'm sorry; I didn't get what you said. You see, I have to adjust it to the different voices. Mostly I hear children, and they're quite different, much higher. It works very well, usually, though. It really doesn't interfere with my teaching at all." She seemed very anxious that they understand this.

Certainly it hadn't interfered with her understanding of any of the conversation up to the time she was asked where she was from. Killian drew his eyebrows down and without appearing to, studied Theodora Meredith closely. Her long dark hair wound in braids around her head looked natural enough, but it might have been pinned on. Her glasses were thick and shaded; they effectively shielded her eyes. She was slightly above average height, but nothing in the telegram had ruled out that possibility concerning Rosa Kincaid.

On the face of it, Theodora appeared to be just what she passed for: a schoolteacher in a small town, past her first youth and slightly bitter about it, quiet, retiring, a bit eccentric. Still, Killian could not help feeling that if an actress set out to create the character of a small town teacher, the results would not be far from Theodora Meredith. She was a shade too perfectly in character to be genuine.

He repeated his question. Theodora smiled vaguely. "I've lived in a lot of places," she said. "Too many to say I'm from anywhere. At the moment I'm from Cognac."

Killian leaned forward suddenly. "Why did you tell the police you saw Ethan in the hotel corridor this morning?"

Theodora met his gaze coldly. "Because I did see him."

"Did you meet him face to face?"

"No. I was outside my door and I saw him going around the corner to the back stairs. I think there was a woman with him. I saw the flare of a skirt."

"You just saw his back?"

"Yes."

"How can you be so sure who it was, the length of the hall away?"

"I tell you I saw him. I saw his wooden leg. I know it was Ethan Droom."

"There is a possibility you are making a mistake," said Killian very quietly and ominously. "You should be very careful in identifying people in a murder case—particularly when you wear glasses and are the full length of the hall from them."

"It was Ethan Droom," said Theodora, her conviction unshaken. "I'm absolutely positive it was Ethan Droom."

"Suppose I tell you that I'm positive it wasn't? Suppose I say Ethan was asleep in our back room when I left, that I went directly to the hotel by the only route and he didn't pass me? Do you expect me to believe that he woke up just as I entered the hotel, tore down The Road and up the back stairs and killed Bennet Farr and got out before I finished talking to Aunty Pliny? Remember I don't have a wooden leg, and I'm some years younger than Ethan."

"I saw Ethan Droom in the Metropole corridor when I went up after talking to you and Irene," said Theodora, her lips set in a thin firm line. "He couldn't have been in your back room when you left, because he was in the corridor when I got there, and he was leaving."

"Don't forget that that story also places you in the corridor alone at approximately the time of the murder," said Killian. "It may incriminate Ethan, but it also incriminates you."

"Mr. McBean!" gasped Theodora. "Are you implying that you think I murdered Mr. Farr?"

"You left us saying he should be exterminated," Killian pointed out.

Theodora Meredith stood up. She was furious. She glared at Killian. "Mr McBean, if you think for one minute you can intimidate me into telling an untruth to save your one-legged friend, you're badly mistaken! I saw Ethan Droom in the corridor, and I intend to go on saying I saw him in the corridor. It is my simple duty as a good citizen, and I pride myself on being a good citizen." She hesitated, glaring and dragging her coat on. "Thank you for the hamburger. Good night," she said stiffly and left.

"Nasty temper, that girl," Killian caught the gleam of amusement in Irene Hubbard's eye.

"This threesome business was your idea," she pointed out.

"Don't rub it in."

Irene leaned across the table and put one hand over his. "You know," her voice was soft, "I don't think you know much about women."

Killian grinned wryly. "What man does?"

"All you had to do was smile at her, maybe say something a little—affectionate—and she would have done anything you wanted."

"All right," said Killian, "consider yourself smiled at and said something a little—affectionate—to. Now tell me why you cooked up that dream tale about hearing me in the hall this morning."

"I did hear you," said Irene, her eyes twinkling. She shook her straight dark hair. "Didn't you tell the same story?"

"You could get yourself in a lot of trouble telling a story like that," Killian pointed out. "Suppose I murdered him? You'd be an accessory after the fact, you know."

Irene smiled at him as at a child. "You didn't murder him." Her voice became confidential. "Did you?"

"No," said Killian in the same tone, "did you?"

"Why, Killian McBean!"

Killian was frowning across the room. "Seems to be old home week."

Leslie Landis had just entered on the arm of Dennis Farr. She wore a tunic of green wool over a black skirt. Her blonde hair was brushed softly back from her forehead and her brown eyes were bright with excitement. Every man in the room turned to look. Dennis Farr never took his eyes off her. He was devotion itself.

Leslie smiled at Killian, spoke to Dennis. Then they both came over.

"Hello," Leslie included Irene in the greeting, but actually spoke only to Killian. "Any orders, boss?"

"Don't eat dinner with strange men. Especially the day their fathers are murdered," said Killian coldly. "I got some more information about you this afternoon."

She tightened her hold on Dennis' arm. "You did? Tell me. What was it?"

"You worked for a San Francisco newspaper for eleven years," said Killian McBean. "And you have no known family."

She thought about this, the excitement fading from her face and the stunned, bewildered look taking its place. She shook her head hopelessly. "It doesn't mean a thing to me. If there had been some relatives—isn't there anyone at all?"

"Apparently not."

She sighed heavily and put her hand to her head. "Do you think I'll ever remember?"

"Maybe," said Killian McBean.

"Of course." Dennis Farr patted her indulgently.

"I hope you're right," she said doubtfully. For a moment she looked frightened and lost. Then she smiled bravely up at Dennis. "How about that steak?"

"You'll take hamburger and like it." Soon afterwards Killian and Irene rose to leave. As Killian stopped at the cash register to pay their bill, he happened to glance out the window. For an instant he saw the face of Celia Austen. She did not see him, because she was looking in at her fiancé, Dennis Farr, and Leslie Landis. Killian muttered an excuse to Irene, asked her to wait a minute, and started for the street door. He did not have to go out, however, for Celia Austen came in, on the arm of Terrence Gillespie. The young state's attorney bowed stiffly to Irene, without smiling, and accidentally looked through Killian. Celia smiled and spoke, but did not see them. Her heart-shaped chin was high, her small mouth even more firm than usual. In her eyes was a look that could only be described as murderous.

"Let's have another cup of coffee," said Irene Hubbard to Killian.

He took her by the arm. "Let's go home."

"Now we've missed all the fun," Irene complained as they went into The Road.

Killian McBean did not change his expression. "What fun?"

Nearly an hour later, Killian sat at his desk, typing out a later story on the Farr murder case for the Chicago paper he had promised coverage. Smoky prowled endlessly around the room.

"Settle down," he told her crossly. "Why don't you go out?"

Smoky was not interested. She ran up the arm of his chair and gazed with wonder at the movement of the typewriter keys. Presently a soft-looking paw darted out.

Killian sighed, stopped typing and lit his pipe. He blew a puff in the direction of Smoky. She retired to a discreet distance and sat staring at him in offended dignity. He grinned wryly and started typing again.

Smoky continued to fix her eyes on him, unmoving. Presently the intensity of her gaze began to have effect even on Killian McBean. He felt himself sweating.

Finally he gave up. "All right," he swung his chair around. "What do you want, anyway?"

Smoky graciously led the way upstairs to the kitchen, her tail high in the air as she stalked in front of him. She looked over her shoulder once or twice to be sure he kept going in the right direction, and once when he crowded her she spat at him warningly.

In the kitchen she sat expectantly in front of her tin plate. Killian sighed and opened a can of fish.

"No wonder I have to eat hamburgers twice a day in restaurants," he complained.

Downstairs in the front office, something dropped.

Killian listened. He heard the sound of the typewriter, going rapidly.

"That you, Leslie?" he called.

There was no answer. He repeated the question, louder. "Jean? Ethan? Who is it?"

The typewriter stopped. A moment later the lights went out all over the house.

Killian groped his way into his bedroom and found his flashlight. He went downstairs without turning it on, however. He found the fuse box in the front hall by the stairs. All the fuses had been removed. Fortunately he had a box of spare ones nearby and could replace them. Soon the lights were on.

There was no one there. On Killian's desk was a typewritten note.

LESLIE LANDIS: LEAVE COGNAC BEFORE 9 TOMORROW NIGHT OR YOU WILL DIE VIOLENTLY.

X

CHAPTER NINE

Leslie Landis looked at the note, and then at Killian. "I don't believe it," she said uncertainly. Her brown eyes were bewildered, and her usually strong chin quivered slightly. "Why should anyone want to kill me? It's a joke, isn't it? You wrote it yourself, didn't you, Killian."

Killian shook his head. "No."

She sat looking at him, almost blankly. Then she looked back at the note. She seemed to be utterly incapable of grasping the situation, let alone dealing with it. Finally she said again, more uncertainly, "I don't believe it."

Killian McBean wound his long arms in back of his head. He said matter-of-factly, "All right. You said that. You don't believe it. Will you believe it if somebody sticks a knife in you?"

Leslie gave a little shuddering cry and buried her face in her hands. Her blonde hair fell forward in rippling waves. Killian eyed her appreciatively. "Sister, you're good," he said.

"I don't know what you mean."

"Amnesia or no amnesia," he pointed out, "you're a woman with eleven years of varied newspaper experience. You've covered murder trials and hangings and kidnapings and gang wars and sex crimes and God knows what. You must have been in plenty of danger before and got into worse corners than this."

"But I don't remember any of that!" she said dully. Her face was blank and bewildered again.

Killian shrugged.

"You—you're insulting!"

He smiled his aloof disbelieving smile. "You don't say."

She rose, her graceful body tense with rage. "I don't have to stand for this. I won't stand for it. I resign!"

Killian grinned, this time actually amused. He indicated the note. "Take your fan mail with you."

She looked at the note again. Finally she put out a slow, hesitant hand to take it. Her hand dropped and she sat down at the desk, her head on her arms. She was crying, with the deep shuddering sobs of a hurt or lost child.

Killian lit his pipe and sat watching her, not moving, not speaking.

Finally she lifted her white streaked face. Her eyes were still very wet. "Please, Killian," she said. "Please help me. You've got to help me!"

"I didn't say I wouldn't help you."

Somehow she was across the room and in his arms. He kissed her, his lips hard against her mouth, his arms tight around her slender body. She shut her eyes and kissed him back. There was force and power in his kiss, and in hers. He kissed her again. She opened her eyes and looked at him, genuinely startled.

"I didn't know anyone could—kiss like that," she said. Killian McBean swore and shoved her away. He snarled at her. "I said I'd help you," he said, "and I will. I'll take you over to the next town in my car and you can get a train to Chicago in about an hour. By tomorrow night you can be hundreds of miles from here."

She looked at him, her eyes speculative. "You want me to go?"

"Certainly I want you to go!"

Leslie smiled confidently and sat down and combed out her blonde hair with slow, deliberate movements. She took out her compact and redid her mouth. She smiled at herself in the mirror. Finally she smiled again at Killian McBean.

"You're sure you want me to go?" Her eyes were no longer lost; they were laughing too.

He scowled at her ferociously. "Quite sure."

She watched him, smiling.

"Dammit, stop sitting there grinning like a cat!"

She continued to watch him, still smiling. This time it was he who crossed the room.

In a few minutes she disengaged herself, laughing. "Now see what you've done to my lipstick again!" She took out her compact. His hand closed over hers and he took it away from her. "It won't pay you," he said, and tossed it on the desk behind him.

Leslie looked startled. Then she laughed. "Darling," she said and put her arms around his neck.

Killian McBean looked down at her. He put a large hand on either side of her slender waist and lifted her off the ground with one movement. "Listen, Leslie," he said soberly. "This hasn't gone so far yet that it would hurt anyone to stop it. It's for you to say. But I'm warning you. I'm not a man to fool around. One woman played me for a sucker once, and God help any other who ever tries it."

Leslie Landis laughed and beat her hands against his chest. "You terrify me," she said. She put up her face to be kissed.

"Don't forget it," he said shortly. He kissed her.

"You know," she said presently, "that of course I'm not going to take your old train."

"Oh yes you are."

"No, Killian. I can't. Not now."

He grinned at her, a little unsteadily. "There'll be plenty of time later. I'm definitely opposed to my women with knives in their backs."

She shuddered. "Please, Killian. It must have been a joke."

"Joke, nothing."

"Maybe somebody just meant to frighten me."

Killian shook his head. "I don't think so."

"You mean," she asked slowly, "that you really actually think that—that somebody is going to try to kill me?"

"That's right. I'll go even further than that. I think whoever wrote that note has already killed two people today."

This shook even the confident Leslie Landis. Her face went very white, and her hands shook. "Two people? You mean Mr. Bennet Farr and—?"

"And whoever was in that car with you before or at the time of the accident."

She stared at him. "You think there was somebody with me?"

"Certainly there was somebody with you. Where else could all that blood come from?"

"There was a cut on my head," she began uncertainly.

"A scratch," he said. "Whoever's blood was in that car was badly injured and pouring forth blood. Old Doc said it was absolutely impossible it could have been yours. And this morning—." He told her about the incident on his front porch and the blood there.

"But that makes three," she said, in a bewildered fashion. "One with me, and one on your front porch, and Mr. Farr. You don't suppose there could be an escaped lunatic or something around murdering people, do you?"

"No," he said. "Our murderer is no lunatic. And it doesn't necessarily make three. Because the person on my front porch could have been the same one who was in the car with you."

"Do you think it was?"

"Do you?" Killian McBean had lit his pipe again and resumed his cold manner.

She shook her head again, like a bewildered child. "I don't know, Killian, I don't know!"

"I wonder," he reasoned coldly, "if I hit you on the head again—"

"Don't you dare!"

He grinned. "You must admit it's tempting. Here the whole affair is probably right inside your head and you can't get it out. Old Doc says your amnesia is perfectly natural and should wear off in a few days. But we haven't got a few days. Can't you remember anything at all?"

"No, I still wouldn't even know my name if you and Mr. Colvin hadn't found it out for me."

"Doesn't it seem the slightest bit clearer than it did this morning?"

"No. It's still just completely a blank. My head aches and aches when I even think about it. There's just nothing there."

He sat smoking his pipe and thinking. She said almost timidly, "Are you sure I must know about all this, Killian?"

"I don't see how you could help it," he answered. "You must know who was in the car with you. Nobody in town is missing, so whoever was killed must have come with you. You must have been driving nearly all night with him—or her."

"You don't know whether it was a man or a woman?"

"Use your head," he growled at her. "How could I know if it

was a man or a woman? I can't even prove there was such a person, actually."

"Oh," she said.

"Whoever it was, somehow, got killed or at least very badly injured. I don't see how they could lose all that blood and still be alive. Maybe the murderer also meant to kill you, in a faked accident. There doesn't seem to have been much reason, except the rain, for a real accident at Indian Mound. Maybe you were already unconscious when the car hit the tree. Bennet Farr may have frightened the murderer off before he could complete the job of killing you. With the lights of his car, of course; Bennet wasn't the type to frighten him with anything else."

Leslie Landis shivered. "If I could only remember—"

Killian McBean shook his head. "That isn't the correct story, not yet. Of course Bennet Farr is dead; he died before anyone could question him about what he saw. It may be that he died because of what he saw. It would be ironic, if with all the people with good and legitimate reasons for killing Bennet Farr, he died because of what he happened to witness by chance at the scene of an accident. But even so, he had a chance to report it to the police. If he had seen anyone else there, if he had seen the murderer dragging a body away, he would certainly have reported it. All he reported was that he saw the wreck and a girl in the car."

"Everyone says Mr. Farr was very upset and acted strangely afterwards, going to the hotel instead of home and all," Leslie Landis pointed out. "Maybe he saw something he didn't tell."

"It's possible. But unless he had some good and legitimate reason to conceal it—say he knew the murderer—" Killian stopped. "It's possible."

"Or maybe he made the whole story up," said Leslie Landis. "About seeing the wreck and everything. Maybe he had something to do with it. Maybe he killed whoever else was in the car and then tried to kill me and then reported it like an accident."

"No." Killian was positive about this. "Whatever else he was, Bennet Farr wasn't the strong arm type. He was too much of a coward, for one thing. He didn't kill anybody. I don't think he could have, even in a fight. Besides, if Bennet Farr had done the killing, who killed him?"

"There were all kinds of people with motives for killing him," Leslie pointed out. "You told me yourself. Ethan, Mrs. Farr, Celia, Irene Hubbard, Theodora Meredith—"

"Too much coincidence," said Killian. "Bennet Farr kills somebody and tries to kill you and then comes back to town and somebody just happens to kill him, for a totally different reason? I don't believe it. I think whoever killed Bennet Farr killed whoever was in the car with you and wrote that note threatening to kill you."

"But you can't know," the girl pointed out.

"I know pretty well. There hasn't been a killing in Cognac in ten years. Then it was manslaughter. There hasn't been a bad accident. When there are suddenly one known murder and one almost known one and a bad accident that looks phony and a note threatening murder all in one day, it doesn't take any great imagination to decide they're all connected."

"You think Bennet Farr was telling the truth about my accident, then?"

"As far as he went, yes. Probably. He may have been holding something back. In fact, from the way he was acting afterwards, he was almost surely holding something back."

"I still don't see how you know."

"In the first place," said Killian, "if Bennet Farr wasn't telling the truth, and didn't show up in time to scare the murderer off, why didn't he finish killing you?"

"Oh." Leslie Landis swallowed.

"The murderer couldn't have meant to leave you alive," reasoned Killian. "He couldn't count on your having amnesia. The chances were a hundred to one that when you came to you would tell the whole story."

"Killian," said Leslie Landis. "I'm scared!" She looked and sounded it.

He grinned at her. "Good. We just about have time to make that train."

She shook her head slowly. "No, Killian. I'm scared, but I've got to know. Don't you see, the only chance I have of finding out who I am, really—not just my name—lies here in Cognac. Somebody here knows me. If I go away, I'll never know. And whoever the murderer is could follow me any time and kill me. I'd always have it hanging over me, every time I met anybody, every night when it got dark. Wherever I was, whatever I was doing, I couldn't help thinking of it."

"I suppose," said Killian thoughtfully, "that as long as there's a chance you might regain your memory, someday, some place, you are a danger to the murderer, alive, anywhere. Maybe you're right. Maybe he or she would follow you."

She clung to him. "You know I'm right. Here I'm in danger, but at least we know it. We can be on guard. That note even names a time. But if I go away, I won't have even that much protection."

Killian swore, and caught her shoulders so tightly that she cried out. "If anything happens to you—" he said.

She put her face against his chest. "Nothing will happen to me, darling."

"We could go to the police with the note," said Killian, between his teeth. "But it's written on my typewriter by somebody obviously familiar with this office—"

"Why?"

"They knew where the fuse box was, for one thing," Killian pointed out. "Of course anybody in town might know that; it's in plain sight and the door is always open and people run in and out of here all the time. But Amos would probably say we made the thing up out of whole cloth as a story for tomorrow's paper. And even if he believed it, what protection would he be?"

"None," Leslie smiled at him, thinking of Amos Colvin. "Let's not tell him, darling." She hesitated. "I—of course this is only an idea—"

"Well?"

"I had dinner with Dennis Farr," said Leslie Landis. "Of course I was only trying to get the story you wanted for you."

Killian grinned. "Sure."

Leslie opened her golden brown eyes wide. "But I was, Killian. You don't think I would—"

"Never mind what I think. Get on with it."

"I just thought that perhaps Celia Austen might have misunderstood. She might have thought—you don't think she would have threatened me?"

"She might," Killian conceded. "Everybody in town knows how jealous she is of anybody who looks at Dennis. And little as she is, Celia is capable of practically anything where Dennis is concerned."

"You think maybe—?"

"No," said Killian. "I don't think so. I think you know who the murderer is and the murderer thinks you might remember. But it would be just as well not to turn your back on Celia."

Leslie Landis moved contentedly in his arms. "Would you really mind if anything happened to me, darling?"

He looked at her.

"Oh, Killian!" she said. She waited to be kissed. She was. But Killian McBean was looking, not at her, but over her head at his typewriter.

"We've got to get down to business," he said. "Tomorrow's press day. What did you find out from Dennis Farr? Did he say anything about quarreling with his father? What about the will?" He looked at her as if seeing her from a distance and for the first time. A fire began to burn behind his eyes.

"Whatta story!" he said. "Whatta story!"

CHAPTER TEN

"What," asked Killian McBean the next morning, holding the paper out at arm's length, "is this thing?"

Leslie Landis smiled sweetly. "It's the story you asked me to do about the church rummage sale."

Killian looked at her. "I never did hold with female reporters," he said. He crumpled the paper and dropped it in the wastebasket. Then he began to type furiously.

Leslie laughed. She got up and came over and kissed him on the back of the neck.

"This is a newspaper office," he growled furiously. "Don't do that again."

"Why, darling, you sound as if you actually mean that."

"I do actually mean it! Don't do it again!"

"Maybe I've made a mistake," said Leslie Landis. "Maybe this isn't the Killian McBean who was here last night, who—"

"This isn't last night. It's today. Thursday. And this is a newspaper office."

Leslie laughed contentedly. "You haven't changed your mind about me, have you, Killian?"

Killian finished the article, snapped the paper release, and pulled it out of the typewriter with one swift movement. He hung it on the late copy hook.

"I haven't changed my mind," he said matter-of-factly. "And you know damn well I haven't. But this is a newspaper office and it's going to be run like one."

"There's no one here but us—and Ethan out in back, of course."

"There's a large bay window," Killian pointed out, "through which half the town can see. Sometimes I think they use telescopes. By this time Aunty Pliny is no doubt on the wire telling half Cognac that that awful Killian McBean is taking advantage of that poor girl who is queer in the head, the one in the accident, you know."

"Nosey busybodies."

"No," said Killian. "It isn't that at all. In a small town everybody's business is everybody else's business. It's too small to be otherwise. That's why the country newspaper is a going concern. Obviously we can't compete with the city newspapers in world news and pictures and famous correspondents and the like. But people in Cognac are interested in Cognac first and the world afterwards. They read the daily city paper to supplement the *Courier* not the *Courier* to supplement it."

"All right, Killian," said Leslie. "Cognac is a great little town and the *Courier* is a great little paper and the people aren't really nosey, just interested in other people's business. Now let's talk about us."

Killian took out his handkerchief and wiped the back of his neck. It came out smeared with Leslie's bright red lipstick.

"Do you buy that stuff by the ton?" he asked coldly.

She smiled sweetly. "You should know." She turned back to her desk. Almost immediately she shrieked.

"Get that horrid beast out of my chair!" she said.

Killian grinned. Smoky was curled up in a tight circle on the cushion of the chair, her tail wound carefully around her black body, her head buried and turned upside down, so that only one ear showed.

"That isn't your chair, it's Smoky's," he replied. "She's always liked that chair."

"It's my chair now. It goes with my desk. Get her out!"

"Not me."

Leslie advanced determinedly on the sleeping ball of black fur. With each step she grew a little less determined. Killian lit his pipe and leaned back in his chair, smiling broadly.

Leslie flicked her skirt at Smoky. "Shoo!" she said uncertainly. "Scat!"

Smoky did not even move her ear.

"Scat!" yelled the girl.

Smoky righted her head, and opened sleepy eyes to stare in disapproval at the noise-maker. Then she shut her eyes, tucked her head carefully under her front leg in reversed position, and was asleep again.

Killian McBean laughed.

"You!" said the girl. "You would keep a cat!"

"Don't be silly. Nobody can keep a cat. If they're lucky, a cat will keep them, as long as they behave."

Leslie glared at him. "Please get her off my chair, Killian."

"Not me."

She stretched a hand out at arm's length and shoved. Smoky came to with a warning growl, far down in her throat. In a split second's time she was unwound, thoroughly awake, and battling for her rights. One of her black velvet paws shot out and speared Leslie's hand with the accuracy of a harpooner. Blood showed distinctly the path of each of her claws. Leslie screamed and tried to slap her; Smoky spat and did slap Leslie, with the other paw. Leslie retired, bloody and infuriated. Smoky, unruffled, curled up and went to sleep again.

"Get another chair," advised Killian.

"I will not!" Leslie washed her hands with soap and water, then with disinfectant. "No cat is going to shove me around." Going out into the hall, she got a broom from the hall closet.

"Don't hurt her," warned Killian McBean.

"I suppose it doesn't matter what she does to me!"

"You're a big girl."

Leslie did not deign to answer this. Holding the broom out full length, she swept Smoky from the chair and plopped herself triumphantly into it. "You see!" she said.

Killian McBean just grinned. Smoky climbed up the arm of his chair and he stroked her back. She purred loudly, her eyes fixed on Leslie.

"How long is she going to sit looking at me like that?"

"Until she gets her chair."

"It's absolutely ridiculous," said Leslie, "and she isn't going to get it."

Smoky continued to look at her, purring.

"The first week that Smoky came here," Killian McBean reflected, "she had kittens. We didn't particularly want a cat, and certainly we didn't want kittens, but there she was on the doorstep and in she came and she's been here ever since. Do you know where she decided to have that first batch of kittens? On my desk. Right on top of the blotter. Of course when I got home and saw them, I put them in a basket in the basement. There were five of them, three yellow and two black. Smoky spent all day every day bringing them up and putting them back on my desk blotter. She could only bring them one at a time, of course, so it took her five trips every time. She was pretty weak, but she did it. As fast as she brought them up, I took them down. And she brought them up again. I said no cat was going to use my desk as a maternity ward and we'd fight it out if it took all year. So I took them down and she brought them up."

"What happened?"

Killian smiled wryly. "I wore out. I used a table for a desk until Smoky was through with mine. Ever since then, whenever the event occurs, I just move automatically to the table and forget it."

"It's absurd. You spoil her."

"You," observed Killian, "just don't know cats. Or Smoky."

Smoky climbed on to his desk now and sat trimly, her tail curled around her, her four paws together, her eyes fixed on Leslie.

Killian laughed.

Jean slammed in through the door, banging it in front and behind her. Her cheeks had gotten back some of their rosiness and she could laugh again. She laughed now.

"Well, my mellow mouses, chop me up and call me suey!" she spoke rapidly and cheerily. "Wait until you hear what I have to tell you. You'll think I'm shooting the Ferdinand, but honestly if I were your cuddle cookie and we were star-dusting—"

"English spoken here," said Killian McBean coldly. "What in heaven's name have you done to your mouth?"

"It's Orange Flare," Jean explained, "guaranteed to make me a potent pigeon. Leslie gave it to me."

Killian gave Leslie a malignant stare. "I might have known," he said. "It's repulsive. Wipe it off and wash your face."

"Uncle Killian!"

He looked at her. "It won't be the first time I've washed your face."

"I'll do it! But you don't have to treat me like a child! I'm a young lady. Leslie said so."

"Leslie," Killian stated, "is apparently half-witted. You're sixteen. You have beautiful coloring. You have no more need for Orange Flare than you have for a mink evening wrap. And even if you did—in Cognac any girl who paints like that at your age is considered fast. You know that. Don't you want to be invited places and have people like you?" He patted her on the shoulder in fatherly fashion. "Be a good girl and wash your face. What did you want to tell me?"

"If I'm such a child," said Jean, "maybe I can't be trusted to be an assistant reporter. Maybe I'd better not tell you."

Killian waited, looking at her, his eyes momentarily softened.

"Bennet Farr left half his money to his wife and half to Celia! He disinherited Dennis!"

Killian exploded in all directions. "Get his lawyer on the phone! Tom, it is. Tell Ethan to stop Gwen! Hold up the front page! Why didn't you tell me? Sitting around here prattling about lipstick!" He ran into the pressroom. Jean got the lawyer on the phone and told him to wait. She went slowly over to the washstand and washed her face.

"Uncles are such a trial. Even make-believe uncles like Killian," she explained to Leslie.

"Never mind, dear, you'll get out of this jerk town some day."

Jean opened her eyes wide. "Oh, I wouldn't want to leave Cognac. I love Cognac!"

Leslie Landis shrugged.

"But do you suppose," Jean's voice was wistful, "that if I try real hard, and stop eating candy, that someday I could be neatly stacked whistle bait like you?"

Killian ran back in, picked up the phone and barked questions into it at a mile a minute. "New will? Made when? A few hours before his death? You don't say. Perfectly legal and binding, of course? Did he give any reason for disinheriting Dennis? Oh, damn your legal ethics. Oh. All right. I'll be right down. We're holding up the presses, you know." He hung up. "Tom doesn't want to talk on the phone. Jean, go back and tell Ethan I have to go down to Tom's office. I'll be right back." He put a strong hand on her shoulder and swung her around to look at her lips. "Good girl." Jean went back to give her father the message. Killian flung his coat on and took his hat.

"You'd better stand by the telephone," he said to Leslie. "I suppose you know shorthand."

"I really don't know whether I do or not."

"You've got the damnedest case of amnesia I ever saw." He pulled her to her feet and kissed her.

She smiled up at him. "It's still the newspaper office. There's still the bay window. Aunty Pliny is probably on the party line right now saying—"

"Look, Leslie," he was suddenly serious. "Jean's a nice kid, a very nice kid. She hasn't any mother now, and it's plain to see she thinks you're what she calls out of this world. Try to use your influence for the good, won't you?"

"It was only a little lipstick!"

"In Cognac it's more than that."

She put her arms around his shoulders. Suddenly she shrieked, "Killian McBean, that cat is in my chair again!"

CHAPTER ELEVEN

"Tom says Bennet Farr called him up about nine o'clock night before last and said he wanted to make a new will this afternoon," Killian was tossing off his overcoat and hat while talking a mile a minute. "Then yesterday morning Bennet stopped at Tom's house and routed him out of bed and made the new will before he went to the hotel, with Tom's family as witnesses. Cut Dennis off with a dollar, just to make it legal. Everything else goes to Frances and Celia, half and half, except for a couple of small bequests. And he got the clipping about Rosa Kincaid from Tom. Made him hunt it up at dawn in the old files he keeps in his attic.

"One of the small bequests," he added, frowning at Jean, "was a thousand dollars to Ethan."

"To Father?"

"Yes."

"But—Bennet Farr always said he wouldn't pay him a cent for his leg!"

"I know," said Killian wearily. He sat down and began to type rapidly. "Tell Ethan this'll be ready in a minute. I'll set it up for him, if that'll help."

"Gnats! It had better be ready!" shrilled Ethan from the doorway. "And I'll set it up myself!"

Killian grinned at him. The two men exchanged a sober look over Jean's head, but neither said anything further about Ethan's legacy. Killian went on with his story and Ethan went back to the pressroom.

"Leslie went to wash her hair," Jean explained to Killian. "Isn't she a Queen of the May, though, Uncle Killian?"

"Definitely." Killian put his pipe in his mouth. "You know better than to talk when I'm writing a rush story, Jean."

"Sorry." Jean came over and stood behind him, watching the story as he wrote it. She did not say anything until he had finished, however. Then she sighed. "You're a wonderful reporter, Uncle Killian. Do you think I'll ever be as good as you are?"

"Take it out to your father," said Killian without removing the pipe from his mouth. "I think he can still get his paper out on time."

Jean ran back with the story. She returned almost immediately. "Father threw me out," she laughed. "And he said to tell you he and Gwen had never put a *Courier* out late yet and if the end of the world came now, it would just have to wait for next week's issue."

Killian grinned, but his mind was not on it.

"Don't look so cross, Uncle Killian," said Jean. "You're always like a bear on press day. First you sit around pawing envelopes in your pockets and chewing that red pencil and checking things to be sure you haven't left anything out. You've done it all a couple of times before, of course, but you do it again. And then you think and think. And finally about when Father starts folding the papers you decide everything is in and you relax a little, for about thirty seconds, maybe, before you start to worry about next week's *Courier*."

The phone rang. Killian answered it, pencil in hand. "Hello. Oh. O.K., Jack, read it to me, will you? Oh. Yes. Wait a minute till I take that down. Yes. A little slower, please. Yes. Yes. I think I've got it now. I'll read it back to be sure it's straight. Here goes: 'No further information A and C but working on them. Their trails seem too well covered to be accidental. D's trail also well covered, except for incident in question. Am sending this P.M. or tomorrow A.M. occupational picture of D. Taken five years ago, but supposed to be clear. Only thing we can pick up on D's subsequent career is a trick under the big top under another name to beat blackball. Ornament in sharp throwing act. Did a trick herself. Man half of act billed brother, but generally believed not. D became very skilled at trade in question there. D known to have violent temper and to have threatened subsequent corpse. Tests on two samples prove both human, O type and meet all other tests for same types; identical in tests depending on presence of agglutinogens and following Mendelian pattern. Medic says are same beyond all reasonable doubt. Still checking. Steve.' O.K., thanks, Jack. Yes, you might send an answer: 'Good work. Will look for photo. Please continue investigation ACD. Additional information vitally needed. Also make absolutely certain no doubt B's whereabouts date in question. New threat. Killian.' Read that back, will you? Yes. That's right. Thanks, Jack. Good-bye."

Jean's eyes were round with excitement. "More secrets, Uncle Killian? I didn't tell anybody about the other, honest. Please tell me about this."

"You heard it, didn't you?"

"But I don't know what it means!"

Killian laughed. "With all that double-talk you torment me with, you can't understand a simple telegram?"

"That isn't a simple telegram. It sounds like code."

"It isn't code. It's just camouflaged a little to keep anybody who shouldn't from understanding it."

"Please tell me!"

"A and C are Theodora and Irene. Steve hasn't been able to get anything further on them, and it looks as if they were trying to cover up their pasts. Still, they couldn't both be Rosa Kincaid, so with at least one of them, there's nothing suspicious about it. He has only two more things on Rosa Kincaid—a picture taken of her in the chorus five years ago—"

"Is that what he means by occupational picture?"

"Sure. He's sending it special delivery tonight or tomorrow morning. Probably he has to get it from the east. Maybe it'll help us, and maybe it won't. But the other fact certainly does."

"What other fact?"

"That Rosa Kincaid subsequently worked in the circus—that's the trick under the big top—as the girl in a knife throwing act."

"What's the girl in a knife throwing act?"

"She stands up against the target and the man throws knives around her and outlines her shape."

"Isn't it terribly dangerous?"

"Well, it would certainly take steady nerves. Of course those men are pretty good, and they rarely miss, but there's always the chance of an accident, and if the girl herself moved—"

"How horrible!"

"Not necessarily horrible. But it does show Rosa Kincaid's settlement from Bennet Farr in exchange for not contesting the divorce couldn't have been very substantial. Also that the black-ball Bennet Farr initiated against her was pretty effective. Otherwise she wouldn't have been engaging in such a dangerous occupation under an assumed name; there would be no other reason for her to do it except that she needed money badly. Certainly it would explain a lasting hatred of Bennet Farr."

"I don't know quite what you mean, Uncle Killian."

"Bennet Farr was a rich man," Killian explained. "By the law of averages, his son would be a rich man too. If it hadn't been for Bennet Farr, Rosa Kincaid would be Mrs. Dennis Farr. She would be sitting pretty with everything money could buy. Or, if Bennet Farr hadn't caused her to be blackballed, she might have been a theatrical star, in the lights and big money. Apparently she had talent. Instead she was down and out and had to assume another name to even get a job in the circus standing up and letting a man throw knives at her, and throwing them at him. Steve says she became quite expert at it. He also says she is known to have a violent temper, and to have threatened Bennet Farr, I suppose to some of her colleagues. Steve must have questioned them.

"All during the knife-throwing episode and God knows what else she went through, she was thinking about where she could have been and what she could have had if it hadn't been for Bennet Farr's meanness. She must have been relatively inexperienced when she married Dennis, and she let Bennet Farr bluff her into a divorce and a small settlement. As she got older, she realized what she could have had. She saw the pure spite of the blackball against her. All the time she got madder and madder and finally she worked herself up to a white-hot rage. She hated Bennet Farr more and more and finally she hated him enough to kill him, and she came to Cognac and did. It's that simple. I suppose essentially that's why anybody kills anybody else. They get to hate them too much to let them live.

"There's the brother angle, too. Maybe the other half of the knife act was her brother, maybe her husband or sweetheart. Steve apparently doesn't think he was her brother. But whoever he was, being close to Rosa Kincaid, he had the same motive she did. Maybe he did it, instead of her. Maybe our killer is a man."

"But what did Rosa or her brother have to gain by killing him?"

"Revenge, pure and simple. Old Gluts spoiled Rosa's life and prospects, so she ended his. Maybe they had the outside hope of getting a blackmail settlement out of Dennis Farr in exchange for going away, but that was secondary."

"But," Jean pointed out, "now Dennis Farr won't have any money."

Killian nodded. "I've been thinking about that. What I want to know is: what will Rosa Kincaid do now?" He cranked the phone. "Hello. Oh, hello, Jenny. When did you get back? Just the one day, huh? How's your mother? Betsy told me. That's good. Tell her there's a little notice in the *Courier* about her. Sure. Sure. Say, Jenny, get me Amos Colvin, will you? Oh, he is. Couldn't find him anywhere? Well, try Terry then. Terrence Gillespie. The barber shop? Thanks."

He hung up and said to Jean. "Amos is so busy giving out stories to the visiting reporters and having his pictures taken for the city papers that he can't be found. Jenny's been trying for fifteen minutes. Terry wants him. Terry's getting a haircut. Jenny says he ought to be pretty nearly through; he's been at the barber shop quite a while. Keep an eye on the street and nab him when he comes out, will you? Ask him to come in a minute."

Killian poked his head into the pressroom, but speedily withdrew it. A stream of shrill invective followed him, above the noise. The words were not distinguishable, but the meaning was.

Killian grinned. "I wasn't going to change anything, Ethan!" he shouted. "Not a word. I just wanted to tell you—all right, all right. I'm going."

He went.

He stopped to pet Smoky, sleeping comfortably on the disputed chair. Smoky accepted his affection without opening her eyes; she merely stretched out her front paws lazily.

"There he is," Jean reported. "Mr. Gillespie! Mr. Gillespie!"

Terry responded to her signal somewhat unwillingly and came in and stood stiffly against the door. His attitude was unquestionably hostile, although still characteristically apologetic.

"Sit down, sit down," said Killian. "Have a cup of coffee. This may take a while."

"I'm in rather a hurry."

"All right, stand up. But just because you have the potentialities of a damn fool doesn't mean you have to be one. Irene Hubbard is nothing to me but a suspect, and you ought to know it. Besides, what were you doing out with Celia?"

Terrence Gillespie did not relax. "I just happened to meet her and one thing led to another. I wanted to ask her a few questions. Are you sure you're not interested in Irene?"

"Positive."

"She—she's very attractive," said Terry doubtfully. "It isn't that I blame you."

"Look, Terry, for the last time: there's one thing that interests me about Irene, and only one. Is she Rosa Kincaid?"

Terrence Gillespie jumped. "You can't mean that!" he said indignantly.

Killian shrugged. "It's got to be her or Theodora. I'd prefer Theodora myself. But it could be Irene."

"Amos and I," Terrence Gillespie stated firmly, "don't hold

with your theory about Rosa Kincaid. Just because there was that clipping about her in Bennet Farr's wallet—it doesn't prove a thing. Certainly it doesn't prove that Farr's death was the result of an elaborate plot involving assumed identities and such. It's pretty fantastic, Killian, and we don't hold with it. We don't hold with it at all."

"Hell. Hold with anything you like," said Killian. "I want to ask you something. How did the knife get in Bennet Farr's back?"

Terry stared. "Somebody stuck it in. How else could a knife get into somebody's back?"

"It could have been thrown."

"Thrown! But that would mean a professional. No amateur starting out to kill somebody with a knife would throw it. They might in a fight or something, but whoever killed Bennet Farr stole the knife from the kitchen beforehand. It was planned. He was stabbed in the back and there was no sign of any struggle."

"I don't think he was stabbed," said Killian. "I doubt if he ever saw the person who killed him. I think the knife was thrown, by a professional, as you say, when his back was turned. You remember Old Doc said it took quite a force to get it in so deep. Throwing would give it that force."

"There aren't any professional knife-throwers in Cognac!"

"That's why I'm telling you Rosa Kincaid is here." Briefly Killian explained Rosa's connection with the circus knife-throwing act and her proven skill at the trade.

"How did you find that out?"

"You can check it if you like," Killian pointed out politely. "I'll be glad to get you the dates and places."

"Just because she was in such an act," stubbornly insisted the young state's attorney, "and because Bennet Farr was killed with a knife, doesn't prove she's here in Cognac and that she killed him."

"Just because you get sunburn when you stay in the sun," replied Killian, "doesn't prove the sun causes it, but it's a very likely supposition."

"We won't get anywhere arguing about it." Terry started to open the door. "You think Rosa Kincaid did it and we don't. You think she's here in Cognac and we don't. All right. If you can prove she's here and that she did it, go ahead. Meantime you'll understand if we proceed along the lines of our own conclusions."

"Just a minute," snapped Killian McBean. "I'm not through with you. I had blood analyses made of the stains in Leslie's car and those on my front porch. They not only proved to be the same general type, O, but they were identical in all other more specific tests. The doctors who made the analysis said there is practically no chance that two people with absolutely identical blood would turn up in such a short space of time. Also, the blood was not of the same type as Leslie's: Old Doc typed hers, for a possible transfusion for shock and she's AB type. There's about one chance in a million of the two samples I sent being from more than one person. In other words, someone besides Leslie was definitely bleeding in her car and also on my front porch."

"If you will submit a copy of your doctor's reports," said Terrence Gillespie formally, "and proof, of course, that the blood tested was actually taken from your porch and the car, we will be glad to study them."

"My word is pretty generally accepted in Cognac." Killian was dangerously calm.

"I'm sorry, Killian, but in a matter of law we've got to have proof. Nobody's word can be taken."

"All right, Terry," said Killian. "If you want to fight, we'll fight. It looks to me as if you were more interested in pinning Bennet Farr's murder on somebody who didn't do it than in finding out who actually did, and who else was murdered."

"You're entitled to your own opinion."

"Thanks. My own opinion is that Mr. Terrence Gillespie, alias the People's Friend, the state's attorney who last week stood for reform and purity, now that he is elected has sold out to the highest bidder."

"Who is—?"

"Probably Dennis Farr. No doubt he's taking up where Bennet left off."

Terry looked at him apologetically. "I can't help what you think, Killian. I just don't hold with this Rosa Kincaid story. Certainly if there is anything in it, I don't believe she is either Irene or Theodora."

"Who else could she be?"

"She might have taken an entirely different identity: maybe even a man."

"Now who's thinking up fantastic stories? Why should she go to all that trouble? What makes you think she could do it? It takes quite a lot of acting ability for a woman to impersonate a man. And besides, what young men have come to Cognac lately? Nobody in five years except you. You're not Rosa Kincaid, are you?"

"She might have come to town and killed Farr and left."

"Don't be a complete fool. The knifing occurred in the middle of town in broad daylight. Nobody saw any stranger in Cognac until after the noon train. No strange cars or pedestrians left, either; I checked it with the Miltons. You know, they live at the entrance to The Road and would have seen anybody getting to the highway after Farr was killed. There wasn't a train out until noon, and the station master says nobody left by that. Just where would a stranger Rosa Kincaid have been in the meantime? Where would she go? And how did she manage to get down The Road and into the hotel and out again without anybody seeing her? A stranger here is as conspicuous as a man with horns and a tail. The hotel was searched afterwards, you know. At least Amos thought of it an hour or so later."

"I didn't say a stranger Rosa Kincaid did it. I said I don't hold she has anything to do with it. And as for this theory of yours about somebody concealing a body—we've had a most complete search of the woods by the scene of the accident made. There is positively no body there."

"Are you sure there isn't one buried there?"

"As sure as it's humanly possible to be. The ground is frozen, you know, and it would be pretty hard to dig without showing some traces afterwards."

Killian shook his head. "I tell you there's another body somewhere. There's got to be."

"Let me know when you find it," Terry used the same sceptically polite tone. He opened the door and went out.

"What's the matter with him, Uncle Killian?" asked Jean, in a somewhat scared tone.

Killian frowned. "It may be just swelled head, or being overly impressed with his new authority. He is an awfully *new* state's attorney, you know. Not dry behind the ears. Or it may be something more than that. I didn't like that crack about understanding if they proceed along the lines of their own conclusions."

"What did it mean?"

"We'll no doubt find out shortly. I'd like to know why he's been looking for Amos."

Jean sat watching him with clouded eyes. "It isn't good to have him mad at us, is it?"

Killian gave her a long glance, and grinned. "Well, it's better to know he's mad if he's mad. Maybe if we find out why, we'll get somewhere."

"You took his girl to dinner."

"Irene isn't his girl. Anyhow I took two of them, Irene and Theodora. That shouldn't make him this sore. There's something behind this. Personally I think Terry knows more about this than he's telling. I'm not even sure he isn't afraid of something. He's certainly acting peculiarly. There's something mighty queer about him anyhow."

"About who?" Leslie came in, shaking her fresh blonde hair.

"Very nice," Killian noted. "But you ought to know better than wash your hair the day after an accident like you had. Old Doc says you should still be in bed. He was furious when he heard you were up yesterday."

"It smelled of mercurochrome."

"I hadn't noticed."

Leslie smiled at him.

"Besides," said Killian, "a newspaper woman like you ought to know that when you're left in charge of an office on press day, even for a few minutes, you're not expected to go off and wash your hair."

Leslie shook her head. "I tell you it's gone, darling. Completely gone. I don't remember being a newspaper woman, and while I don't remember being one, I'm not."

"I'll say you're not!"

"Get that beast out of my chair."

"Not me."

Jean was watching them. "Why, Uncle Killian! You mean you and Leslie—oh, it's wonderful!"

"Now what did I say," asked Killian, "to lead you to jump at any such conclusion?"

"It wasn't anything you said, or did. It's just in the way you look at her and she looks at you. It is true, isn't it?"

"Um," grunted Killian.

"Now you can rebuild your life!" said Jean. "Now you can be the man you should have been!"

Killian laughed. "I am the man I should have been."

"No, but I mean, everybody knows what wonderful offers you've had from city newspapers and things—"

"Really, Killian?" asked Leslie.

"I'm the editor of the *Cognac Courier*," he said firmly. "I like being editor of the *Cognac Courier* and I intend to go on being the editor of the *Cognac Courier* as long as I can fend off the mortgage."

Celia Austen opened the door. "Killian, I just heard. It's all over town. It can't be true. Tell me it isn't true."

"It isn't true." Killian obliged. "What isn't?"

"That they're going to arrest Ethan."

"No!" Jean stood up.

"I'm sorry." Celia Austen was. "I didn't see you, Jean."

"It wouldn't hurt you any to look around," growled Killian. "As long as you've started it, finish."

"Good morning, darling," said Leslie Landis.

Celia favored her with a stare. "Hello."

"The story, kid." Killian was not wasting any time.

"It isn't a story, really. But Aunty Pliny had it from Amos Colvin's wife, Jane—just that they had proof Ethan did it and they were going to arrest him."

"Proceeding along the lines of their own conclusions," murmured Killian McBean thoughtfully. "Any details, kid?"

"No. Killian, don't just sit there. There must be something you can do! You know Ethan didn't kill him. You know it!"

"You sound awfully positive."

Celia Austen shook her red hair. She put her heart-shaped chin up and looked squarely at the editor of the *Cognac Courier*. "Killian—where is your raincoat?"

Killian McBean returned her look without changing expression. "Out in the hall, I imagine."

"Oh no, Uncle Killian!" Jean began.

"Want to see it, kid?" He ignored Jean.

Celia Austen's eyes were puzzled. "You're sure?"

"Want me to get it?"

"No," Celia got up. "Never mind, Killian. I—I'm sorry I bothered you."

"You never bother me, kid," Killian assured her. He watched her go toward the door. The question he put was casual, almost idle. "How much did Dennis Farr tell you to offer Terrence Gillespie last night, Celia?"

She flushed, then grew pale under her freckles. "You listened?"

"You know better than that."

"Then how did you—you tricked me!"

Killian shrugged. "How does it feel to be an heiress?"

"It isn't my money. It's Dennis'. You know that. No matter who Father Farr left it to, it's Dennis'."

"Don't be a fool, Celia. He'll share it with you after you're married, of course, but right now it's yours."

"We're going to be married soon. Almost immediately."

Killian McBean did not change his expression. "Good luck, kid."

Her chin trembled. Impulsively she put out one of her small firm hands. Killian put a large one over it. "Killian—" she said and turned and ran out of the office.

Jean was looking pretty shaken, too. "What's the matter with her, Uncle Killian? What was she crying about?"

He shook his head. "I'm afraid she thinks I murdered Bennet Farr. But that isn't the main point. *What was Celia doing at the hotel on the morning Bennet Farr was murdered?*"

CHAPTER TWELVE

Theodora Meredith came awkwardly into the newspaper office and stood looking very uncomfortable.

"Hello, Theodora. Have a cup of coffee?" asked Killian.

"No, thank you," she said stiffly. "I—never drink coffee."

"People have been known to give up the habit after trying ours," Killian admitted. "It usually starts the day out tasting very good, but whenever the pot gets low, anybody who happens to be around uses his own judgment about adding more coffee or more water. Sometimes three people in a row add coffee, and other times a half dozen add only water. It makes for a varied strength and taste."

"Oh." She took her glasses off and wiped them carefully on an immaculate white handkerchief. "They steam, coming in out of the cold."

"Sit down, won't you?"

After putting her glasses back on, she sat very straight on the edge of the folding chair. "I came to tell you—I wanted—." She stopped suddenly. Leslie Landis came into the room.

"Haven't you got a home?" asked Killian coldly.

"I just wanted to get some carbon paper."

"Well, get it. You know Miss Meredith."

"Hello, darling," said Leslie Landis.

"How do you do."

A dead silence descended on the room while Leslie ran her graceful fingers through the contents of her desk drawer. "No carbon."

"Certainly there is." Killian got up to look. "I guess there isn't, at that. You must eat it. Come out back and I'll show you where the supply cabinet is. Back in a minute, Theodora."

"I'm in no hurry," she said politely. "The children are in assembly, and I got excused."

When he came back, Theodora was gingerly petting Smoky, comfortably encircled on Leslie's chair.

"Like cats?"

"I—don't know very many," said Theodora, accurately and without a trace of humor. She sat down in the straight chair again. "Mr. McBean—"

Killian waited, but no more came. Theodora flushed an embarrassed red but did not seem to be able to get the words out.

"Is it about Tommy?" he asked more gently than was his custom.

She nodded gratefully. Her words came in a sudden rush. "I just heard what you did. I mean about calling the governor to try to get Tommy out of reform school and that they're going to send him back here for a real hearing with the judge from the next county and if enough people speak up for him he'll be put on probation."

"That's right," Killian answered. "I haven't had time yet to do anything but talk that once to the governor, but I don't think there'll be much difficulty once we get an honest hearing. A few apples don't stack up well against a boy's life."

"He won't get in any more trouble, Mr. McBean. I promise you."

"A big promise." Killian grinned. "Tommy was born to mischief. And never having any family except an old aunt hasn't been any restraining influence. Sure he'll get in more trouble. But when he does just send him around. A little firmness in the right places will do Tommy a lot of good."

"You don't mean you'd strike him!"

"Look," said Killian, "when I was about Tommy's age, I took some of Bennet Farr's apples, too. I was like Tommy; I knew it was stealing, and I shouldn't do it, and I would get in trouble if I got caught. There were plenty of other places I could have gotten all the apples I wanted, like Tommy. But I climbed over the same stone wall he did and got the same apples. Bennet Farr didn't catch me, but my father did." He shook his head. "It was years before I would look at an apple."

"It isn't right. You must reason with a child."

"When a child knows something is wrong and does it anyway, he doesn't need to be reasoned with. He's testing us out. He needs to be shown that the consequences of doing wrong are painful and not to be desired."

"But the progressive method says—"

"I'm not progressive. Neither is Tommy. Send him along the next time he gets in trouble."

Theodora adjusted her ear-piece nervously. She giggled suddenly. "It would be nice to have a man's advice with him," she gulped. She stood up with a jerk. "I—will it be all right—I mean could I—stop in sometimes and just talk about him?"

"The *Courier* is always glad to see its friends and subscribers. You are a subscriber, aren't you?"

"Oh yes!"

"Drop in any time."

Theodora started to go, stopped. "Thank you again, Mr. McBean. It was wonderful of you!" She blushed, but her face was serious. "Mr. Gillespie and Mr. Colvin were questioning me again this morning. I'm sorry. I've thought and thought, but I'm still sure it was Ethan Droom I saw in the hall of the hotel."

Killian looked at her sceptically and shook his head. "Who else do you think you saw?"

"Why, nobody." But there was a noticeable hesitation in her voice. She opened the door and bolted suddenly out it.

"Quite the little lady's man, aren't you?" asked Leslie, from the doorway.

"Do you make a habit of listening to other people's conversations?"

"Only when they interest me, darling. Do I need to fear the rivalry of the adoring Theodora?"

"What do you mean by that crack?"

"Only what's plain to be seen, darling. Theodora thinks you're God's gift to women."

"As insane a remark as I ever heard," said Killian McBean. He looked after Theodora, however, with a slightly changed expression.

"It's obvious." Leslie was fixing her lips. "The poor girl."

"I told you putting that stuff on was a waste of time."

"Why, Killian! This is a newspaper office! With a window through which half Cognac can see. By now Aunty Pliny—"

A few minutes later Jean came in. She did not look embarrassed, only interested.

"Father says he's nearly through," she announced, "and he thinks the *Courier* will get out on time after all, no thanks to you.

And Irene Hubbard is coming down the street and it looks to me like she was heading for here."

"Thanks." Killian grinned.

When Irene got there, Killian was seated at his desk, apparently deeply buried in his accounts. Leslie and Jean were working at Leslie's desk.

"Hello, city girl," said Killian.

"Hello." Irene winked at him and smiled sweetly at Leslie and Jean. "Good morning. How is your head this morning, Leslie?"

"Much better, thank you. It hardly aches at all."

"But I suppose your mind, I mean your memory, hasn't come back?"

"Not yet."

"Dear me," said Irene to Killian. "Of course I suppose it's all right, but doesn't it give you a queer feeling? I mean, she might be anybody. She might do anything."

"It's pretty definitely established who she is," said Killian coldly. "Though now you mention it, she does give me a queer feeling." He did not smile or look at Leslie. She laughed.

Irene looked annoyed. "If I might talk to you privately?"

Jean got up immediately, but Leslie lingered.

"Take your carbon paper with you," advised Killian. "What's on your mind, Irene?"

At that moment the front door opened again and Amos Colvin waddled in, followed by Terrence Gillespie. His grim face grew even grimmer at the sight of Irene Hubbard.

"Behold the chief of police and state's attorney," said Killian.

"I've got a warrant for the arrest of Ethan Droom for the murder of Bennet Farr," stated Amos Colvin.

"Oh no!" Jean was horrified.

"I always knew you were crazy," Killian remarked, "but this time you're really out-doing yourself, fat stuff."

"There's no use trying any of your tricks, Killian," Terrence Gillespie put in firmly. "We asked one of the visiting reporters about that different-type fairy tale you gave us. He said he had been in here to look at the files and that the size type found in Bennet Farr's room was the size type formerly used on this paper."

"You don't say. Did he also tell you why Ethan or I should be carrying in our pockets type from a font we haven't used in five years? Remember all the type was the old kind, none the new."

"That ain't the point." Amos poured himself a cup of coffee. "The point is, you got that type here and it could of been in Ethan's pocket. He was heard threatening Bennet Farr's life a few minutes previous to his murder, and he was seen in the corridor of the hotel at practically the time of his death. There was printer's type all over the room. He got a thousand dollars from Bennet Farr's will. Maybe that don't prove he done it, but we'll let the jury decide that. The hell with it."

"Men have been hanged on circumstantial evidence," said Terrence Gillespie. "In the case of—"

"I'm not interested," Killian interrupted coldly. "Dennis Farr has taken up where his father left off. He's told you who he wants the crime pinned on, and you're trying to pin it."

"You can't talk like that to me!" said Terrence Gillespie. "You—." He took a step closer to Killian, who did not move.

"Terry, please!" Irene put a hand on his arm. "Mr. McBean is naturally upset."

"You would defend him."

"You!" boomed Amos Colvin at Jean, who was trying to slip out unnoticed. "You come back here!"

"Sit down," said Killian quietly to her.

"But Uncle Killian, you can't let them!"

"Sit down."

Terrence Gillespie had regained control of his temper. "You may prefer to believe in some fictional assumed identity story, Killian, but we've got to deal in facts. It's our duty to the public. Where's Ethan?"

"I suppose it hasn't occurred to you who has the best motive of all for killing Bennet Farr?"

No one answered. There was a silence until Leslie Landis said, "Who, Killian?"

"Dennis Farr."

Amos Colvin's crafty little eyes peered through his thick glasses. He roared. "I suppose he killed him so he'd be disinherited?"

"Bennet Farr had an appointment with his lawyer for the afternoon to change his will and disinherit Dennis," Killian pointed out. "There is no reason to suppose anybody knew that he hurried his plans and altered the will before going to the hotel. If Dennis Farr killed Bennet that morning, he had every reason to think he would inherit at least half of his father's estate, and no one would be the wiser. Certainly even if after his death yesterday morning it had become known that Bennet Farr was going to change his will yesterday afternoon, it could never have been proved he was going to disinherit his only son."

"You can't even prove Dennis Farr was in the hotel," sneered Amos Colvin.

"You have no way of telling what I can prove. And you can't prove he wasn't."

"Anyway," snarled Amos Colvin, running a fat hand over his well-greased hair, "you can't prove that Dennis Farr stood to gain a thousand dollars by Bennet Farr's death. Ethan did. Everybody knew how much Ethan needed the money. He's still in debt from his accident and his wife's illness, and with Jean getting ready for college—"

"Ethan," stated Killian coldly, "is the beneficiary in my life insurance. It's considerably more than a thousand dollars. I also willed him my interest in the paper. Why didn't he kill me?"

"Too bad he didn't."

"I have a scholarship to college," said Jean fearfully. "Father wouldn't have to k-kill anybody for money for me!"

Terrence Gillespie looked rather unhappily at her young face. "There is no use in prolonging this. Will you ask Ethan to come out here, or shall we go in and get him?"

Jean's wail brought Killian McBean to his feet, his face grimly set. "I'll get him."

"Uncle Killian!"

Leslie Landis put a soothing hand on Jean's shoulder as Killian went into the press room.

The noise of the press had stopped, and Ethan was sitting down at his desk.

"Terry and Amos are here, Ethan," said Killian quietly.

"For me?"

"I'm afraid so. They've found out about the old type and I guess the inheritance cinched it."

Ethan spat tobacco juice reflectively. "Gnats. You know, I think Old Gluts Farr thought maybe something was going to happen to him and just put that in his will for spite, just so I'd be suspected. He couldn't help being mean even after he's dead."

"I can't think of any other explanation," agreed Killian. "Certainly he had no conscience to bother him. Look, Ethan, you haven't changed your mind? You don't want to tell me about it?"

"No," said Ethan positively.

Killian frowned. "Well," he said, "a friend of mine is coming down from Chicago to defend you. I talked to him yesterday; I was afraid this would happen. He's a fine lawyer. Right at the moment he's tied up on another case, but he expects to be finished tomorrow morning at the latest. Fortunately he owes me some money from a long time ago. He'll try to get here tomorrow night. If he doesn't, it'll be Saturday morning. In the meantime, don't do any talking. No matter what they try, don't do any talking."

"Not a word?"

"Use all the words you like. Only keep them on the weather. Nothing else."

"Can I ask them to pass the salt at mealtimes? Jane Colvin never uses enough salt in her vittles."

Killian grinned. "I sometimes think the reason you get run in so often is that you like Jane's cooking."

"I don't get run in," said Ethan with dignity. "Just taken into protective custody. But Jane is a good cook. Best in Cognac."

"How many times have you been arrested—taken into protective custody?"

"Only eight," Ethan said.

Killian shook his head. "The evils of hard drink. Remind me to do an editorial about it."

"Gnats." Ethan grinned, too, but his mouth was tight and frightened.

The two men looked at each other. They looked around the familiar room. Ethan patted Gwen. Finally he said shrilly, "Well, come on!"

"Remember," warned Killian, "stick to the weather." He put his hand on the older man's shoulder, then dropped it and opened the door. The grin he gave Amos Colvin and Terrence Gillespie was broad and unconcerned. Ethan hobbled along quite cheerfully on his wooden leg.

"She's all done!" he shrilled triumphantly. "Just the trimming and folding and addressing left. I guess you can attend to that, Killian. Mind you do it careful now. I never sent out a sloppy looking *Courier* yet."

"Don't worry, Ethan," Killian grinned at him. "I'm the best runner of the folding machine you ever saw. And Leslie here was born with an addresser in her hand."

"Mmm," Ethan was doubtful. "Amateurs. Probably take me a week to get Gwen back in good humor, just from associating with you."

"F-father!" Jean got up and came over to him now.

Ethan patted her briskly and cheerfully on the shoulder. "Don't you fret, Jean. Mrs. Colvin is a real good cook. This isn't the first time I've been in that calaboose, you know. Now you be a good girl and do like I told you."

"But, Father—"

"You heard me." Ethan hesitated, then kissed the girl's cheek almost defiantly. He turned to Amos Colvin. "All right, all right. Let's go."

They went.

For a few minutes nobody in the newspaper office said anything. Then Killian got to his feet. "This isn't getting the *Courier* folded and addressed. Come on. Let's get busy."

"You—you're heartless!" Jean threw at him. "I—I hate you! You aren't going to help Father at all!"

"You can show Leslie about the addresser," Killian answered, "while I'm folding." He paused a minute, running his tongue over his gold tooth. Awkwardly he shifted from one foot to the other. He cleared his throat. Finally, "I think it'll be all right, Jean. It may take a little time, but I think it'll be all right."

Jean's tears were spilling down her smooth round cheeks. "You d-do?"

Killian sighed. "I'm going to call you my handkerchief girl. Not pin up, but wipe up." He took a clean handkerchief and wiped her face.

"That wasn't f-funny!"

"No," he admitted. "But I tried. Blow."

Jean blew.

"You—think you can find that Rosa Kincaid?" she asked.

Killian's eyes, as hard as diamonds, were fixed firmly on Irene Hubbard. She did not move. "Who's that?"

"Why, Uncle Killian," Jean protested frantically, "you know!" She too looked at Irene. "Oh!"

Irene Hubbard got up. "If there's anything I can do," she said to Killian and Jean, "just ask me. If you'd like to come down to the Metropole and stay with me for a few days, Jean—"

"Oh, no thank you. I'm not afraid to stay at home alone. I often stay there alone when Father is—out. Thank you just the same."

"Can whatever you wanted to see me about wait?" Killian asked Irene.

She nodded her dark bobbed head. "Easily. It wasn't important. More—personal." Her good-bye smile included Leslie, if her conversation did not. The door closed behind her.

"There's something strange about that librarian," said Leslie Landis. "I don't trust her."

"Why not?"

"I don't know. She—she's sly, somehow."

"Come on," said Killian. "You're going to run the addresser."

"But, Killian—"

"All right?" asked Killian of Jean. He gave her a fatherly pat.

"I g-guess so."

"Don't worry," he spoke in a low tone. "Ethan is only going to talk about the weather until his lawyer gets here."

"His lawyer?"

"A friend of mine is coming from Chicago."

"Why do we have to have a foreigner?"

"There's only one other lawyer besides Terry in Cognac," Killian pointed out. "And he's handling Bennet Farr's estate. He couldn't defend a man charged with his murder too."

"Oh." Jean looked up at him and smiled a trifle damply. "I—I'm sorry I said you were heartless, Uncle Killian. You're really hep with helium." She reached up and kissed him, perfectly naturally, without a trace of coquettishness.

"I suppose hep with helium is a compliment," growled Killian. "Get going on that addresser."

"Killian!" Leslie Landis nearly screamed. "Look! On my desk!"

He took the typed sheet she handed him and swore as he read it.

FINAL WARNING, LESLIE LANDIS. LEAVE COGNAC BEFORE NINE TONIGHT OR YOU WILL DIE VIOLENTLY. X

"That wasn't there a little while ago!" said Leslie, very pale. "Someone must have brought it."

"But if it was Rosa Kincaid," Jean was excited, "we must have seen her!"

"Sure." Killian sighed wearily. "Somebody who was here today left the note. And who was here? The whole list of suspects, except Aunty Pliny. Leslie and Jean and Ethan and I work here. Celia was in, and she would have brought it for Dennis Farr if he asked her to. Theodora, Irene, Terry twice, and Amos Colvin. One of us is the murderer, Rosa Kincaid or not. It narrows the field down nicely. Maybe we ought to draw lots."

"Uncle Killian!"

"What puzzles me," said Killian, "isn't how the note got here. Anyone who was here this morning had plenty of chance to leave it without being seen. But what I want to know is, how did the murderer have the chance to write it on our office typewriter?"

"Maybe he wrote the two notes last night and just left one," offered Leslie Landis.

"It's possible," Killian admitted. "But I didn't hear but one sheet of paper being taken out of the machine."

"Where were you?"

"Upstairs."

"Then how could you be sure? Anyhow, how do you know it was written on the office typewriter?"

"I'd know its E's in the south Pacific. And its T's are pretty unmistakable too. There isn't any question it was written on the office machine."

"I don't care what it was written on!" Leslie Landis cried. "What are you going to do to keep me from being killed?"

Killian grinned grimly. "I think we'll be here in the office tonight at nine. Maybe we can prepare a little reception for our murdering visitor."

CHAPTER THIRTEEN

Leslie Landis shivered and pulled her trim brown suit more closely about her. "Why do we have to stay here? It's cold."

"Fuel conservation," Killian pointed out.

"I don't care. If I'm going to be murdered, you might at least make me comfortable while I'm waiting!"

"O.K.," Killian sat down at his desk and put his feet up on it. "When you're going to be murdered, I will."

"You don't think whoever it is will try—?"

"I certainly hope they try," Killian lit his pipe. "I've got to get Ethan out of jail by next Tuesday at the latest. He sets up the ads Tuesday."

"Sometimes I don't understand you, Killian. You look positively contented!"

"It's the let-down after press day," Killian explained. "The *Cognac Courier* is out! It's written and set up and copy-read and made up and printed and folded and delivered or mailed! It's a wonderful feeling. At first I used to get drunk every Thursday night, but now—" he stretched comfortably. "Now I just do what Ethan calls bide."

"Don't let me interfere with your *biding*." Leslie was angry. She let out a little shriek. "Get that beast out of my chair!"

Smoky was curled up in a dark indistinguishable ball. Killian laughed. Leslie reached for the broom and swept vigorously. Smoky landed on her feet on the floor, hissing and glaring. She circled Leslie Landis' legs, glaring malevolently, looking for an opening. Leslie kicked at her.

"Don't do that!" Killian put down his pipe and went over to gather up the still battling black cat. Smoky growled a little in her throat, but finally consented to being picked up. He sat down with her, stroking the length of her back and rubbing under her chin and the sides of her face under her ears. All this Smoky accepted indifferently, still glaring at Leslie. Presently, however, she turned her head ever so slightly to facilitate his rubbing, and at last she began to purr, rumbling deeply and contentedly. Her eyes were half closed, for comfort, but the slit that remained was still watching Leslie—and the chair. Killian, seeing the direction of her glance, grinned.

"Killian, it's after eight-thirty!"

"I don't think we'll have any trouble until nine."

"You don't? How do you know?"

"Manly intuition. Anyhow, the notes said nine. If anything happens to you before nine o'clock, I'll be very much surprised."

"Oh you will!"

Killian put Smoky down carefully on his green desk blotter. She walked daintily to the edge of it and sat primly, her four black paws together, her tail curled neatly around her, her green eyes never wavering from Leslie Landis.

"Keep your shirt on, Leslie," said Killian. "I'm not just letting you sit here as bait, you know. I've taken precautions."

"What?"

"The doors and windows are all locked, for one thing. And the various entrances through them are all blockaded so we can't be surprised from the rear."

"What do you mean, blockaded?"

"Oh, pots and pans, strings, that sort of thing. The only way anybody can get in here is through the doors and windows of this room."

"They only need to get in one way!"

Killian put his hand in his pocket and took out his revolver. Without any apparent care, he fired across the room. The bullet hit a fat sheep grazing at the exact center of a calendar hanging on the hall.

"Did you aim at that sheep?"

"Certainly."

"You must have had an awful lot of experience with guns." Leslie Landis was thoughtful.

"I did have, once," Killian answered briefly. He checked the gun carefully before replacing it. "Are you still worried about the intruder?"

"Of course."

"Your confidence is most touching." Killian grinned and came over to her. Without hesitation she moved into his arms. Their kiss was a long one. When he released her, Lesile smiled up at him more steadily.

"That's better." He ran his lips down her throat and kissed the pulse at the base of it. She snuggled her blonde head against his shoulder and he kissed the soft cloud of hair. For a minute or two they just stood there, his long arms tight around her slender body. Then Killian let her go, with a gentle shove.

"Go way, wench. What are you trying to do, disturb my reporter's objectivity?"

"Oh?" Leslie's eyes were wide and laughing. "Is that what it is?" She began to re-do her red lips in front of her mirror.

"I hope that stuff isn't made of any critical materials," observed Killian. "I'd hate to have you rationed."

"If I'm going to be murdered, I might as well look my best."

Killian glared at her. "It's ten of nine. We'd better stop playing around. Our caller's watch might be fast."

"What preparations are we going to make?"

"We're going to turn out the lights, and—"

"All of them?"

"Certainly. Then if anyone tries to come in, our eyes will be accustomed to the darkness and his won't. Anyhow, the way the street light shines on the bay window, we should be able to see at least the shape of whoever comes in. I hardly think they'll try the doors."

Leslie Landis shivered. "It's terribly—risky, isn't it, Killian?"

"So is crossing the street." Killian McBean's eyes were hard now, and his movements crisp and efficient. He checked the gun again.

"Do you suppose whoever it is will know we're here?"

"I imagine so. We didn't take any pains to conceal our whereabouts. Everybody in Cognac usually knows pretty well where everybody else is, anyhow. If they don't, they can always ask Aunty Pliny. Hurry up, now. I want you to get in the kneehole of your desk."

"You want me to what?"

"You heard me."

"But, Killian, I'd be so scared!"

"I've got to know where you are," Killian pointed out. "Otherwise if I start shooting at moving objects, you might get hit. Now get in there and stay there."

"All right," said Leslie Landis resignedly. She shrieked. "Killian, that cat!"

Smoky was sound asleep in the disputed chair, looking as if she had grown roots.

"We haven't time for that now," Killian looked at his watch. The back of it snapped open and revealed the young woman's picture. He closed it with an angry gesture. "Hurry up."

Leslie stooped and crawled somewhat gingerly into the space.

"It's a good thing you're no bigger. Another inch and you'd bulge," Killian pointed out practically. He put her chair between the opening and the rest of the room. "Now stay there. Don't come out under any circumstances. Get that?"

"Yes. But, Killian, suppose whoever it is should get to me here? I can't move."

"Don't worry," Killian's tone was even grimmer than usual. "Nobody will get to you. Just stay there and keep quiet and you'll be all right."

"Whatever you say, darling."

Killian grinned appreciatively. "Sister, you're good."

"I don't see why you always say that."

"I'm going to turn out the lights now." He did. The room was in its first utter blackness, before their eyes were accustomed enough to it to even see the outline of the windows.

"Killian! I'm scared."

"Shut up. So am I."

"You don't sound scared."

"You do."

There was a moment's silence, broken only by the ticking of the grandfather's clock and a short, abrupt murmur.

"What's that?" Leslie hissed.

Killian chuckled. "It's Smoky purring on your chair."

"Get her out of there!"

Another silence. Then there were quiet moving sounds.

"Is that you, Killian?"

"Yes."

"What are you doing?"

"Knocking my shins, principally."

"Can you see anything?"

"No."

"What time is it?"

"It must be nearly nine. Now quit talking."

Killian put Smoky out and closed and locked the hall door behind her. They waited in the darkness, not moving, not speaking, scarcely breathing. The outline of the triple bay window was clear now, and the street light beyond gave a faint background of light. The room itself was still very dark, however. The outline of the heavier pieces of furniture was scarcely distinguishable, and Killian's figure, crouching by the windows, was only part of the shadows.

Outside, there was a stealthy sound, silence, and then another.

"Somebody's walking very quietly up to the windows," Killian whispered.

"Oh!" said Leslie, under the desk.

There was another silence. For a full minute nothing moved. Then the sliding steps began. They came along the north side wall, where there were no windows, gradually approaching the front bay window, but not yet reaching it. A step or two, sliding almost noiselessly, a pause, then another step.

Killian waited, not moving, his gun in his hand, his eyes on the windows.

Suddenly there was a shattering crash, then another, and a

third. They seemed to come from all directions, and the light from the streetlight became slightly brighter.

The tall figure of a man appeared in the central window, knocking out the jagged glass with something metallic. Killian did not fire, but sprang as the figure entered the room. Though Killian was much the smaller of the two, the force of his attack knocked the other man down. The taller man fought back instantly, however; they wrestled and crashed across the floor, with one on top, then the other. Leslie screamed; the men swore and grunted and fought on.

Killian got his fingers on the other's throat, only to be knocked back by a vicious elbow driven into his stomach. Winded, he landed on his back, with the other man on top of him, fingers at his throat. Gasping, Killian doubled his feet up and sent the other man crashing back against the wall. Killian rolled under the table, waiting and trying to get his breath.

Apparently his opponent was either stunned or winded, for no sound of movement came from him, except his heavy, labored breathing. Killian reached in his pocket for his flashlight, but his hand brought out only the case and a handful of shattered glass. Swearing, he start to crawl along the floor toward the light plug.

The other man groaned, and began to thrash noisily. Killian crawled back to where his opponent lay, felt for his head, and brought his gun butt solidly down on it. The man stopped thrashing, noisily or otherwise. Only his heavy, uneven breathing continued.

Winded again, Killian lay flat on the floor and rested. The fight had been more exhausting than he had realized. It was several minutes before he could edge along the floor toward the light plug again.

At that moment, another and bulkier figure entered the room through the window, having a little difficulty squeezing through. Killian raised his gun.

"I've got you covered," he said. "Don't move or I'll shoot. And I won't miss."

"I won't move!" shrilled the figure.

Disgust gave Killian added strength. He staggered to his feet and turned on the lights.

"Too bad I didn't shoot first and talk afterwards," he snapped. "You and Bennet Farr could have had a double funeral."

Amos Colvin's small rat-like eyes peered uneasily through his thick glasses, blinking in the sudden light. "Where's Terry?"

Killian leaned against his desk and straightened his tie. He nodded casually in the direction of his opponent's unconscious form.

"You've killed him!" Amos Colvin's voice went up and broke hysterically. He rushed over to the prostrate state's attorney.

"Oh, I don't think so," Killian protested. "I didn't hit him that hard," he added modestly. He looked at himself in the mirror. His lip was cut, and there was a large bruise on his forehead and fingermarks lightly bruising his neck. One of his hands was cut. He looked at Terrence Gillespie. The young state's attorney's two blackening eyes stood out prominently, as did a large bump on his head. His throat was so bruised it was swelling, so was the left side of his jaw.

Killian smiled at himself in the mirror. He winked at Leslie Landis, emerging from the cubbyhole of the desk.

"Darling, I thought you were being killed at least!"

"Who, me?" Killian was politely surprised.

"Was that Mr. Gillespie you were fighting? Why were you fighting him?"

"I'm peculiar that way. I always fight people when they break my windows and come in through them."

"We didn't break your windows!" Amos Colvin's voice was less shaky now, and came down an octave and boomed. "We were standing outside that wall there when they crashed. Sounded like somebody threw rocks through them. So we came in to see what the trouble was."

"What were you doing here in the first place?"

"We got a note saying there was going to be trouble." Amos Colvin fished in his pants pocket with a fleshy hand and brought out a sheet of paper with typewriting on. "And there sure was!"

Killian studied the note, pulling his eyebrows down. "'Be at the newspaper office tonight at nine o'clock. There will be trouble. A Friend.' When did you get this?"

"Found it under my door tonight about an hour ago. Don't know when it got put there, of course. The hell with it. Are you going to let that boy lay there and die? Get Old Doc!"

Killian moved away from the desk, steadying himself unobtrusively with his hand. He held his head rather stiffly, but otherwise gave no indication that the room was wobbling from side to side. He walked a reasonably straight line to the sink, filled a pitcher with water and came back and tossed it full on Mr. Gillespie's unmoving countenance.

"No use bothering Old Doc," he said. "He was up all last night with the Miller baby. Came at four this morning," he said.

Terrence Gillespie groaned and moved his aching head from side to side. He came to rather convulsively, his hands and arms moving first in swinging movements, as if the fight were still going on. Finally he opened his eyes. "Oh!" He groaned and shut them again.

"It's all right, Terry," said Amos Colvin encouragingly. "It's all right. I got the situation under control."

Killian McBean did not change his expression. Without looking at Leslie Landis, however, he winked.

"What—what hit me?" Terry tried to sit up and thought better of it. He groaned again and put a hand to his head.

"I did," Killian admitted modestly.

"You?" It took a minute or two for this to percolate slowly through to Terrence Gillespie's brain. He looked at Killian disbelievingly. "Didn't I hit you at all?"

"Oh, yes." Killian grinned. "Nothing to speak of. Don't worry about it."

Terry groaned and shut his eyes again. "Thanks." He became conscious of the water around his head on the floor. "What were you trying to do, finish me off by drowning?"

Killian reached down and offered his hand. Terry took it and laboriously hauled himself up on his elbows. Killian did not wince, but the room wobbled again.

This time Terry managed to get on one knee and lean against the desk. Amos Colvin waddled over and between them, he and Killian got Terry into the room's only easy chair.

"Oh!" he moaned. "Have I really only got one head? What do you fight with, brass knuckles?"

Killian went over to the blue metal coffee-pot and poured four mugs of coffee. The first he gave to Leslie, the second to Terry. Amos Colvin grasped his eagerly. Killian himself was gladder than he would have admitted to drink the hot liquid.

"You're not much of a nurse, are you?" he asked Leslie.

"Why should I nurse him? He came here to kill me, didn't he?"

Amos Colvin exploded like an oversized milkweed pod, wrath

going in all directions. It was some time before he calmed down enough to be shown the threatening letters Leslie had received. Even then he was only partially mollified.

"That's all the thanks officers of the law get for risking their lives to protect you!" he boomed at Leslie Landis.

"You weren't trying to protect her," Killian pointed out. "You didn't even know she was threatened. That note you got just said to expect trouble here. You only came because you hoped to get something on me."

"Besides," said Leslie Landis, "how do we know you ever even got that note? How do we know you didn't write it yourselves to use in case we caught you trying to kill me?"

The glance Killian gave her was admiring but noncommittal.

"C'mon, Terry," Amos growled. "Let's get out of this joint."

"If I can move."

"Better have another cup of coffee first." Politely Killian got him one. "Want to wash your face?"

"I don't ever want to touch it!"

Finally, somehow, with Amos Colvin's wrathful help, Terrence Gillespie managed to stagger out to his car. The state's attorney and chief of police drove away.

Killian McBean stood dusting his bruised knuckles in pleased fashion as he surveyed the office. There was a quantity of shattered glass directly under the window, outside as well as inside, a few blood stains and some water on the floor where Terrence Gillespie had lain, a couple of overturned chairs. Otherwise everything seemed unchanged.

It was very cold. Leslie Landis shivered as she put her hand over Killian's bruised ones. "Poor darling." She hesitated. "Do you think they came to kill me?"

Killian shook his head. "I doubt it. If Amos Colvin wanted

to kill somebody, he wouldn't give them advance warning of the exact hour and then try to sneak up on them. After all, Amos knows his own bulk. A knife in the back unexpectedly would be more like Amos."

"Isn't that what happened to Bennet Farr?"

"Yes," Killian McBean was thoughtful. "It is."

There was a pause before Leslie Landis asked, "Do you think Terry might have been trying to kill me?"

"I doubt it. Whatever else Terry is, and I'm by no means sure, he's smart. Too smart to take an elephant like Amos Colvin along if he wanted to commit a murder."

"But he left Mr. Colvin outside. Maybe he just brought him along for an alibi in case anything happened."

"Maybe, but it isn't likely. I don't think Terry left Amos outside purposely. I think Amos' own concern for Amos' hide kept him outside until his curiosity brought him in after he thought the fight was over."

Leslie Landis pursed her freshly-lipsticked mouth and shook her blonde head. "I still think they wrote themselves the note."

Killian frowned. "Not unless they wrote the notes threatening you too. All three were written on the same machine, the one here in the office."

"They were?"

"Yes. I don't see very well how either Amos or Terry could use my typewriter without being seen, do you?"

"Maybe whoever was here last night when you were upstairs—"

Killian shook his head. "There wasn't time. The typewriter wasn't used long enough. Besides that third note was written today, after we made our plans to be here at the office tonight. Even then, I don't see how the murderer knew we were going to be here. Where were you when I went down to see Ethan this afternoon?"

"I did go down to the grill for a few minutes."

"And left the door open with nobody here?"

"Yes. I'm sorry. I didn't think."

"So the murderer came in then and wrote the note. That doesn't prove much, except that he or she is someone who can come and go here without attracting attention if anyone saw them from the street. But almost anybody could have a good reason for being in the *Courier* office. On press day, like today, they could be wanting to buy a paper."

Leslie Landis shrieked suddenly. Killian jumped. He looked in the direction of her shaking finger.

In the seat of her chair, firmly fixing the cushion to the wood and deeply impaled beyond, was a long sharp knife.

Leslie threw herself at Killian, sobbing hysterically. His own hands were far from steady. He put an arm around her, staring angrily at the knife.

"That's why the windows were broken." His voice was unsteady, too. "So the murderer could stand outside and throw the knife. I should have thought of that. The note to Terry and Amos was a blind to distract our attention." He growled. "And I fell into it and jumped Terry. While we were rolling around, the murderer stood a few feet from us outside the window—and we never looked up! I suppose Amos didn't see him or her because Amos ran the other way at the first sound of fighting. He must have. Unless—"

He shook his head. "It couldn't have been Amos. It had to be a professional knife-thrower, and a mighty good one at that to aim the knife in practically total darkness and hit the one spot they wanted, like that."

He continued to sooth Leslie, still looking at the chair. "Whoever it was must have seen you in that chair some time today. It's a good thing I put Smoky out. That knife would have cut her in two!"

"D-damn Smoky!" said Leslie Landis. "That's my chair! That knife was aimed at *me* and I must say I think you take it pretty calmly!"

Killian smiled grimly at her. She clung to him, and put her face up to be kissed. She was, on the cheek.

"Killian McBean!" she said. "When you kiss a girl, think about it!"

"Sorry." He did not sound it. "I was thinking about a girl, though. I was wondering what Rosa Kincaid, or her brother, will try next."

CHAPTER FOURTEEN

THE WEATHER was still very cold and there was snow on the ground, but the sun was shining brightly as Killian and Smoky emerged from the *Courier* office the next morning, Friday. Smoky gave a low warning cat growl in her throat.

A lean yellow dog with a long nondescript tail was nosing around the open porch. There was a long bloody cut on his head. He snarled viciously at the man and cat.

"Now, Smoky," said Killian resignedly. He tried to reach her, but failed.

Smoky shut her eyes and walked an absolutely straight line. It ended up under the surprised mongrel's face. Leisurely Smoky opened her eyes and swung a barbed paw. It hit the yellow dog on the shoulder. Probably he was not hurt much, but he was insulted. Baring his teeth and snarling ferociously, he leaped at the black cat. Without apparent haste, Smoky balanced daintily on her hind paws and cracked him beautifully across the nose. Blood showed distinctly the path of each of her claws. She arched up her back, blew out her tail like a balloon, and leisurely waited his reactions.

Killian and the dog leaped for Smoky at the same time, but

somehow the man landed on the floor of the porch, the dog leaping over him. This time Smoky hit him with both front paws, simultaneously. The dog leaped back, yelping, and landed full on Killian's stomach. Smoky came sailing out of nowhere and landed on the mongrel's back, digging in with all her four needled paws. In an instant the porch became an inferno of swinging paws, hissing cat, yelping dog and yelling man. Bedlam reigned unchallenged.

Finally Killian succeeded in grabbing the dog and dragging him off by main force. Finding himself miraculously freed, the yellow dog did not stop to question the circumstances. He went down the street at a speed few dogs ever achieve. Killian looked after him, grinning. He wiped some blood from his hands, straightened his tie, and turned to view the dog's antagonist.

Smoky was sitting, unruffled, on the porch railing, looking absently into the street. Not a hair was out of place. As her owner watched, fascinated, she daintily lifted one black paw and began to wash it with her small, rough tongue. She purred loudly and contentedly.

Killian sighed. He tucked her under one arm and spoke to her sternly. "We're going to see Ethan," he said. "Now behave yourself. Even if you don't like dogs, I won't be pulling you out of fights all the way down The Road and back, do you understand?"

Smoky stopped purring and moved her hind paws against his hip bone to indicate her dissatisfaction with her position. Accidentally, several of her claws came out. Killian hastily doubled his arm higher, supporting her with the full length of it. Smoky settled down comfortably, her eyes shut, her purr beginning softly and unevenly.

The Cognac jail was a low white frame building, distinguished only by some frail-looking bars on a couple of the back windows. Upstairs Amos Colvin and his wife lived in a small apartment. Killian walked up the steps and in the front door without knocking. Amos Colvin sat at his desk in the front room, scowling forbiddingly.

"You get out of here," he growled. "Assassin!"

Killian McBean smiled. "Terry doesn't feel so good?"

"Get out of here! You can't see Ethan, and that's that."

"Now, fat stuff." Killian shifted Smoky to his left arm. "You'd better let what's past stay past. After all, I could press charges of illegal entry and assault with intent to kill. You didn't have any warrant last night, you know. And Terry certainly wasn't playing tiddledy-winks. You were both armed."

Amos Colvin's small eyes studied him malevolently through the thick glasses. Finally he heaved his bulky body out of his chair.

"The hell with it. I'll find out if Ethan wants to see you." Amos took a bunchy string of keys from his pocket and dangled them officiously. "You wait here."

Killian stood behind the chief of police, and when Amos opened the door to the iron grill, he and Smoky followed him in.

"You—" growled Amos Colvin.

"Come on, fat stuff. I can't sit around all day on the tax-payers' money, the way you can."

They went down a short corridor, turned right, and came to the expanse of Cognac's jail: two cells. In one of them Ethan Droom reclined, his wooden leg braced comfortably against the wall, his body stretched out on an iron cot. Terrence Gillespie, his right hand bandaged, his eyes both black over a considerable area, was pacing up and down furiously beside him.

"There's no use in denying it," he said angrily. "We know you were there."

"Gnats!" Ethan's eyes were closed. "Nice day, isn't it?"

"We not only know you were there, we know what you were doing there."

"A mite cold though," Ethan murmured pleasantly. "Wouldn't be surprised if it snowed up a real blizzard, either."

"It will pay you to tell the truth!"

"Snow would be mighty good for the winter wheat. We've had a pretty dry spell lately. Cold, but dry."

Terrence Gillespie glared at Killian and Amos. "Amos, I told you," he began furiously.

Ethan did not open his eyes. A long stream of tobacco juice, however, hit the cuspidor dangerously near Terry's feet. "Breakfast?" he inquired hopefully.

"You had breakfast!"

"No harm in trying," Ethan complained plaintively. "Jane's getting a mite sparse with her vittles, seems to me. Gnats! Only one breakfast?"

Killian put Smoky down. She sniffed disdainfully, shook her paws daintily and crossed the floor to jump up on the cot, landing full on Ethan's stomach. He put out a lean wrinkled hand to stroke her. The black cat settled down comfortably on his chest, tucking her paws under her.

"That you, Killian?" Ethan still did not open his eyes.

"That's right. 'Morning, Terry. Aren't you starting your official duties a little early?"

Terrence Gillespie tried to get up with dignity, but his joints were noticeably stiff. Killian grinned a little too broadly, for the young state's attorney snarled at him. Killian's own injuries had been considerably improved by a good night's sleep.

"T-t-t-," Killian disapproved. "Such language for an officer of the law. The People's Friend, too."

"I'll get you for this, McBean, if it's the last thing I ever do!" Terrence Gillespie's long lean body limped down the hall, followed by the waddling Amos Colvin.

Ethan chuckled deep in his throat. "What hit him, anyway?"

"I did."

"Gnats!" Ethan's enthusiasm was unlimited. "No wonder he's so mad. What happened?"

Briefly Killian recounted the happenings of the evening before. The older man whistled delightedly and insisted on having all the details of the fight repeated several times. Finally he got up and began to stump around the cell, excitedly re-enacting the story. Smoky curled up on the warmest spot of the cot and watched him with distant, half-closed eyes.

"Too bad you didn't plug Amos," Ethan shrilled.

"It would have been quite satisfying," Killian admitted. "But it would be pretty hard to get up in front of a jury with a straight face and claim you didn't recognize fat stuff's silhouette."

"They wouldn't have hung you," Ethan was confident. "Even if they did, it would have been worth it. Gnats!"

Killian pulled his eyebrows down and frowned at his printer. "A fine attitude, I must say."

Old Ethan laughed his shrill laugh. "You sure got that Gillespie guy mad. Gnats! He was here before breakfast, plugging at me."

"You stuck to the weather, didn't you?"

"Sure. Didn't tell him a thing."

"See that you don't. Remember, no statement of any kind until your lawyer gets here."

"Don't worry," Ethan said confidently. "I can talk about the weather for a week."

"Be very careful. Terry's pretty sore. And he's smart. He's liable to try something."

Ethan straightened his slight stooped body and stamped his wooden leg. "Gnats! I suppose you think I'm not smart?"

"I didn't say that. I said—"

"I heard you. Let me tell you, Killian McBean, I'm smarter than Terry'll ever be. If it wasn't for my leg, I'd be a commando!"

"Sure you would, Ethan. Only remember, even commandos have to be careful. Want me to leave Smoky?"

"You know how she hates to be shut up. In half an hour she'd be tearing the bars out of the window."

Killian admitted there was something to the theory. He picked Smoky up carefully. Ethan moved his wooden leg as noiselessly as possible and looked carefully up and down the corridor.

He spoke in an elaborate stage whisper. "I think there's something going on around here. Something, mighty suspicious. Should be reported to the F.B.I. Last night somebody came to see Amos in the middle of the night. I heard 'em. And he and Amos went out and Amos didn't come back for a couple of hours. Four o'clock, it was."

"Was it a man or a woman?"

"A man."

"How do you know?"

"I heard his footsteps, coming in and going out."

"Fast or slow?"

"Fast."

"A young man, you think?"

"Sounded like it. I heard their voices when they went out, too. Not the words, just the voices. There was something familiar about the other man's voice, but I couldn't quite place it."

"Maybe Terry?"

Ethan thought. "I don't think so. No. Not Terry."

"Then Dennis Farr?"

Ethan's piercing brown eyes quickened with excitement as he thought back. "Could be. What makes you think it was him?"

"Nobody else could have gotten Amos out of bed and out into the cold. The point is, what were they up to?"

"Probably a poker game."

Killian grinned, but his heart was not in it. He made a pretense at nonchalance as he prepared to go. "Anything you want?"

"A drink," said Ethan.

"No. Not a drop. Now remember that."

"I couldn't very well forget it. Gnats!"

Killian picked up Smoky and banged on the door. Amos' timid assistant, Jones, came to let him out. As he went down the corridor he heard Ethan, determinedly singing "Over There" off-key as he beat time with his wooden leg. The din was terrific.

The telegram was clear and to the point.

> ABSOLUTELY NO QUESTION B'S WHEREABOUTS DATE IN QUESTION. CAN PRODUCE A DOZEN NEWSPAPER MEN AS WITNESSES, ALL ABSOLUTELY RELIABLE. AT MORNING AND AFTERNOON SESSIONS OF COURT IN LOS ANGELES ON THAT DAY. WITH REPORTERS IN EVENING AND COURT THE NEXT MORNING. NO FURTHER DATA ON A OR C. CHECKING NEW LEAD ON D, BUT NOTHING CONCLUSIVE YET. BELIEVED TO HAVE RECENTLY BEEN IN CHICAGO, UNDER ANOTHER NAME. ANYHOW APPARENTLY NOT HERE NOW. CLOSING IN ON SO-CALLED BROTHER. WILL LET YOU KNOW. SENDING PICTURE THIS A.M., SPECIAL.

"But Uncle Killian, you've had Leslie investigated before!" said Jean. "She was in California the day Dennis Farr was married. The telegram says there isn't any question about it."

"I guess a dozen reliable newspaper men would satisfy even Amos. But it never does any harm to be sure."

Jean was looking very unhappy. "Uncle Killian, why don't you want me to go to see Father?"

"Because Ethan doesn't want you to. I've told you that a dozen times."

"B-but, Uncle K-killian!"

"I'm going down to the hotel," he said abruptly. "Stay here and answer the phone till I get back. Here," he thrust a clean handkerchief into her hand and went out without looking at her. As he strode down the street his face was grim, and he did not stop for his usual chats with everyone he met.

"Miss Meredith, please," was all he said to Aunty Pliny, who was at the desk in a bright green dress, red earrings and high heeled sandals.

"I hear they've arrested Ethan," she said triumphantly.

"Is she in?"

"Of course not. She's at school."

"Holiday this morning. Kids are rehearsing music for Bennet Farr's funeral. The school chorus is going to sing his praises."

"I forgot about that." Aunty Pliny wrinkled her sharp nose. Plainly she was a little upset. "Trash. Say, Killian, was there anything to that story in the *Courier* about all those goings-on on your front porch Wednesday morning, I mean the blood and all?"

"Gospel truth. I guess I'll just see if Theodora is in myself."

Before the astonished Mrs. Pliny had time to more than gasp shrilly. Killian was going up the stairs three at a time. At the top he paused to see if Aunty's sense of chaperonage would overcome her stiffening joints' dislike of climbing. It did not; she did not follow him.

Killian looked up and down the hall. No one was in sight. He opened the door of the broom closet. It contained nothing more suspicious than two mops and a broom. He knocked on the door of the room which had been vacant at the time of Bennet Farr's murder. A sleepy groan came from within; presently a half-awake reporter for a Chicago paper appeared.

"This your room?"

"Sure. Who the hell's room do you think it is?"

"Just checking," replied Killian. "Gallup poll."

The sleepy reporter banged the door in his face. Killian tried the door of the room which had been Bennet Farr's. It was unlocked, and empty. It had been scoured of all traces of blood, but apparently from a sense of propriety or superstition, not rented. A careful search of the bureau, closet, and desk revealed nothing except complete barrenness.

Out in the hall once more, Killian hesitated, tried Irene Hubbard's door. At this hour, he knew, she was at the library. Swiftly he took some keys from his pocket and chose one which unlocked the clumsy lock. He shut it carefully behind him. In a few seconds he was going through the desk. It contained nothing except hotel paper, blank; envelopes, also blank; stamps; a pencil and pen. There were no letters, no papers of any kind. The bureau drawers were equally impersonal. Lingerie, handkerchiefs, sweaters, gloves, a few pieces of costume jewelry, pajamas, stockings—everything there might have belonged to any woman anywhere. There were no initials, no personal keepsakes or trinkets, just the standard minimum essentials which could be bought anywhere. Killian swore, and looked around the rest of the room. He pulled back the rug, felt down in the chair, lifted the mattress and patted the bed. Nothing anywhere seemed in any way out of the ordinary.

Finally he looked at the closet. There were several coats of different weights and about a dozen dresses and skirts. On the shelf above were four hats. None of the clothes seemed particularly expensive; they were moderately priced dresses of somewhat standard styles, all of them carefully kept but plainly showing signs of wear. It was only after looking at them several times that Killian realized what was out of the way about them: all of the dress labels had been carefully cut out. Their origin was as anonymous as everything else the room contained.

Killian looked to make sure that everything was as nearly as possible the way he had found it. He listened at the door, heard nothing, and stepped boldly out into the hall, locking the door behind him. He knocked on Theodora Meredith's door.

After a moment, it opened an inch or two to reveal Theodora Meredith, in a long red chiffon negligee, her face cold-creamed, her hair done up tightly on small metallic curlers.

She gave a slight scream. "Oh! Oh dear me!" She shut the door. Killian waited for her to open it again. When she did not, he sat down, grinning, on a chair in the hall. It was a good ten minutes before further signs of activity came from Theodora. Then her door opened cautiously an inch or two and she peered out. She was fully dressed now, in her usual prim black, and her face shone righteously from soap and water alone. She wore her glasses and ear-piece, and her hair, having been removed from the curlers while still wet, was pinned straight back in a tight knot. She looked very confused at the sight of Killian McBean. For a moment he thought she was going back into the room, but she did not.

"Good morning," she said uncertainly.

"Good morning," Killian looked at her thoughtfully. "You should wear more red, Theodora. That negligee was good on you, cold cream or no cold cream!"

"Oh!" Her face was nearly the same color as the negligee. "I—suppose you think it's scandalous—for a schoolteacher, I mean. But I only wear it—in my room. I—had it, when I—at something I did before I came here."

Killian waited for her to continue, but she did not. Instead she looked at him steadily and said efficiently, "What was it you wanted to see me about, Mr. McBean?"

"About the woman you say you saw with Ethan here at the hotel the morning Bennet Farr was murdered."

Theodora Meredith did not flinch. Her tone was brisk and to the point. "What about her?"

"You're sure there was one?"

"Yes."

"What did she look like?"

Theodora Meredith sat down in a chair in the hall. So did Killian. It was a moment before she answered. "I've told you. I didn't see her. Only a swish of skirt."

"What kind of skirt?"

"I—don't remember. Just a skirt."

"You profess to be such a good citizen that you can't withhold information from the police," Killian pointed out coldly, "and you are obviously holding back information about another suspect. You couldn't possibly see a piece of skirt and nothing else. You'd have to see a leg, or shoulder, or hair, or something. I think you did. I think you know what kind of skirt it was. I think you know who wore it."

There was a silence, broken finally by Killian. "Well?"

"Well?"

"Are you in the habit, Theodora," asked Killian, "of giving faked references to schoolboards?"

She gasped and sprang to her feet. "You—that's blackmail!"

"Not at all. I'm merely a good citizen like yourself inquiring into the records of the teachers of our youth."

"Look, Mr. McBean. There wasn't anything wrong about it, really. I've always wanted to be a teacher, but I never had a chance to get the credits. So of course I could never get a job. But now when there is such a shortage of teachers—and I knew I would make a good one—I just told them I had the credits and faked a record of them. Please don't tell the Board!"

"Everyone says you've made a good teacher," admitted Killian. "Your principal, the parents, the children. I don't know how you got around the state certificate requirement, and don't tell me." He paused, then added, "Who was with Ethan?"

Theodora Meredith met his eyes steadily. "What were you doing in Irene's room just now when she wasn't there?"

"So you aren't really deaf."

"Not that deaf."

"But if you could hear me just now in Irene's room *you must have heard what went on in Bennet Farr's room the day he was murdered.*"

"I did."

CHAPTER FIFTEEN

KILLIAN MCBEAN did not take his sceptical eyes from Theodora Meredith's face. "What did you hear?"

She hesitated. "I couldn't hear everything, of course. But I heard Mr. Farr quarreling with some one, pretty violently."

"Who was it?"

"I don't know. Some man."

"You're sure it was a man?"

"Yes. I couldn't hear what he said, or distinguish the voice well enough to recognize it, but I'm sure it was a man."

"You don't think it was Ethan, do you?"

"N-o, I don't think so. I can't be sure, but I think it was lower than his voice. It was still pretty early in the morning, you see, and I was in bed and didn't have my ear-piece on. I didn't even know it was Mr. Farr until later on."

"How early was it then?"

"I don't know. I didn't look at the clock. I got up at seven, though, and it was some time before that."

"But Bennet Farr wasn't killed then!"

"I know. He was alive when we came back from breakfast."

"How do you know?"

"I heard him talking to Irene."

"To Irene?"

"Yes. She must have been either in his room or the doorway. I couldn't hear the whole conversation, but I did hear him tell her to get out. He sounded pretty angry."

"Didn't you ask her about it?"

"Of course not. Nobody knows I can hear that well."

"Why do you want to pretend to a handicap you don't have?"

"I'm not pretending. I really have an ear injury. I got it in an accident last year. At first I was nearly totally deaf, except for lip-reading and my ear-piece. I put that on my application. They took me anyway. After I got the job here, my hearing began to improve. I couldn't tell them right away that I wasn't deaf any more; it would have looked suspicious, and they might have checked me more thoroughly. Besides, I still do need the ear-piece, you know."

"Mmm." Killian McBean was sceptical. "What happened after you say you heard Bennet Farr tell Irene to get out?"

"Nothing. In a minute or two she knocked on my door and suggested we go for a little walk, and we went."

"That was when you met me?"

"Yes. We'd been out once to breakfast and came back and did our beds and then went out again. After I left you and Irene on The Road I came upstairs."

"The front stairs?"

"Yes."

"How did it happen Aunty Pliny didn't see you?"

"She wasn't at the desk."

"She claims not to have left it," Killian reminded her.

"She wasn't there," Theodora insisted stubbornly.

"All right. What happened then?"

"I came upstairs and went into my room. I heard voices in Mr. Farr's room, but I don't know who was there. Then I heard something heavy fall. I was thinking about Tommy and—crying, I guess, but after a few minutes I began to wonder what had fallen and I went out in the hall to find out."

"What did you see?"

"I saw Ethan Droom down at the other end of the hall, going toward the back stairs."

"Nothing else?"

"No. That is, I didn't see anyone but Mr. Droom. But Irene's door was closing."

"In the wind, maybe?"

"No." Theodora was positive. "There was someone there. I saw the handle turning."

"Then what happened?"

"Then I heard Mr. Farr moan and his door was open and I looked in there and saw him with the knife in his back."

"You did what?"

"It's true, Mr. McBean. I saw him. He was just dying. He died while I was looking at him."

"How do you know? Did you feel his pulse?"

"N-o. But I saw him. He died. One minute he was alive and the next he was dead. I know he was dead."

"You didn't go into the room?"

"No. I knew he was dead, and there was nothing I could do for him and I couldn't get mixed up in a murder case. I just couldn't!"

"Was there anybody else in the room when you looked in?"

"No. At least I didn't see anybody."

"You didn't look in the closet, did you? Or behind the door?"

"No. I didn't look anywhere. I just saw Mr. Farr and ran in my room."

"Old Doc says Bennet Farr died practically instantaneously. If your story is true and you saw him dying, the murderer couldn't have been far away."

Theodora pursed her lips determinedly. "That's why I felt I had to tell the police about seeing Ethan Droom in the hall. He was the only person in sight. He must have been the murderer."

"If Ethan had been the murderer," Killian pointed out, "he wouldn't have been in sight. The murderer undoubtedly hid when he or she heard you coming out your door."

"Where could he hide?"

"Maybe in Bennet Farr's room," said Killian, "behind the door or in the closet. Maybe in the broom closet. Maybe in Irene's room. That door wasn't closing without a reason. And there was the empty room, 207, at the back of the corridor, don't forget. Or he could have gone up the stairs to the third floor. Always supposing, of course, that your story is true and you didn't kill Farr yourself."

"Mr. McBean!"

"The time element is important. If your story is true and if the time after you came upstairs was short enough, it completely clears Irene and me. Bennet Farr must have been killed while we were talking on the street."

Theodora hesitated. "He was dead before you came up, yes. But, you said you stopped and talked to Mrs. Pliny in the lobby and Irene said she heard you come up and knock on Bennet Farr's door. You came up right after I saw Mr. Farr, so Irene must have been here."

"Could you have heard Irene's door open?"

Theodora shook her head. "No. I didn't hear her come up. I never do."

Killian thought about this for a minute or two. He switched his attack. He said abruptly. "When were you in the kitchen?"

"I wasn't."

"I understand," Killian did not give Aunty Pliny as the source of his information, "that you usually are there every day in the morning, fixing your sandwiches for lunch."

"Not every day, but pretty often. I have an arrangement with the cook. I just didn't happen to go Wednesday."

"Who is in the kitchen in the morning?"

"Nobody. Nobody ever is. The hotel doesn't serve breakfast, you know."

Killian frowned. "But the kitchen is wide open?"

"The cook leaves it open for me to make my lunch. I guess she locks it later. I don't know. It's always been open whenever I've wanted to get in."

"You used a bread knife?"

Theodora Meredith hesitated. "Yes," she admitted finally.

"I thought bread came sliced these days. Mine does."

"Not homemade bread. The cook always leaves the wrapped loaf and knife there for me."

"What kind of a knife is the bread knife?"

"It's long steel, very sharp, with a plastic handle."

"Just like the one in Bennet Farr's back?"

Theodora Meredith shuddered. "I didn't look at that very closely. And I couldn't see the blade, of course. But the handle looked the same. I remember thinking: there's the bread knife."

"Which brings us back to our original point. Who was with Ethan?"

Theodora was silent.

Killian's tone could not have been more matter-of-fact. "If you prefer to tell the state's attorney—"

"I couldn't!"

"Who was with Ethan?"

"It—was his daughter."

"Jean?"

"Yes. But, Mr. McBean, she couldn't possibly have had anything to do with it. Surely you won't force me to drag her name into it. She's just a young girl. I'm not her teacher, but I am a teacher in the same school system and I feel a responsibility toward her—"

"Forget it," said Killian harshly. "If you're telling the truth and it was really Jean you saw, forget it. Completely."

Theodora's eyes filled with tears. "You're really very good, Mr. McBean."

Killian glared at her. "Was there any type in the room when you saw Bennet Farr?"

"T-type?"

"Printer's type. Like this." Killian produced a pocketful.

"I didn't see any."

"You would have seen it if a lot of it had been scattered around the room, wouldn't you? You weren't that excited?"

"I wasn't excited at all. Just scared. I would have seen it."

Killian nodded. He got up, looking thoughtfully at Theodora Meredith. "I hope for your sake you're telling the truth. You're in a pretty difficult spot, remember. You threatened the deceased, you're here under false pretenses, you pretend to a degree of handicap you don't have, you admit being familiar with the kitchen and murder weapon. In fact, you were apparently the only person who knew the kitchen was open then and that the knife would be there."

Theodora Meredith put her head up. "But I didn't kill him!"

"Neither did Ethan." Killian studied her. Theodora was a poor liar, and it was evident she was lying, at least in some degree. She would not meet his eyes.

Killian grinned at Irene Hubbard as she came up the stairs. "Hello, city girl."

Irene looked at him and Theodora coldly. "Don't let me interrupt your tête-à-tête."

Theodora looked guilty. "I thought you were at the library."

"So it seems." Irene Hubbard went into her room and slammed the door.

Killian looked after her thoughtfully, realizing two things: Irene's usually gay disposition was very much on the surface, and there was no love lost between Irene Hubbard and Theodora Meredith.

"Hello, Ethan," said Terrence Gillespie affably.

"Nice day," Ethan did not open his eyes.

"I hope you have everything you want here."

Ethan did open his eyes, suspiciously. "Gnats! Since when did you care what I wanted?"

"Why, Ethan," Terry's voice was smooth and soothing. "We always want our guests to be comfortable."

Ethan spat across the cell, narrowly missing the state's attorney's feet, but hitting the receptacle. He shut his eyes again and began to hum, beating time on the wall with his wooden leg.

"It isn't any too warm in here," Terry was saying.

"Warm enough. Cold day out. Damn cold. Been cold all week. Damn cold."

"It's too bad the stove is so far away."

"Sun's shining, though. Folks don't mind the cold so much when the sun's shining."

"I thought maybe a little of this would warm you up." Terrence Gillespie took a bottle and two small glasses from his pocket.

Ethan opened his eyes, goggled, and shut them quickly. "Wouldn't be surprised if it blew up a blizzard, though."

Terry clanked the glasses rather louder than necessary, and made quite a popping sound with the cork. He poured two drinks. One he took over to Ethan.

Ethan opened his eyes, hesitated, shook his head virtuously. "Haven't had much rain in quite a spell, it being so cold."

"Whatever you like, of course," the young state's attorney was indifferent. He put the glass down on the floor beside Ethan's cot. "You don't mind if I have one?" He did, making a smacking sound with his lips.

"I knew today would be clear by last night's sunset," said Ethan, looking again at the glass. He shut his eyes quickly. "But it's sure likely to blow up a blizzard tonight."

"Good stuff," Terrence Gillespie smacked his lips again. "Don't get it like this very often these days."

Ethan opened his eyes again and looked at the glass His tongue circled his lips nervously. "Pretty cold out."

"You don't mind if I have another?"

Ethan's sharp brown eyes watched him pour it, his wooden leg beating a nervous tattoo against the wall. He shut his eyes again, but only momentarily. "It is a mite cold in here," he said weakly. "Gnats! I guess maybe one—"

He took the glass. Terrence Gillespie drained his second, his expression unchanged except for his eyes, which were bruised but triumphant.

"'Morning, Aunty Pliny." Killian leaned on her desk.

The old lady fluttered uncomfortably. "You want to see somebody?"

"Yes. You."

"Trash. This is only Friday. It isn't time for you to be snooping around pumping people for next week's edition."

"No," Killian reclined lazily against the hotel desk and watched her closely.

Aunty Pliny fussed among some papers, unable to conceal her nervousness. Finally she snapped, "Get on about your business, Killian McBean. Trash. You can't loiter in the Metropole."

Killian's gray eyes wandered about the lobby. They took in the two brown plush sofas, the three green plush chairs, the ashstand, the cuspidors. Suddenly they came back to the face of the old lady beside him. "Why did you kill Bennet Farr, Auntie?"

Her gasp was a minor shriek. "I didn't!"

The newspaper editor shook his head regretfully.

"I tell you I didn't kill him, Killian McBean! He was dead as a mackerel when I found him!"

"His door must have been locked," he said, "if he came here because he was afraid of something. Nobody but you had the key. It's that simple. You were alone in the hotel with Bennet Farr when Irene and Theodora were out on the street talking to me. You've hated him for years, ever since your husband mortgaged his soul to him. This was the first time you'd ever had a chance alone with him. So you went out into the kitchen, took the bread knife, and went up to his room. You let yourself in with the pass key, sneaked up behind Bennet Farr, and stuck the knife in his back."

"No! I didn't! No!"

Killian ran his tongue over his gold tooth. "I wouldn't have known if you hadn't left the one clue that pointed directly to you."

"To me? What clue?"

"The printers' type."

"That didn't point to me," she nearly screamed. "It pointed to you and that no-good drunken printer of yours. Trash! Everybody knows you both carry a pocketful of type."

"Not that kind of type."

"What do you mean, not that kind of type?"

Briefly Killian explained to her the difference in size between the old ten point type and the new seven point now used by the *Courier*. "So you see neither Ethan or I could possibly have had the other type. But if you, being a printer's widow, happened to carry some of his type for luck or habit or sentiment or some other reason, it would be the old size in use when your husband owned the *Courier*, the ten point."

"I didn't kill him!" she gasped.

"There's no other way to explain the type."

"I'll tell you. I put the type there, but he was stone dead. I didn't kill him!"

"You mean you went in and found Bennet Farr dead and then scattered the type around? What did you do that for?"

Aunty Pliny had enough conscience to look ashamed. "I knew you'd done it, that's why, and I didn't want you to get away with it like you got away with my husband's newspaper!"

"Where did you get the type?"

"I've carried it in my handbag for years. My husband gave it to me the day he bought the *Courier* from your father."

Killian thought. "How did you happen to take your handbag up to Bennet Farr's room?"

"I couldn't leave it here," she said, scandalized. "Nothing locks!"

Killian shook his head. "How do feel now that your faked clue has Ethan in jail?"

"I wasn't pointing it at Ethan," she said primly. "Although I did see him leave. But they wouldn't arrest him if he hadn't done it. And if you didn't, he must have."

"That's not for you to say. It so happens that neither of us did it. But you might hang Ethan with your meddling!"

Aunty Pliny's sharp chin trembled suddenly. "I'm sorry, Killian. I really am sorry. I haven't been able to sleep since I did it. I don't know why I did!"

"It'll be a great comfort to Ethan while hanging to know you're sorry and can't sleep," snapped Killian.

The old lady sniffled. Killian looked alarmed. "You didn't do it entirely for spite, did you?" His tone was slightly softer. "It was partly because you didn't want anyone to know Celia was here, wasn't it?"

Aunty Pliny's eyes darted fire. "Trash. She was not!"

"It's all right," said Killian. "Even you couldn't accuse me of intending Celia any harm. I just wish you'd taken some other method of distracting attention from her, that's all. Couldn't you have pinned it on Dennis Farr?"

Aunty Pliny stiffened still more. "Dennis Farr was gone hours before his father was killed?"

Killian asked casually, "You mean after the quarrel they had early in the morning?"

"Yes. I stopped by the Metropole after that crazy girl's accident. Usually I'm not here that early, but I was wide awake and I had some accounts I wanted to catch up on. Dennis Farr left before seven o'clock. At least an hour before I found the body, and old Doc said Bennet Farr hadn't been dead much over ten minutes when I found him."

"Did it ever occur to you he could have come back, by the rear entrance?"

"Yes," Aunty Pliny admitted. "It occurred to me. But there's a sight of difference between occurring and proving. Nobody saw him."

"Celia won't tell you what she was doing here?"

"No. She doesn't even know I saw her. She won't talk about it at all. And don't you go pestering her, either! She's unhappy enough, with Dennis Farr trying to hurry her into marriage with his father hardly cold, him that was always postponing it before she got the money, and all the time making sheep's eyes at that crazy girl you have in your office and that librarian and everything else in skirts in town."

"Did you ever think about what probably brought Celia to the hotel at all that morning at about the time Bennet Farr was murdered?"

"I told you I don't know!"

"Who has been the cause of all the trouble Celia ever got into?" Killian asked. "Who would she be here trying to shield, to keep from an action she thought he would regret?"

"Dennis Farr! Trash! I'll bet that's why she won't talk about it, either. Wild horses couldn't make her say anything to get that worthless no-good chaser in trouble."

"Personally I'm afraid he didn't murder his father," Killian regretted. "But it's a nice idea."

The front doors of the hotel banged open and Jean came running in, coatless and screaming.

"Uncle Killian!" she said. "Uncle Killian! Mrs. Colvin just told Celia that Terrence Gillespie has a signed confession from Father saying he killed Bennet Farr!"

Stunned, Killian automatically took off his overcoat and put it around Jean's shoulders. Behind him he heard Aunty Pliny's malicious cackle. "Planting evidence, am I?"

CHAPTER SIXTEEN

"I don't see the use in worrying about it, darling," said Leslie Landis. "If Ethan did it, he did it, that's all."

"I tell you he didn't do it!"

She lit a cigarette with a graceful gesture. "But he signed a confession!"

"He was drunk. Terry probably told him it was a report to the F.B.I."

"I still don't think Mr. Gillespie would dare to fake the whole thing."

Killian let his pipe go out in his hand, not seeing it. "That's the whole difficulty. Probably any lawyer could get that confession thrown out; Ethan was plainly not competent. But he's admitted at the very least that he was at the Metropole at the time of the murder, and that his previous statements denying his presence are false. I don't think Terry would dare fake the whole confession, either. Ethan must have said *something*. And whether or not the confession is admitted as evidence, everybody knows about it. How can we get a coroner's jury or any other jury that won't already have its mind made up as to Ethan's guilt?"

"I don't understand."

"Oh, they always ask jurors if they've made up their minds about the case," Killian explained, "the same here as everywhere else. Only most places people don't like to serve on juries. In Cognac, we don't have very many, and we love it. Nobody is going to take a chance on getting disqualified for jury service by admitting he's already made up his mind."

"Your lawyer can get a change of court or something."

"Sure. It would be easy to arrange a change of venue. But Ethan's whole life is here in Cognac. Except for the last war, he's never left it. Even if he were tried somewhere else and acquitted, everybody in Cognac would still believe him guilty. He couldn't come back here. If he did, he'd be ostracized. Cognac didn't like Bennet Farr, and they do like Ethan, but murder is murder. It's wicked. Black is black and white is white, to Cognac. Nobody would read a paper printed by a murderer. Nobody would let their children associate with his daughter."

"He'll be lucky if he gets off," said Leslie Landis. "He doesn't have to live in Cognac. There's the whole world to live in!"

"Not for Ethan."

"Oh, darling," said Leslie. "Let the lawyer worry about it. Let's talk about us."

Killian got up abruptly. "Some day," he said coldly, "some man is going to strangle you by that beautiful blonde hair."

"Why, darling! Where are you going?"

"Out!"

Killian strode down The Road, conscious of the whispers which marked his progress. People turned suddenly into doors or had some vital errand across the street, trying embarrassedly to avoid the issue. The newspaper editor looked them all coldly and clearly in the eye. At first this seemed to rather surprise them, then they whispered among themselves. Finally they spoke to Killian McBean, still embarrassed, but for the large part friendly.

Cognac had decided that, after all, it wasn't Paul McBean's son's fault, whatever his father's printer turned out to be. And they could hardly blame him for sticking by the old man under the circumstances. Everybody knew Killian McBean was as fond of Jean, Ethan's daughter, as if she had been his own. Though the child would probably come to a bad end, like her drunken father.

Killian returned the greetings he received, neither hurrying nor lingering in the process. He walked straight down the street and up the steps of the jail.

"Who's so smart now?" Amos Colvin jeered at him.

"Out of my way, fat stuff. I want to see Ethan."

"You can't. Terry said he's to be held incommunicado."

"All right, fat stuff. You've used the big word. Now open that door before I pull it down."

"You can't talk to the chief of police that way!"

"Get moving."

Amos Colvin met Killian McBean's eyes for a fraction of a second. The anger there startled and confused him. "Look, McBean, I can't help it if your printer goes around murdering people," he whined. "I—oh, all right, you can see him. But Terry is going to be awful mad."

"Terry's going to be more than that, before I get through with him. So are you."

"Now, McBean—"

"Open the door!"

Amos Colvin opened the door. He waddled wordlessly down the hall and let Killian into Ethan's cell. "Just holler." He locked the door behind them.

Ethan still lay on the cot, but his wooden leg was not braced against the wall. He had a towel over his face, and his slight body was limp and uncomfortable.

Without speaking, Killian strode across the cell and pulled the towel off. Ethan opened one eye, cautiously, shut it instantly as if struck by a sudden pain.

"Gnats. My head aches," he complained.

"I don't doubt it."

"Your paw would never jump on a man when he was down," said Ethan shrilly and reproachfully.

"It was my fault." Killian shook his head. "I should have known better than to wait for a lawyer. I could have gotten you one from the next town and had you let out on bail. I knew we couldn't trust that Terrence Gillespie. But it never occurred to me he'd pull anything like this."

"You talk too much," Ethan moaned. "What'd you do with my towel?"

Killian dipped the towel in the pitcher of water, wrung it out and dropped it none too gently on the old printer's face. He moaned.

"I know," said Killian. "Don't tell me. My paw would never have done that. But what I want to know is, what would my paw have done?"

"Let me sleep."

"Look, Ethan: I've got to know. What did you tell that shyster?"

"It isn't very clear right now," Ethan admitted, "but I guess pretty nearly the whole thing. We were singing and one thing led to another—gnats! I guess I didn't leave much out."

"You told him you heard Celia and Dennis Farr tell me Bennet Farr was at the hotel and you went there?"

"Yeah. Sure."

"Did you tell him you were in Bennet Farr's room?"

"Yeah. I told him the whole thing. Even about the knife."

"What about the knife?"

Ethan wriggled uncomfortably around his wooden leg. "I was the one who took it from the hotel kitchen."

"*You were what?*"

Killian got up and paced up and down the cell savagely.

"Sit down. You hurt my head."

"Good!" said Killian.

Ethan moaned and turned over on the cot, his towel falling to the floor. Killian McBean wet it again and slapped it on his face without wringing it. Ethan sat up and stared at him reproachfully.

"What in heaven's name did you take the knife for?"

"It isn't exactly plain," Ethan held his head with both hands. "I—wasn't quite clear. All I can remember is being in the kitchen and later being on the stairs with the knife in my hand. And then I was in Bennet Farr's room and he was yelling at me and the next thing he was dead on the floor with the knife in him."

"That doesn't prove you killed him."

"There wasn't anybody else there," said Ethan.

"There must have been. You don't remember actually killing him, do you!"

"No."

"You would have, if you'd done it. If you remembered any of it, and you had killed him, you would have remembered that."

Ethan put his head carefully back on the pillow and eased the rest of his body down with extreme caution. Even so, he groaned.

"You're sure there wasn't anybody else there?"

"I'm not sure about anything," Ethan's shrill voice cracked. "I don't remember anybody else being there, that's all. I think there was somebody in the hall, somewhere. Gnats. I can't remember."

"One more case of amnesia," said Killian, "and I'm going to lose my mind, not my memory. Can't you remember anything else?"

Ethan just groaned. Killian got up and wrung the towel out and carefully eased it down on his head. He put one hand on the old man's shoulder. "Don't worry, Ethan. We'll think of something."

Ethan shook his head painfully. "Don't bother about me, Killian. I'm nothing but an old drunken bum, anyway."

"Best damn printer in the state, my father always said."

Ethan grinned, briefly. "Any jobs come in since—?"

"Nothing that can't wait until you get back."

"Maybe," said Ethan reluctantly, "you ought to see about getting someone else."

Killian laughed. "I thought about Bert Miller."

"Bert Miller! That four-flusher doesn't know a press from a linotype! Don't you dare let him touch Gwen!"

"Why should I care who touches Gwen? You say yourself you're nothing but an old drunken bum."

"Now you see here, Killian McBean! I've licked you plenty of times when you were a kid and I'm not so old I couldn't do it again!"

Killian grinned at him. "Just wanted to be sure you had the old fighting spirit left." He banged on the door. "I couldn't bring Smoky. She's too busy patrolling the front porch against a yellow dog that keeps hanging around. Never saw anything so persistent, unless it was Smoky. Hurry up, fat stuff. I haven't got all day."

Ethan cheered him down the hall with a feeble rendition of "Look for the Silver Lining."

"Mr. Gillespie isn't in."

"He's in to me." Killian opened the door and went into the inner office. The secretary followed him, protesting.

"It's all right, Mary," the young state's attorney was affable in the extreme. "We're always at home to the press."

"When you say that, smile," snarled Killian. "You may not be here long enough to find out."

Terrence Gillespie smiled and leaned back in his chair. His face, carefully covered with white plaster and some sort of powder, looked strange but not badly bruised. "Threatening the state's attorney?"

"I've been in plenty of fights, some of them none too clean. But I never encountered anybody quite so low and sneaking and two-faced and crooked as you. Taking advantage of an old man's weaknesses, pretending to be his friend—"

"Of course you realize I can't discuss Ethan's case with you. It's unethical. But you may quote me as saying an indictment is absolutely certain—and so is a conviction. We adjourned the coroner's inquest until Monday."

"Pretty sure of yourself, aren't you, Terry?"

"Positive." Terrence Gillespie folded his hands over his lean stomach and leaned back in his chair, smiling.

"Whatever deal you made with Dennis Farr may look pretty good to you now, from where you sit," said Killian McBean. "But it won't look so good before I get through with you."

Terry laughed. "You terrify me."

"You tell Dennis Farr and Amos Colvin and all his other stooges that they're through. This time I'm going to run the whole rotten lot of you out of Cognac. We've had enough."

"Strange words for a newspaper editor preaching law and order."

"Not half so strange as the reform speeches you made before you were elected to office. The People's Friend. And don't worry about law and order. Tell Dennis Farr it'll be so legal he can dot the I's on the court order!" Killian slammed the door behind him.

"Temper," said Leslie Landis, who was sitting in the outer office, "never got anybody anywhere, darling."

"What are you doing here?"

"I'm going to lunch with Mr. Gillespie."

"I thought you specialized in Dennis Farr," Killian said nastily.

Leslie Landis smiled. "He's nice too. Of course you understand this is all in the line of duty. I'll give you all the details when I get back."

"Don't bother!" Killian McBean banged the outer office door behind him.

Jean was sitting in the dining room of their small frame cottage, staring disconsolately at the table. It was heaped with food: plates with cakes, others with cookies, one with a pineapple upside down cake, one with a small cooked ham. There were loaves of homemade bread, and plates covered with immaculate white napkins and bulging with inviting mystery.

"Mmm," Killian began to turn back the napkins and look at the food. "Your birthday?"

"You know it isn't. I was sixteen two weeks ago. People just brought them. They ring the bell, and leave the food and go away. Like—when somebody dies. Only nobody talks to me!"

"Me either," said Killian with a cheerfulness he did not feel. "They mean well, Jean. The fact that they go to all this trouble shows that. They're just afraid to face a condemning public opinion alone, by being publicly friendly. But that's Aunty Pliny's best cookie recipe, and Jane Colvin's maple layer cake—all their specialties."

"I don't want their old food!" said Jean. "I don't want their sympathy either. They think my father is a murderer!"

Killian asked very gently, "Do you?"

Jean looked at him and put her face down on her arms, sobbing.

"I should have known better," said Killian. He got up and gave her his handkerchief. "If we were in England, it would take my year's clothing ration points just to get enough handkerchiefs to keep you mopped up."

Jean continued to cry. He patted her a couple of times, and finally picked her up bodily and sat down with her on his lap. "The last time I did this you were four and skinned your knee," he said. "You always were quite a howler." Jean snuggled her head against his chest and cried bitterly. Killian's eyes became colder and harder than ever.

Gradually her sobs became longer and more gasping. She submitted to having her nose blown and her face wiped. Then she put her arms around Killian's neck very tightly. "Oh, Uncle Killian!"

"I don't think he did it," said Killian suddenly.

Jean's reddened eyes opened very wide. "You don't?"

"No. I don't." Killian put her down gently. "All we've got to do is prove it."

"Can we?" There was doubt in her voice. She pushed back her short hair with an unheeding gesture.

"We can try."

"Do you still think this Rosa Kincaid—"

He frowned. "I don't know. Amos and Terry, obviously, figure that the fact that Ethan brought the knife up from the kitchen proves that there was no such person as Rosa Kincaid involved. If she had come there planning to kill Bennet Farr with a knife, she would have brought one. She couldn't count on somebody else being there in the room with one waiting for her.

"Unless, of course," he continued thoughtfully, "Rosa Kincaid was already there, or came after Ethan, with another weapon, and decided on the spur of the moment to use the bread knife instead. For instance, if Rosa Kincaid lived in the hotel and saw Ethan with the knife and heard him threatening Bennet Farr, it would be the perfect chance for her to get her revenge without attaching the slightest suspicion to anybody but Ethan."

"But, Uncle Killian—" Jean stopped.

"Well?"

"Nothing."

Killian watched her carefully. "Don't you think you could tell me now about what you were doing at the hotel that morning?"

She gasped. "Did Father—?"

"No. As far as I can gather, he either doesn't remember it, or for reasons of his own isn't telling. He knew you were there, didn't he?"

"Yes, of course. I took him home."

Killian shook his head. "How did you get there?"

"Somebody called me up and told me he was there. It wasn't very long after you called me and said he was all right. I didn't know anything was wrong. I just thought he—well, wasn't feeling good—and might need me to get him home."

"Who was it that called?"

"I don't know. She didn't say. I've tried to think, since then. It was somebody I know, because I've heard the voice before, but I can't quite place it."

"What did she say?"

"Just that Father was at the hotel in room 210 and the back door was open."

"And you came right down?"

"Yes. The back door was open and I went upstairs and down the hall to 210 and—"

"Did you see anybody?"

"No. Nobody at all. Not until I saw—Father and Bennet Farr."

"What were they doing?"

"Mr. Farr was on the floor—with the knife—in his back. Father was—oh, it was awful, Uncle Killian!"

"What was Ethan doing?" Killian's voice was gentle.

"He was sitting in a chair looking at Mr. Farr and laughing."

"Laughing?"

"Yes."

Killian digested this slowly. "Which way was Ethan's chair facing? Toward the door or away from it?"

"It had its back to the door."

"So if someone had stood in the doorway and thrown the knife while Ethan was sitting in that chair, he wouldn't have seen them?"

"No, he wouldn't have seen them. But, Uncle Killian, Father had the knife!"

"Just because he started up from the kitchen with it doesn't prove he had it when he got to Bennet Farr's room. According to his story, the last place he remembered having it was on the stairs. If he dropped it somewhere, anyone could have picked it up, followed him along the hall, waited until he sat down in Bennet Farr's room and then thrown the knife from the doorway behind him."

"But there wasn't anyone in the hall when I came along," said Jean doubtfully. "And wouldn't there have been, if that happened?"

"Not necessarily. The killer couldn't have been very far away, that's certain. But there was a vacant room to step into, or if Irene or Theodora did it, there were their own rooms. The stairs to the third floor are practically by Bennet Farr's room, and there was nobody up there. When did you put my raincoat in the broom closet?"

Jean gasped. "Oh, Uncle Killian! I never thought about their finding it. I—tried to help Mr. Farr, and it got some blood on it. I couldn't wear it out on the street, so I just left it."

"It's too late to worry about that now," Killian said. "No harm was done anyway. Now tell me, was Mr. Farr dead when you got there?"

"Yes."

"Quite dead? You're sure?"

"Oh, yes. I'm sure. He was dead."

"Theodora Meredith says he was still alive when you and Ethan were at the other end of the hall. She claims to have seen him die."

Jean stared. "He couldn't have been alive then."

"If Bennet Farr was dead when she entered his room, it would seem to clear Theodora, certainly," Killian reasoned. "It would also account for her insistence on reporting that she saw Ethan. Seeing him gave her an alibi, because Bennet Farr was dead when Ethan left his room, before she claims to have entered it. Though why she should claim he was alive when he wasn't is beyond me. You didn't see Celia anywhere around, did you?"

"Celia? No. Uncle Killian, you don't think she's Rosa Kincaid, do you?"

"Of course not. Celia was here in Cognac when Dennis Farr married Rosa Kincaid. She does have red hair, but that's just coincidence."

"Do you know she was here in Cognac then?"

"I wasn't here, and I didn't see her personally, if that's what you mean," said Killian. "But I've always assumed she was. Though, now you mention it, I can't remember anybody's ever saying she was. She was away for a couple of years afterwards of course. Most of the time, that is. Anyhow, why should Celia go east and dance in a chorus and marry Dennis Farr under an assumed name? She was engaged to him; his father was crazy for the match."

"Leslie said Dennis Farr told her he was so drunk he doesn't even remember what his wife looked like. When he came to the next day he was on a plane with his father, going home."

"But Bennet Farr saw Rosa Kincaid. At least we've always assumed he did. He knew what she looked like. If it were Celia, he wouldn't have wanted the divorce. And when did she learn to throw knives in the circus?"

"Celia's always going up to the city for a couple of months at a time. The last time was when she took that nurse's aide course. There would have been plenty of time."

"If Celia wanted to kill Bennet Farr, why would she wait five years?"

"Well, I certainly wish somebody would turn out to be Rosa Kincaid," sighed Jean.

"Just one more question," said Killian. "And remember, if you can't answer it, don't. But if you do answer it, tell the truth. Do you have anything to do with killing Bennet Farr?"

"Uncle Killian!" she gasped. "Of course not! Do you think I look like a *murderess?*"

Killian grinned. "Not exactly. I just had to be sure."

Jean looked at her plump tear-streaked cheeks in the mirror with new interest. "Did you really think I could have?" she asked. She drew her mouth down and slanted her eyebrows up with her fingers. "I look more wicked that way, don't I?"

"Infinitely," he assured her cheerfully. "Is all that food just for looks, or could we try it? I haven't had anything but hamburgers since Wednesday when this affair started."

"Uncle Killian, we couldn't *eat,* with poor Father in that horrid jail!"

"Why not? It hasn't affected Ethan's appetite. Let's try that upside-down cake."

Jean eyed it cautiously. "Well, if you think it's all right."

When they actually started, they found it impossible to show strict partiality toward the upside-down cake. They sampled the cookies and cake, too. Killian finished off with a ham sandwich.

"You're king-sized, Uncle Killian," Jean said. "Eating your dessert first and then your sandwich! If you and Leslie weren't a gruesome twosome I might try to draft you myself."

"How nice," he said politely. "Unintelligible, of course, but nice. Now look, Jean. I don't want you staying here alone. I'll call Celia and you can go up and stay with her and Aunty Pliny for a few days."

"Don't be silly, Uncle Killian. I'm not a child! I'm a woman of the world. I can take care of myself."

"Celia isn't going to put you back on a bottle," Killian assured her. "You can still take care of yourself—at Celia's."

"Why can't I go to the hotel?"

"Because you're going to Celia's."

"Uncle Killian, you know it's perfectly safe here in Cognac! Most people never even lock their doors! I was here alone last night."

"You shouldn't have been."

Jean stopped suddenly. "I forgot to tell you about my burglar!"

"Your what?"

"Somebody tried to get in last night. They must have had a key or something, because they unlocked the door. But the chain was on the inside, so I guess they went away. It was probably just somebody leaving food or something. I didn't find it until this morning."

"You're sure you locked the door?"

"Yes, of course I'm sure. I always lock the door. Father says I have a suspicious nature."

"Was there any food left then?"

"Of course not, silly. It was freezing cold out. Nobody would leave food out in the cold! Probably they thought they could leave it without waking me, and when they found the chain on they went away and came back later."

"People don't come bringing food in the middle of the night and just happen to have keys to fit other people's doors. Don't forget whoever murdered Bennet Farr probably had a pass key to his door. Unless, of course, Bennet Farr opened it for Ethan and left it unlocked. Which seems unlikely, if Farr was afraid of something."

"Uncle Killian, you don't think—?"

"You're not to take any more chances," he said grimly. "You've been too many places and you may have seen too many things. Maybe you know something dangerous to the murderer. Anyhow, you're to go up to Celia's and stay there. Understand?"

"You shred it, wheat," she promised meekly.

"Can't you think of anything you haven't told me? Anything you saw at the hotel or—wait a minute. You were at the newspaper office Wednesday morning a few minutes after that incident of the blood on the front porch. Did you see anything then?"

For the first time Jean hesitated. "No. Nothing important, Uncle Killian! Nothing that had anything to do with—any of this. It was just something I found by your porch early Wednesday morning when that man was there."

"Why didn't you tell me about it then?"

"I thought you knew. I mean—I thought—well, Uncle Killian, everybody in Cognac thinks maybe you have a secret life, and I thought if there was a woman in it and I was the one to discover it—"

"*What did you find on my porch Wednesday morning?*"

"I can't tell."

"Show it to me."

"No."

"It was something connected with a woman, apparently."

Jean was silent.

"A particular woman. Who was it?" Patiently Killian persisted, but Jean continued to refuse and insist that what she found had nothing to do with the murder, anyway. Finally Killian said, "All right. Go up to Celia's. I'll be up to see you tonight and I want you to tell me then whatever it is you're holding back."

"I'll think about it, Uncle Killian. If I can figure out any way it could possibly be connected, I'll show you what I found."

They went out of the house together. Neither of them saw the door of the pantry, just off the dining room, open, or the person who came out.

CHAPTER SEVENTEEN

"But Uncle Killian's coming!" said Jean for the tenth time to Celia.

"I'll tell him where you are. He can go and bring you home, if he wants to. You know Killian; he may be working on a story or something and not show up for hours. You need some fresh air and exercise. You're losing those beautiful cheeks. Now run along."

"But Father—"

"You can't help your father by moping," said Celia firmly. "He wouldn't want you to."

"But the other kids won't want me!"

"Nonsense. Of course they'll want you. You'll have to see them all at school Monday anyway. It'll be more natural this way. You're a beautiful skater, and they're all your friends. Now run along."

"If you say so," said Jean politely but forlornly. She dawdled hopefully about her dressing until Celia came into her room again.

"Not ready yet?"

"You want to get rid of me, don't you, Celia?" the girl asked abruptly.

Celia flushed under her freckles and pushed back her auburn hair. "Of course not, honey. It's just that Denny is coming tonight, and well, his father's funeral is tomorrow and all, and I just thought it would be better if he didn't run into Killian. For both their sakes."

"Oh," said Jean. "Can't I just go to the library or something? Do I have to go skating? Everybody'll be there."

Celia's chin softened when she smiled. She wore a light turquoise blue, with white collar and cuffs, which showed her slight figure to its best advantage. "It won't be bad, Jean. You'll see."

"You don't know those drips," observed Jean glumly.

"You look lovely," Celia encouraged her. "That skating outfit is beautiful."

"Uncle Killian gave it to me when I won the junior racing championship." Jean smoothed the short red skirt carefully, and buttoned the quilted red jacket. Her sturdy legs were bare above her knee-length woolen socks.

Celia shivered. "Won't they get cold?"

"Of course not," said Jean a little scornfully. She gathered up her mittens, scarf and white figure skates. "I hope you treat most of your guests better than you do me!"

"Bring your friends back later and you can make cocoa," coaxed Celia.

"What friends?"

"Someday," said Celia, "you'll be in love. Then you'll know that nothing, nobody, else matters. You'll lie for him, steal for him, kill for him—"

"I will not!" said Jean. She went out without looking back.

Once outside, she stopped to wind her scarf around her neck

and then turned slowly, draggingly toward the river, which was across the fields and down The Road, just south of Cognac. Celia's was the last house, so the way was dark and lonely.

She did not see the figure standing on the shadow side of the oak tree. But she looked back at the lighted house uneasily and reluctantly quickened her footsteps.

The figure followed her, moving from shadow to shadow, soundlessly. Its outlines were black and indistinct, but human. It moved quickly and easily.

Jean swung her skates, and slowed down again. She looked over her shoulder just as the figure moved into a shadow.

"Is there someone here?" she asked uncertainly. Her voice echoed across the field. Jean hesitated, then walked faster. By the time she reached the road she was nearly, running. She stopped for a moment to get her breath. The figure, which was close behind her, reached for her scarf. It pulled tightly around her throat. Jean flung up an arm and broke its strangling tug. She screamed and swung her skates backwards. The figure jumped clear, and faded into a group of trees. When Jean turned, there was no one there.

The girl screamed again and ran down The Road. Her feet pounded heavily; her skates banged against her body, but she did not stop to ease the bruising pressure. She arrived at a small shack beside the river and flung herself breathlessly into the warm, heated room.

A group of high school students were sitting on the narrow wooden benches of the shack. They were lacing up their skates and fastening the straps at the ankles. As Jean burst into the room, they looked up, then down hastily. They became deeply absorbed in their skates, keeping their eyes rigidly at floor level. The girls began to nudge each other and mutter remarks in low tones, punctuated now and then by a gale of titters. The boys looked more uncomfortable; they fidgeted on the benches and laced their skates very tightly.

Jean opened her mouth, then shut it again. She was still gasping for breath as she sat down, alone, at the extreme edge of one of the benches.

A long blond boy of about sixteen, whose joints were not very well coordinated and whose feet were several sizes bigger than the rest of him, cleared his throat nervously. He looked around at his classmates, absorbed in their skates. His homely, pimpled face grew redder than the heat of the stove warranted. Finally he got up and flopped awkwardly over the wooden floor on the points of his skates.

"Hello, Jean," he said.

Jean's color, too, was very high, as was her head. But the smile she gave the boy was dazzling. "Hello, Willie."

Several of the other students put their heads up to watch, then down instantly. They met each other's eyes with difficulty.

"Lace your skates for you, Jean?" asked Willie.

"Thank you." Jean put her foot up on the bench, her leg flat and straight. Willie began to lace the white figure skates.

"Too tight?"

"No. I like them tight."

By now the undercurrent of conversations and laughter had stopped, and there was silence in the skating shack, broken only by Jean's bright voice and Willie's quiet one. Jean's voice was a little too bright, a little too loud and gay. She looked straight ahead, and gave no indication there was anybody else in the world but her and Willie.

"You're plenty potent, superman!"

"Latch your lashes at these skates," said Willie, helpfully.

"Tell me another while that one's still warm."

Willie looked a little bewildered, but kept trying. "You're on the beam, main queen."

Fortunately Willie laced fast. Jean's skates were on almost as soon as she had her breath. "Thanks, Willie."

"All right if I skate with you?"

Jean gulped a little, for the first time. "Maybe you'd better not."

Willie was magnificently oblivious. "Why not? I'm no drip."

"Well, for a little while."

Jean and Willie rose to the tips of their skates and went across the wooden floor and out the door on to the ice. Behind the door, they heard the instant burst of excited conversation which followed their departure.

"Thanks, Willie," Jean's tone strained to be bright and unconcerned. "You—don't have to stay."

"I'll stick around."

Jean hesitated, then crossed her hands and joined them with his crossed ones. They skated the width of the river in silence.

"We can't go very far up river," said Willie. "It isn't frozen over the rapids."

"No. There was a notice in the *Courier*. Anyhow, it never freezes there."

Another silence. Then Willie ventured, "What were you running for? I mean when you came in?"

"I—thought someone was chasing me. It felt like somebody grabbed my scarf and tried to—choke me."

"I thought your old man was still in jail," Willie blurted.

Jean yanked her mittened hand from his, pulled off the mitten and slapped his face as hard as she could. Willie looked more bewildered than injured. "Look, Jean, I didn't mean—"

"Don't speak to me!" Jean turned her back and skated away from him, fast. Willie plowed awkwardly behind her. "Wait, Jean," he called.

Jean tossed her short hair and whirled airily on. She got back across the river just in time to meet the rest of the skaters, emerging from the shack with their skates on. Jean gave no indication of seeing them. She turned, with a graceful movement of her hips, her full skirt flying up. While the others stood dumbly looking on, she went into an exhibition, beginning with simple figure eights and ending with elaborate backward leaps and glides which left her audience amazed and wilted.

One girl finally got her voice. "Showing off," she said quite audibly. "Come on, Willie. We're going to build a fire and toast some marshmallows."

Willie hesitated, one eye on Jean. She tossed her head and looked haughtily through him.

"Marshmallows, Willie. Your favorites."

Willie sighed, and went.

Jean occupied herself elaborately practicing her figures, back and forth, up and down, back and forth. The fire, however, was only a short distance down the river from the shack and the sound of gay voices and the good smell of toasting sweets was a little too much. Jean gulped back the tears, hesitated, skated on. Gradually she began to work her way upstream, further and further from the fire and the sound of voices. Presently she went around the bend and was completely out of sight.

The dark figure followed her along the bank, soundlessly.

"Don't be silly, Aunty Pliny. Of course she's here. I told her to stay here, and she knew I was coming."

"Don't you call me silly, Killian McBean. Trash. I tell you she's gone skating!"

"Where's Celia?"

"She went out."

Killian swore, quite audibly. "Jean didn't go alone, did she?"

"As far as I know she did."

There was no formality of good-bye. Killian left, and Aunty Pliny shut the door. The man strode down the driveway with long, quick steps. He crossed the field at a pace which was nearly a trot. At the edge of The Road he found the bright striped scarf which he had many times seen around Jean's young throat or head. Thoughtfully, he stopped to pick it up. The speed of his walking increased.

The skating shack was deserted when he got there. He called impatiently toward a group of young skaters. "Where's Jean?"

They stopped skating, but did not answer. They looked up and down and to each side—everywhere but at him.

"She—was skating up near the bend just a little while ago, Mr. McBean," Willie finally volunteered miserably.

Killian tossed a few choice remarks in the general direction of Jean's classmates which left them red and shamefaced. He started up the ice as fast as he could go without falling. Willie trailed him at a discreet distance. The other skaters compromised by merely skating in circles which gradually took them up river, as if by accident.

As he rounded the bend in the river, Killian shouted. Ahead of him, by the slight light of the crescent moon he saw a dark figure crossing the ice.

"Jean!" he shouted. "The rapids! You know the rapids are up there!"

"That's not Jean, Mr. McBean," Willie pointed out. "Whoever

that is isn't skating. They're walking. Kind of funny walking too. And they're going right for the rapids!"

Killian shouted again and regardless of the dark and slippery ice, began to run. Willie plowed doggedly along behind him on his skates. He would have passed the man if he had not twice tripped over his own feet.

"They're dragging something, Mr. McBean!" he shouted. "It looks like a body!"

This time the dark figure heard Killian's shout. It turned and saw him. A few more steps forward and it stooped for an instant. Then it was scuttling across the river in the opposite direction, over the firm ice.

"I can catch him, Mr. McBean!" shouted Willie.

Killian's hand moved instinctively into his right pocket, but his gun was not there. It was a good many years since it had been. "Never mind him! We've got to get Jean! Whoever that was threw her into the river! I saw her red jacket!"

"G-gosh!" said Willie. Manfully he redoubled his awkward skating strides.

As he ran, Killian pulled off his overcoat and suit coat and sweater, tossing them wherever they fell. As he got near the hole in the ice he kicked off his shoes. In another moment he had jumped into the icy water and disappeared.

"G-gosh!" said Willie again. He stood uncertainly. Finally he decided to yell. He did, a bellow that did full justice to his sense of the emergency.

Killian came up for air, his teeth chattering. He shouted at Willie. "I can't find her! Get the fire department! Get Old Doc! Get some blankets!" And he dove under again.

"Y-yes, sir!" said Willie obediently but doubtfully. Some of his classmates, summoned by his bellow, appeared. He shouted at them. "Get the fire department! Get Old Doc! Get some blankets!"

They flew in all directions.

Killian came up again, his face blue. "She's caught on a log!" he gasped. "I think I can get her this time! Get a board or something!"

"Yes, sir!" The fastest skater of the group tore back across the ice for one of the benches in the shack. Others began to arrive breathlessly with blankets and extra coats.

This time when Killian broke the icy surface he could hardly get his breath. But he had Jean's unconscious form in his arms. Willie lay down flat on the ice and wiggled cautiously towards the edge.

Killian had about enough energy to say, "You'll f-fall in, you little f-fool," to him.

Willie showed unexpected spirit. "You'll drown, you big fool!" he replied. He caught Jean's limp wrists and began to inch back across the ice. Several times the weight of Jean's body broke the edge back dangerously close to where Willie was, but somehow he did not fall in. Finally the bench arrived, and he was able to get Jean on it. By grasping the other end, his classmates quickly pulled her to safety. Willie went to work on the newspaper editor, who by now was clinging to almost anything with a glazed look in his eye. At last Killian, too, was pulled to safety on the bench.

"Got—to give her—artificial—respiration," Killian was barely able to mutter.

"It's all attended to, Mr. McBean," said Willie politely. "We're scouts, you know. Now I'm going to do you."

Killian felt himself turned over on his stomach, wrapped in blankets, and his head put on his arm, facing one side.

"I don't need any artificial respiration!"

"Oh yes you *do*, Mr. McBean," said Willie firmly.

His weight was solidly astride the back of Killian's hips. He began to count. "One—two—three—release. One—two—three—release."

Killian gave up.

CHAPTER EIGHTEEN

"What does Old Doc say?" Killian propped his head up on his elbow and sat up in bed.

"He doesn't know yet. She's still unconscious. He said he'd stop in here as soon as he could. I told you," Amos Colvin replied patiently. "McBean, you *must* know whether it was a man or a woman."

"I tell you I don't. The figure was quite a distance away from me, and it had on something long and black and floating. At least that's the way it looked to me. I didn't have time to look very closely, you know. It was moving away with its back to us most of the time."

"You didn't see the face?"

"I saw a white blur when it turned around and saw us. That's all."

"Don't you have any idea," asked Amos Colvin. "Didn't it impress you one way or the other—male or female?"

"No. It didn't. All I thought about was that Jean was under that ice and if the current ever caught her, she wouldn't have a chance."

"I don't see how she had a chance anyhow," Amos Colvin

shook his bulbous head on his thick neck. "Dumped in that ice-cold water unconscious with a lump on her head like a pineapple. She must've been under a couple of minutes, too, before you got there and found her."

Killian shivered. "I thought I never would get there. And when I went under twice and couldn't find her—"

"Lucky those kids knew what they were doing. Red Cross training, I guess, and scouts. Even so, the fire department had to work on her an hour before they got her breathing. And she's still unconscious."

Killian humped his lean tough body among the bedclothes. "What's Old Doc doing, anyway? What's taking him so long?"

"Nobody ever accused Old Doc of being a speed demon," Amos pointed out. "But he's good. Who do you suppose would want to kill Jean anyway?"

The newspaper editor just shook his head. He was trusting no one, especially Cognac's chief of police. "Whoever it was was pretty energetic. Of course he or she was running for his life, but he covered that ice pretty fast. Must've been somebody fairly young and active. I guess we can eliminate you and Ethan and Aunty Pliny, Amos. Otherwise, as far as I'm concerned, any of the rest of the suspects could have done it. And I'm going to find out who did!"

"You and me both," said Amos Colvin. "There's been entirely too much rough stuff going on around here. The hell with it. It's got to stop!"

"A fine time for you to be figuring that out!"

Old Doc came into the room now and looked at Killean McBean critically. "Nothing seems to hurt you," he said finally.

"Willie was pretty hard on my ribs," Killian winced. "How's Jean?"

"Still unconscious. I think her skull is fractured. It may be a couple of days before she comes to."

"But she will come to? She'll be all right?"

"I guess so," Old Doc advanced cautiously. "Can't see any reason why she shouldn't, if she doesn't get pneumonia or something. Pretty tough kid, Jean."

Killian McBean relaxed. "Sure," he said. "I knew she'd be all right."

Old Doc opened his mouth, thought a moment, and closed it. He compromised by winking at the astonished Amos Colvin. "You'd better keep some sort of a guard here," he said. "She'll have a nurse, of course, and I don't think the murderer would try anything right here in Celia's house, but it won't do any harm to be sure."

"O.K., Old Doc," Amos Colvin promised.

"I'll be here most of the time," said Killian McBean. "Celia doesn't know it yet, but she's got two guests."

"Jean's not to see anybody but Ethan," ordered Old Doc.

"Ethan's in jail!" roared Amos Colvin.

Old Doc raised a firm white eyebrow. "Doctor's orders," he said. This time he winked at Killian.

"Oh, all right," sulked Amos Colvin. "But Terry won't like it!"

Killian McBean made a growling noise in his throat, not unlike Smoky at the sight of the yellow dog.

"Now, McBean," said the chief of police quickly. He heaved himself uneasily around in his chair.

Old Doc took Killian's pulse, shook his head. "You ought to be dead. I can't account for it. A couple of days in bed and you ought to be as good as new."

"Mmm," said Killian McBean noncommittally. He closed his eyes and feigned exhaustion. Old Doc motioned to Amos Colvin, who rose and tiptoed from the room with the approximate sublety of an elephant.

When the door had closed behind him, Killian McBean sat up with some effort and looked around for his clothes. His ribs ached, and his head, but aside from being generally very tired and stiff, he found himself able to move with reasonable ease. His clothes were nowhere to be found, so he wrapped himself in a blanket Indian style and went out into the hall.

"Killian McBean, you go right back to bed this minute!" said Celia.

Killian frowned at her. "I'm mad at you. Good and mad. I sent Jean up here to keep her safe. You knew that. So you send her out skating, alone, at night!"

"I'm sorry, Killian," Celia's small face was worried and unhappy. "I didn't dream anything would happen to her. You see, Denny was coming and we were going to plan our wedding—just a simple one, of course, because of Father Farr—don't you see how terribly important it was, Killian? And if Denny had seen Jean here he would have known you sent her, and it makes him furious when I have anything to do with you and anyway he thinks Ethan killed his father. I just couldn't spoil tonight, Killian. I've waited so long for it, I couldn't!"

"Very touching. Where are my clothes?"

"They're drying in the kitchen by the stove. Killian, you can't go out tonight. You'll catch pneumonia. I'll tell Old Doc!"

Killian turned toward the stairs, without answering. Celia trailed down after him, still protesting. He whirled on her. "What do you mean, *if* Denny had seen Jean here, and we *were* going to plan our wedding? Didn't Dennis Farr show up?"

Red spots appeared on either of Celia's white cheeks. "No. He didn't even call!"

"Where were you when I called here for Jean?"

"I got worried," said Celia, "when I knew Denny wasn't coming, or at least wasn't coming anywhere near on time, I thought I'd better go and see how Jean was getting along and bring her home. I drove around the long way and got there just when they were working on you. I had them bring you both here, of course. It's closest, and anyway—"

"A little late for you to worry about Jean, wasn't it?"

"Killian, please stop!" Celia wailed. "I tell you I didn't mean to have anything happen to her! I still don't see how anything could have!"

Killian McBean opened the door to the kitchen and saw his clothes and Jean's drying on lines over the stove. He felt his. "They're dry. Most of them I tossed off while I was running, of course, so they never got wet."

He pulled them off the line and retired into the small breakfast room, leaving the door open between. The blanket he threw out to Celia, who folded it and stood holding it forlornly.

"Killian please!"

"How often are you going to let that Dennis Farr stand you up?" he asked cautiously. "Haven't you any backbone at all?"

Celia did not answer.

"All right, be a sucker. But next time don't kill other people doing it."

He heard Celia sobbing. "I didn't think you could cry," he said coldly. "I thought you were one of those patient noble women who bore their crosses without complaint." He came out, fully dressed. "What were you doing at the hotel the day Bennet Farr was killed?"

Celia's freckled, tear-stained face looked up at him, startled. "How did you know—?"

"You thought I did it," said Killian McBean. "Even though Irene Hubbard gave me a perfect, if false, alibi. That meant you had either seen me go into Bennet Farr's room or you saw my raincoat hanging in the broom closet, and the bloodstain on it. Which was it?"

"We saw the raincoat," she admitted.

He pounced on the pronoun. "We?"

Celia dropped her eyes and lowered her auburn head.

"You and Dennis Farr," prompted Killian, "saw my raincoat. Where were you?"

"I was alone."

Killian glared at her. "All right," he asked finally. "Where were you alone?"

"In the empty bedroom at the hotel."

"How long were you there?"

"We—I left right after Jean and Ethan."

"You didn't see me come in?"

"No."

"Then how could you have thought I did it? Weren't you there when the murder was committed?"

"I don't know. I was there when Ethan came. I didn't see you or Irene or Theodora come in. I couldn't see the front stairs. Father Farr was alive when Ethan came, because he unlocked the door to let him in. I heard him."

"Did he lock it again behind Ethan?"

"Yes."

"You're sure?"

"Positive. I heard him."

"Who unlocked it to let Jean in, when she came for Ethan?"

Celia's eyes were surprised as she thought. "Why—no one. It was unlocked."

"Don't you see what that means?" asked Killian. "It means Ethan didn't kill Bennet Farr! He dropped the knife somewhere in the hall and the murderer picked it up. Farr never unlocked his door after he locked it after letting Ethan in. The key was still on his desk. The murderer had a key which would open Bennet Farr's door; practically any good pass key would open those locks. He opened the door quietly when Farr and Ethan were arguing, threw the knife over Ethan's head into Bennet Farr's back, and disappeared again."

"But where did he go?"

"Probably into Irene or Theodora's room. Otherwise he or she must have gone up to the third floor and either down the back stairs from there or down the front stairs while Aunty Pliny was in Farr's room. It would take plenty of nerve, but our murderer seems to have plenty. Nobody came down the back stairs while you were in the empty hotel room?"

"No."

"Why were you hiding anyway?"

Celia's small upturned nose went further into the air. "I wanted to see Father Farr about—something private. When I heard Ethan coming, I went into the empty room, 207, to keep from being seen. I was going to see Father Farr when Ethan was through. I didn't think he'd let Ethan in, anyway."

"He wouldn't have," said Killian, "if he hadn't been more afraid of somebody else than he was of Ethan. Why didn't you go to see him after Ethan and Jean left?"

Celia Austen hesitated. Her auburn hair has slipped from its usual coil low on her neck and hung down her back in soft curls. She looked like a twelve year old, and rather small for her size at that.

"I—changed my mind about seeing Father Farr," she said.

"Why?"

Celia was silent.

"You realize, of course," Killian McBean watched her closely, "that by your own story you yourself had a perfect opportunity to slip down the hall and throw the knife over Ethan's head?"

She met his eyes steadily. "You don't really believe that, Killian. No matter how mad you are at me, you can't believe that."

"I'm a hard man. I can believe anything."

Celia lifted her determined chin. "You're no more hard than I am."

Killian McBean glared at her. She laughed suddenly. He grinned reluctantly. "I'm sorry to have to ask you this, Celia, but I've got to. Did Dennis Farr ever speak to you about his wife, Rosa Kincaid?"

Her laughter was gone, and her eyes were hurt. "No. He didn't."

"You expect me to believe you never asked him about her, kid?"

"I—did once. He said he didn't even remember what she looked like."

"That," said Killian McBean, "is exactly what I wanted to know." He bent down and kissed her gently on the forehead. Pulling his overcoat on, he made for the door.

"Killian McBean, you'll catch pneumonia!"

"I've got to send a telegram."

"You can use the phone to send a telegram from here."

"Not this telegram, kid."

"I'm coming with you. You're not strong enough. Please, Killian."

"I'm leaving you in charge of Jean, kid," he said slowly. "I wouldn't trust her with anyone else. And you're responsible for her safety. Don't trust anyone. Do you understand that, Celia? Anyone."

"I understand, Killian."

He held her tiny shoulders for an instant, then enveloped her in a careless bear-hug. "Sorry I had to get tough, kid. You wouldn't have talked at all, otherwise. You weren't exactly garrulous, as it was."

"I know," she said. She stood on tiptoe and pulled his overcoat collar up. "Be careful, Killian."

"I'm tough."

She laughed again. "Sure you are. But be careful anyway."

The man eased himself quietly up to the door of the newspaper office and tried several keys, before one fitted the door. Smoky, who was waiting patiently on the doorsill, brushed past him as he went in. The man jumped, and kicked out in the darkness. Smoky spat and leaped clear.

He did not turn on the lights, only his flashlight. With it, he made straight for Killian McBean's desk. He began to go through the drawers, frantically, pushing and pulling papers this way and that. Not finding what he was looking for, he got up and flashed the light around the room. It lit on the files, and he made for them. He began to paw through them, throwing papers to the floor, hurrying, hurrying, but not finding what he was seeking.

Another idea struck him. He went over to the mail chute, installed alongside the front door. There was one letter in it, which he seized and tore open. It contained only a gloss photograph. This he stuffed hastily into his pocket. As he made for the door, he heard Killian McBean coming up the front steps. In a panic, he turned out the flashlight and blundered back down the hall in the darkness, looking for the back door. When Killian McBean turned his key in the lock, the man flattened himself against the hall wall, behind the stairs.

The first things Killian saw, coming into the dark house, were Smoky's green eyes shining at him from where she sat on the post at the bottom of the stairs.

"Hello, Smoky," he said automatically. Then it clicked. *Smoky's in; I left Smoky out. Somebody must have let her in. Somebody may be here now.*

Regretfully his right hand closed over the space in his right pocket. Lacking a gun, he tried something he was long at: patience. He backed carefully into the dark hall corner, where nothing could creep up on him on either side, and waited.

One minute. Two minutes. Still he waited, even breathing cautiously. Then, further down the hall, he heard a sliding step, edging toward the back. A pause, then another step. There was a soft thump. Smoky's eyes were gone from the stair post. Another footstep. Killian himself began to edge quietly toward the hall light.

Suddenly bedlam broke loose. There was a squawk, a piercing cry of anger, and a number of crashing sounds from the other end of the hall. Killian switched the lights on suddenly.

"You should know better than to step on Smoky's tail, Farr," he said. "Smoky is very sensitive about her tail."

Dennis Farr, nursing a battered shin which, presumably, Smoky had attacked either with her teeth or claws, or both, snarled angrily. He pointed a gun at Killian. "Don't move."

"Aren't you a little out of your field, with a gun?" asked Killian indifferently. "I thought knives were more to your liking."

A sweat broke out on Dennis Farr's handsome, selfish face. "I didn't kill him!" he said. "I didn't kill him!"

"Maybe," Killian admitted reluctantly. "But if you didn't, you certainly know who did."

"No!" Dennis Farr's voice was near hysteria. "I don't! I don't!"

"Better put that gun down before you hurt yourself," said Killian McBean. He walked over to him and took the gun from his limp hand. "Who are you afraid of?"

Dennis Farr buried his face in his hands and sobbed hysterically.

Killian turned on the office lights. After a disgusted look at the mess which had been made of his desk and files, he went over and poured two mugs of coffee. One he thrust at Dennis Farr with scant ceremony and no sympathy. "Drink it!"

Dennis Farr did. He grew more like his usual arrogant and bellicose self.

"All right," said Killian, "it'll probably be a lie, but let's have it. What were you doing burglarizing my office?"

"Prove it," snarled Dennis Farr. "I guess my word is as good as yours in Cognac."

"Who killed your father?"

Dennis Farr sneered at him.

"Was it Rosa Kincaid?"

This brought young Farr to his feet, swinging. "Why, you—!"

"O.K," said Killian, "if you don't want to talk, run along. You'll talk before I'm through with you. Take your gun." He shoved it across the desk to him, and turned his back.

Dennis Farr put the gun in his pocket and walked jauntily to the front door and let himself out. He hesitated only a moment before going out into the cold darkness. Under the street light in front of the *Courier* office, he took out the picture he had taken from Killian's mail and began to study it closely.

He never saw the person who threw the knife. He felt it only for a fraction of a second as it entered his back. When they found his body there was no picture in his hand. He was quite dead.

CHAPTER NINETEEN

Killian sneezed again. His eyes were red, and his nose was purple. He blew this offending object vigorously.

Leslie Landis laughed. He glared at her.

"I'm so sorry, darling," she said. "But you do look so funny." She got up and came over to kiss him. "There. Feel better?"

"Germs," he warned thickly.

"Love laughs at germs, darling." She kissed him again, thoroughly. "Like that?"

"Yes," he admitted, "as much as I could like anything today. Do you think I have pneumonia?"

"I wouldn't be surprised," she agreed cheerfully. "What in heaven's name is so important about this telegram that you have to sit around all morning fuming for it? Why can't you go to bed?"

"It's just my whole story, that's all. And that fool has to go away on Saturday just when I need him!"

"What fool?"

"The one I'm sending the telegram to, of course. What other fools are there?"

Leslie Landis laughed. "I hope your disposition improves after we're married, darling."

Killian McBean frowned ferociously at her. "Did I ever promise to marry you?"

"You'd better, if you want to keep your good name in Cognac. What are you doing, making me an immoral proposition?" She came over and leaned against him, cuddling her blonde hair against his neck. He put an arm around her to steady her. Presently he barked into the telephone again.

"Of course I know his office is open Saturday. Well, then try his home again. He can't still be out. Well, look around. He must be somewhere. Chicago isn't that big!"

"Your telegram sounds important," murmured Leslie.

"It is."

The phone rang and Killian grabbed it eagerly. "Oh, hello, Amos," he said thickly and sourly. "What do you want? Who? She's what? Of course don't let her leave! Oh, tell her anything. Tell her she's a material witness. Only keep her here!"

He slammed down the phone and glared at it.

"Who wants to leave, darling?"

"Theodora Meredith. Amos got her at the railroad station, on an anonymous tip. Irene Hubbard, no doubt."

"Why should she want to leave?" Leslie was fixing her lips with a steady and practiced hand. "She hasn't done anything, has she?"

"I think her conscience is bothering her about her job. But I wish I *knew*," said Killian. "Can't you remember anything yet? Old Doc says you should at least be getting glimmerings by now."

"Sometimes I think maybe I am. Sometimes I see people and think I've seen them before, only I don't know where. But mostly before my accident is all a blank. There isn't anything there."

"Anybody in particular?"

"It's funny," said Leslie slowly, "but it's principally Celia. Celia is awfully familiar to me."

"Mmm." Killian sneezed.

"What I can't understand," said Leslie Landis, "is whatever happened to Jean. Are you sure she didn't just fall in the river?"

"Certainly I'm sure. I saw the murderer dragging her. Willie saw him too. Or her. Besides, what about the bump on her head?"

"What about it?"

"It's very plain," said Killian. "The murderer wanted it to look like an accident, not murder, and especially not a murder connected with Bennet Farr's. That would have made it plain Jean was killed because of what she found on my porch Wednesday morning and make us turn in the very direction we were not meant to. So the murderer couldn't use a knife, but instead threw a rock, or maybe a chunk of ice, and hit her on the head. Once she was unconscious, it was a simple matter to drag her across the ice to the open water by the rapids. If we hadn't happened to see the whole thing, Jean's body would probably not even have been found until spring. Even if it had, there would be no reason to have thought anything but that she just fell in."

He cranked the phone again and barked into it. "What about my telegram? Oh, all right. I *am* waiting. You got him? What did he say? What? Read that again. Slowly. All right. Thanks. No, I'll have to check it before I send an answer. Get me the post office, Betsy. Oh, sure, somebody'll be there even if Dick is getting his hair cut. Hello. This is Killian McBean. I want to check on a special delivery letter that was mailed to me yesterday morning from Chicago. Yes, Friday morning. It should have come in on the six o'clock train last night. What? It did? Well, what happened to it? You delivered it here? You know I never get any mail here—always at my box at the post office. Yes, I know specials are delivered to the door. I also know people sign for them. Who signed for this? Oh, the boy signed it himself? Who was the bright messenger? Oh." He groaned. "Willie. I might have known. No, never mind. No, I'm not complaining. Forget it."

He hung up, feeling his ribs in gingerly reminiscence. Going over to the mail chute by the front door, he stopped to pick up an envelope which lay on the floor beside it. He turned it over disgustedly. It was torn and empty.

"Is that your letter, darling?"

"That's it," Killian replied grimly. "Now I know what Dennis Farr was looking for last night. Apparently he found it. And was killed because he knew too much." He cranked the phone and said, "I'm ready with the answer to that telegram now, Betsy. O.K., here it is. 'Letter arrived, but picture subsequently stolen. Rush duplicate by messenger, also special delivery. Urgent. Killian.' Same address. That's it. Thanks, Betsy. Yes, I've got a cold!" He put up the receiver with a little more than necessary vigor. A sneeze overtook him immediately.

"Darling, maybe a hot lemonade—" said Leslie Landis.

"One more cold cure," he threatened, "and I'll start throwing knives myself." He got up and put on his overcoat. "I'll be back."

"Where are you going?"

"Out to cover my story."

"Can't I come along and help?"

He shook his head. "These are calls on women. Somehow I don't think you'd be much help."

"Are you going to see Jean?"

"No. Nobody can see Jean for a couple of days. She's unconscious, anyway."

Leslie Landis yawned. "What am I going to do while you're gone?"

"Try working on this week's accounts. They should have been done yesterday." Killian sneezed again.

"Oh, Killian! I knew you'd come!" Mrs. Bennet Farr extended her hand graciously and presented her flabby cheek to be kissed. "You aren't the one who's throwing all those dreadful knives, are you?"

Killian said no, he wasn't.

"So dreadfully inconvenient, too," complained Frances fretfully. "We were going to have Bennet's funeral this morning, you know. And now Celia insists that we wait until Monday and combine them. Why couldn't we have two?"

"I really think one would be better, Frances," Killian told her gently.

"You do?" Frances was disapprovingly surprised. "It seems—lacking in respect to me somehow."

"Celia wouldn't want anything lacking in respect, Frances."

"Celia!" she said fretfully. "Nothing but Celia! Celia is a wonderful girl. Celia is this. Celia is that. The only good thing about this whole affair is I'll never have to see Celia again. But why should she have half the money? Tell me, why should she have half the money?"

"Because Bennet wanted it that way in his will," Killian reminded her. "Celia really loved Dennis, you know."

"Oh, I suppose so," she admitted, "in her own way. But he never loved her!"

Killian forebore from pointing out that Bennet Farr never loved Frances either, or that Frances exhibited no noticeable sorrow at the loss of her husband and her son. "How are you feeling today, Frances?" he inquired dutifully. Immediately she launched into an extensive account of her symptoms. The avalanche stopped when Killian inadvertently sneezed.

"My throat spray!" she cried, pulling the bell for her maid. "My nose drops! Oh, I can feel the germs penetrating! Killian, how could you do such a thing?"

In the resulting mêlée Killian escaped relatively unnoticed. He did not go out immediately, however. First he made a careful search of the rooms of Bennet and Dennis Farr. In neither did he find what he was looking for—a picture of Rosa Kincaid. But he did discover one thing: Dennis Farr's desk had been completely swept clean of all personal papers.

He went directly to Celia's house next door.

"May I see Celia, Old Doc?" asked Killian.

Old Doc shook his head. "I finally got her to sleep with a sedative," he said. "She can't be disturbed."

"How did she take it?"

"I can't say. I didn't see her until this morning when I came to see Jean."

"How did Celia look?"

"Stunned, mostly. She was terribly quiet. Of course she's always quiet, but this was something different. She didn't cry, or say anything. She had been crying, though, I guess; her eyes looked like it. Aunty Pliny said she didn't say anything when the news came about Denny; just stood there and took it. Finally she put on her hat and coat and went out, and didn't come back until morning."

"Where was she?"

"I doubt if she knows. She looked as if she might have been walking all night. She was exhausted."

Killian shook his head.

"That fat fool Amos Colvin," said Old Doc contemptuously, "thinks she killed him."

"He thinks Celia killed Dennis Farr? Is he crazy?"

"Just dumb," said Old Doc. "Can you keep a secret?"

"Not if it's news."

Old Doc agreed. "I think you'll keep this one. Go in and see Jean."

"Jean! Is she—?"

"Go in and see for yourself. I told the nurse it was all right."

Killian knocked quietly on the door. A smiling nurse let him in. Jean was still lying flat on her back, but she was conscious. She smiled faintly but cheerfully.

"Well, chop me up and call me suey!" she said.

Killian just grinned down at her. "Good girl."

"Where'd you get that cold, Uncle Killian?" Jean's tone was fading.

"What cold?"

"See my roses?" Jean pointed happily. "Willie sent them. He works for the government!"

"I know." Killian remembered the special delivery letter.

Jean giggled. "He thinks you're wonderful, Uncle Killian. So brave. I guess it must have been important after all."

"What you found on my porch?"

"Yes. Is it still in my purse?"

Jean was asleep. Killian followed the nurse out quietly.

"She isn't entirely clear yet," Old Doc explained. "But she's coming around remarkably. Hasn't even caught a cold."

Killian sneezed.

"You ought to be in bed!" Old Doc barked at him and without waiting for an answer, went down the hall.

Killian found Jean's quilted skating jacket and took the small purse from the zipper pocket. It contained only a quarter and three pennies, a compact, a bright red lipstick, a white button, and a pencil and pad, completely blank.

Leslie Landis opened the *Courier* door a few inches and spoke to Killian, coming up the steps. "Can't you do something about that yellow mongrel? He looks vicious to me. Who does he belong to?"

"I don't know. Must be a stray. I've never seen him around town until a day or so ago. I don't think he's vicious."

The yellow dog growled angrily.

"You see," said Leslie Landis. "He's dangerous!"

"Probably his encounters with Smoky are souring his disposition," Killian grinned. "I've seen her send him yiping down the street at least three times. I wonder why he keeps coming back."

The dog growled again, more threateningly. The cut on his head looked better. But in the back of his eyes was cold misery.

Killian snapped his fingers at him, but was ignored. "The beast's probably hungry. I'll get him something."

"If you feed him he'll never leave!"

"If I don't feed him he'll starve."

Killian went upstairs to his kitchen, trailed by a protesting Leslie.

"Smoky is going to hate me," Killian opened a can of prepared meat. "Next to tuna fish, this is her favorite delicacy."

"Killian, that takes points!"

"The dog is hungry," he pointed out. "I'll get him some dog biscuit this afternoon. What's the matter with you, can't you stand dogs, either?"

Leslie Landis slammed the kitchen door.

Killian mixed the prepared meat with some hot broth and mashed in a few left over vegetables. Grinning, he borrowed Smoky's milk bowl and filled it with warm milk. He carried both dishes down to the front porch and called the yellow mongrel. The dog sat, wet and cold and miserable, near the lattice covering the opening under the porch, but would not come near Killian.

"I hope you're satisfied," said Leslie Landis, through a crack in the door. "All those points!"

"He'll eat it. He just requires privacy." Killian left the dishes and went back into the house. Through the now replaced bay windows of the office they watched the dog. It looked around suspiciously. It tried ignoring the food, although its mouth dripped with longing. Finally it came reluctantly over to sniff the plates. At last it bolted the contents practically whole. It went back under the porch.

At this instant Smoky came prowling around the corner of the house. Unbelievably she stared at her milk bowl. She also stared at the plate. Haughtily she sniffed it to ascertain what its late contents had been. There was blood in her eye when she found out. She ruffled up her tail and furled it straight in the air. Her fur ballooned out, doubling her size. Her ears went back and she started for her objective with a fearsome yowling sound.

The yellow dog trembled under the porch, but this time he did not run. He snarled ferociously. Smoky was only momentarily taken aback. Her size grew larger and her eyes were green pools of hatred. She sprang with the confidence and fury of a lion.

The yellow dog cringed and looked around in panic, but still he did not run. Since he did not run, he was obliged from sheer self-preservation to fight back. This he did. True, his defense sprang from desperation and was more noise than actual bite, but it was nonetheless impressive. It impressed Smoky. Used to having dogs twice the size of the yellow mongrel flee before her fury as a matter of course, Smoky found herself involved in a knock-down-and-drag-out battle which was the more undesirable from being unexpected.

At first Smoky was unbelieving: she struck out with flying paws and claws and teeth and hissed in her most terrifying manner. When the yellow mongrel did not yield ground, but instead seemed to be gaining strength, Smoky took the shortest distance between two points—a straight line up the maple tree in front of the house. Although entirely unpursued, she climbed to the very top and sat there, howling mournfully.

"That dog *is* vicious," said Killian McBean indignantly. He stared disbelievingly at his vanquished black warrior. Then he put on his overcoat and went out the door and down the front steps.

"Come on," he commanded the yellow mongrel. "Out! On your way! Get going! You can't attack my cat and get away with it!"

The dog cringed back, still trembling, but snarled when Killian reached for his collar. The man stooped down to pull him from under the porch. A moment later he straightened up, his face grave. Without further attention to the dog, he ran up the steps and into the office and cranked the phone frantically.

"Hello, Betsy. Get me Amos. Amos Colvin. And hurry, will you? That you, Amos? McBean speaking. You'd better get right over here. I've found your other corpse. It's a man. He's under my front porch."

CHAPTER TWENTY

"You don't have to shoot the dog, Amos," said Killian. "He won't leave the body; apparently he's guarding it. The man must have been his master. But no dog who sticks around guarding his dead master in this bitter cold without food is going to be shot. Use chloroform."

"Oh, all right. The hell with it. But it's only a mongrel," said Amos Colvin.

They used chloroform in considerable quantities before the dog was unconscious; then Killian McBean wrapped him carefully in an old blanket and carried him in by the stove. He washed the cut on the animal's head.

Leslie Landis, by Killian's advice, had gone back to the hotel, white and shaken. Killian had insisted that she look through the window at the corpse, to see if she knew him.

"No," she said faintly. "No, I don't know him. At least I don't remember knowing him. I would, wouldn't I?"

"He was probably killed in your car. You must have been there. Maybe you were unconscious. But how did he get in your car in the first place if you didn't know him? He's a stranger in Cognac."

"I don't know, Killian. I tell you I don't know!"

Killian ruffled her blond hair thoughtfully. "Go on back to the hotel. This won't be very pleasant. Better use the back door. No use stirring the dog up. He nearly took a piece out of me when I tried to look at the man." She left.

"How long has he been dead, Old Doc?" Killian asked now.

"Couple of days anyhow," grumbled the doctor. "That lattice work kept you from seeing him. But if it hadn't been so cold—"

"Could he have been dead since Wednesday morning?"

"It's possible. He's plenty stiff. I'll let you know later. Offhand, a couple of days, two anyway, is as close as I can get."

Terrence Gillespie chose that moment to arrive.

"Who is he? What killed him?" he demanded, stamping his feet in the cold and looking at the body under the porch.

"We don't know, and a knife in his back," said Killian coldly. "Whom are you going to try to pin this one on?"

"Now, Killian," said Old Doc mildly. "It's a rather special kind of knife this time, Terry." He held it up. The knife was long and narrow and almost frail looking. Its handle was intricately carved bone.

Killian looked at it. "It's too strong and sharp to be an ornament and too long and elaborate to be used for cutting anything. I'd say it was made for just about what it was used for—throwing. Perhaps a professional's?"

Terrence Gillespie looked at the knife long and carefully. He cleared his throat nervously. "It looks like it," he admitted cautiously. "Maybe—maybe there is something to this Rosa Kincaid theory of yours, Killian."

"What's that?" demanded Old Doc.

Killian explained briefly.

"You mean the killer is either the librarian or the schoolteacher or that amnesia girl?" asked Old Doc, plainly charmed with the idea.

The librarian or the teacher, Killian explained; it was proved beyond any doubt that Leslie Landis had been in California at the time. "There's always the brother, too, of course," he said. "Or husband or whatever he was. But Terry here is the only man young enough who's come to Cognac within the time limits."

Terrence Gillespie's jaw fell open and he stared at Killian. "You mean you think I threw knives in a circus for a living?" This seemed to insult him more than the implication that he was the murderer.

"It's always possible," Killian sneezed.

"You ought to be in bed!" roared Old Doc.

"What about Ethan?" Killian asked Amos Colvin.

The chief of police shifted his small eyes and enormous body. "Well—he signed a confession—"

"It's plain even to you," Killian pointed out, "that three people all killed by knives in their backs within four days isn't coincidence. They're all professional jobs, and they were done by one person."

"Ethan was in jail when Dennis Farr was killed," Killian continued. "Otherwise he makes an ideal suspect. Except, of course, that he was drunk when Bennet Farr was killed and couldn't have held a knife steadily, let alone throw it."

"I don't think he done any of them, Terry," advanced Amos Colvin.

"Whose side are you on, anyway?" roared the infuriated state's attorney.

"My own." Amos Colvin was at least direct. "We ain't got no Farrs back of us now, don't forget. You're smart, and legal, and all. I'm not either. To hell with it. If you want to go on fighting, all right. Me, I want an armistice. I'm going to let Ethan out. We can always get him again if we want him, and if we don't, McBean here can run his paper and all."

Killian sneezed happily.

The body of the strange man, having been photographed and charted at the insistence of Terrence Gillespie, was now removed from under the porch. The man had been about fifty, around five feet eight inches in height, and moderately heavy. His eyes were blue. On his right cheek near the nose was a large mole. Scars of an operation showed at the side of his neck. He had been lying face down. A search of his pockets revealed only an empty wallet.

"No papers, no money, no nothing," grunted Amos Colvin. "How the hell are we going to identify him? Nobody could have missed him much, or there would have been a squawk before this."

"Fingerprints," said Old Doc. "Probably has a record. People who run around getting murdered generally have."

"I don't hold with them fingerprints," grunted Amos Colvin. "Just because they never found two people with the same ones don't prove there ain't two people, does it?"

Old Doc and Killian McBean and Terrence Gillespie just looked at him.

Amos Colvin was unabashed. "Say!" he pointed. "What's that?"

The corpse was pretty well covered with dried blood, which made observation difficult. But when the body was turned over, there was more blood on the front than there had been on the back. And, where Amos Colvin pointed, there was a small round hole in the man's chest.

Old Doc knelt stiffly on the cold ground. "Shot," he said

briefly. "Bad wound, but not necessarily fatal. Anyway, not immediately. He must have bled a lot."

"That explains what happened on my front porch," said Killian McBean.

"How?" Amos Colvin was growing more respectful of Killian's opinions.

"Somebody shot this man, but not fatally. Probably he was shot while driving Leslie's car and that caused the crash. Leslie was knocked on the head, and with blood all over both of them, the murderer thought they were both dead. Either that, or the murderer was scared away by something after the shooting. Anyhow, this man came to and somehow staggered from the scene of the accident here. Could he have gotten that far, Old Doc?"

"Could be," Old Doc said grudgingly. "He must have lost a lot of blood, though."

"Somehow, he got here. He was bleeding badly. Maybe he stopped to rest on the porch, intending to get help, or maybe he fainted. Anyhow, the murderer went back to the accident while Leslie was still unconscious, missed this man and followed him here. When the murderer caught up with him, he or she finished him off with a knife. The murderer tried to drag the body away, but the noise woke me up. So he or she shoved it under the porch, and it's been so cold ever since nobody found the body. It didn't occur to Amos to look as far as under the porch, of course."

"You could of looked, couldn't you? It's your porch," Amos pointed out.

"Next time I will!" Killian sneezed. "Don't say it, Old Doc. I ought to be in bed."

"I've been wanting to try some of those sulfa drugs on pneumonia," said Old Doc cheerfully.

When the body had been taken away, and Old Doc and

Amos Colvin and Terrence Gillespie had followed it, Killian McBean went wearily back into the *Courier* office. He poured himself three white mugs of coffee and lined them up on the edge of the desk. He put his feet up and sneezed and drank coffee. Mostly he thought intensively.

The phone rang. He got up casually and took it off the receiver. "Hello. Oh, hello, city girl." It was Irene Hubbard.

"Hello," Irene was being sweetly charming. "Say, what's going on up there at the newspaper office, anyway?"

"What makes you think anything is?"

"People," said Irene, "they're standing around there three deep."

"Just waiting for next week's *Courier*."

"Speaking of that, I have an item for you."

"Yes?"

"Terrence Gillespie and I are engaged."

"You don't say! When did all this happen?"

"Last night at dinner. It was pretty sudden, in a way, but still—I think both of us knew it was inevitable, from the moment we met."

"When shall I say the wedding is planned for?"

"Just say our plans as to date are indefinite."

"O.K. Thanks for the item, Irene."

"Have you got a cold? It sounds terrible. You ought to do something for it. Now, hot lemonade—"

He replaced the receiver and poured three more mugs of coffee. He put his feet back up on the desk and thought some more. Outside he could hear Smoky wailing long catcalls from the top of the maple tree. Presently the phone began to ring.

"Yes," he said wearily. "I know my cat is up the tree. She can get down. She goes up and down that tree a dozen times a day. It's her favorite way of getting in the house. I can't help how she sounds. Certainly she can get down. Yes. I do have a cold. All right. I'll try that."

Everybody in town, it appeared, was worried about Smoky. And everybody had a different cold cure.

Beside the stove, the yellow dog began to stir and mutter in its throat. The chloroform was wearing off.

The sound of singing came down the street. It was the hale if somewhat raucous strains of *He's a Jolly Good Fellow*. Presently it was accompanied by the stamp of marching feet. Someone crashed on to the front porch amid sounds of applause and "Speech! Speech!"

"My friends and fellow-citizens," Ethan's voice was somewhat thick, albeit still shrill. "I thank you. Gnats! I thank you one and all. It was a damn dirty trick, you thinking I'd murder anybody, even Old Gluts Farr, but we'll call it square. Gnats! I fought for you in the last war and I will again in this. Monday I intend to enlist in the marines. Gnats! I'll show those Japs and Jerries! I thank you." Probably in this mood, Ethan would have been talking yet, if the cold had not been so extreme. As it was, he came stamping happily in.

"Hello, marine," said Killian McBean sourly.

Ethan beamed and beat his wooden leg on the floor. "Gnats! What rank do you think I'll get?"

"General."

"Oh, I don't know," Ethan was modest. "Maybe they'd want to start me a little lower than that. Just so as not to discourage the others. But you got to hand it to the marines, they know a good man when they see one!"

Killian McBean sneezed.

"You ought to do something for that cold," said the old printer.

"I'll do that. So they let you out?"

"Celia made old lady Pliny tell 'em about putting the type around, last night," said Ethan. "Meddling old bitch. And Celia told 'em about hearing Bennet Farr lock the door after me, and how it was open when Jean came. So that proves somebody else opened it behind me while I was there, and Old Doc says the knife that killed Bennet Farr was absolutely thrown, and in my condition I couldn't possibly have done it, so—" Ethan began to sing *The Battle Hymn of The Republic*.

"I trust you will now see the error of your ways," said Killian glumly.

Ethan opened his sharp brown eyes very wide. "What error?"

Killian sighed. "Did your lawyer show up?"

"Oh, he came this morning," Ethan admitted reluctantly. "Gnats! He yelled at Amos Colvin and told him they didn't have a thing but hot air and he'd have me out as soon as he could get a writ of something or other—"

"Habeas Corpus. It's in the Constitution. They can't hold you without showing reason why."

"They held me illegal!" shouted Ethan, banging his wooden leg violently. "They can't treat a veteran that way! And I'm practically a marine! I'll report 'em to the F.B.I."

"You do that." Killian sneezed. Ethan embarked on the third stanza of *The Battle Hymn of the Republic*. "I saw Jean this morning."

Ethan stopped singing. "She all right?"

"Sure. Fine. Of course if she hadn't been chasing around worrying about you, she wouldn't be practically unconscious now, with a bump on her head and maybe pneumonia coming on, for all we know. She wouldn't have had to go through what she did last night—having her lifelong friends turn on her and—maybe you don't realize what an experience like that means to a kid."

The light faded from Ethan's face. He twisted his slight aging body. "No matter if I did get drunk," he pleaded, "I never meant to do anything to hurt Jean. You know that, Killian!"

"It hurts just as much whether it's intentional or not." Killian's jaw was grim.

"Your paw would never have said that," reproached Ethan.

Outside in the maple tree, Smoky wailed forlornly. The yellow dog stirred again, and opened his eyes. For one instant they were uncomprehending; then they shot fire. He leaped out of the blanket, snarling, to fall uncertainly when his legs failed to hold him. He struggled to his feet again, however, and ran around the room, howling madly. Finally he clawed frantically at the door. Killian McBean got up and let him out. The dog made for the place under the porch where his master's body had lain. Failing to find it, he sat down and bayed his heart out.

Smoky, who had progressed down a branch or two from the top of the tree, instantly ascended again to the uppermost limits, and added her howl to the fray.

"Oh, shut up!" said Killian McBean to her.

Smoky went on howling. Killian went back into the house, put on two sweaters and his overcoat, overshoes, and a muffler. Sneezing, he went out and sat on the top step.

"I never got that drunk!" Ethan taunted through a crack in the door.

Killian McBean huddled into his overcoat and said nothing. Smoky continued to howl. The yellow dog, however, gradually quieted down and became a shivering, whimpering mongrel again, cowering under the porch. Presently he crept out and stood looking at the man on the porch uncertainly. Smoky wailed angrily. The dog sneaked up the steps and sat on his haunches at the extreme end of the top step. Killian McBean did not look at him. Gradually the yellow mongrel sidled closer and closer to him. After a while the man put his hand on the dog's coat. He whimpered and shrank back, but did not snarl. Killian McBean rubbed the lopsided ears. The lost frightened look did not entirely leave the dog's eyes, but it lessened. When Killian got up to go in, sneezing, he snapped his fingers carelessly, and the dog followed hesitantly at his heels.

Smoky shrieked her rage as the door closed behind them.

"All kinds of people are calling up about Smoky," said Ethan reproachfully. "Is that mutt going to stay here?"

"Yes."

"Looks vicious to me. Gnats! Aren't you going to get Smoky down?"

"No. She knows perfectly well how to get down herself. She's just being temperamental."

"She sounds awfully unhappy."

Killian sneezed. "How do I sound?" He made the dog a bed by the stove, but the yellow mongrel kept slipping over to lie at Killian's feet. Finally Killian brought the blanket over there, and the dog went to sleep.

"No license, but he's got a nice collar," said Killian. He went down to examine it. He straightened up to stare unseeingly at Ethan.

"So that's it!" he said.

"Sure," Ethan agreed amiably. "What is?"

Killian was cranking the phone frantically. "Betsy, I want to send a telegram. To the same man as the last one. Well, they'll have to hunt him up again. It's important. All right. Here it is. 'Rush descriptions of ABCD. Include gender. Killian.' It's all right, Betsy. He'll know what it means. No, it isn't against the regulations. It isn't code. Just abbreviations. Thanks. Good-bye."

"Mighty funny sounding telegram," said Ethan mildly.

Killian McBean snapped his watch open and looked at the picture in it for perhaps a minute. Then he turned to his typewriter and began to work furiously, sneezing but not looking up.

"Yes, I know," said Killian McBean for the hundredth time, several hours later. "My cat is up a tree. I can't help how she sounds. She isn't in trouble. Oh, all right, I will do something about it!"

He slammed down the receiver and grumpily got on his sweaters and overcoat again. Ethan also put on his. "I'm going up to see Jean," he said. "You don't think anything of catching pneumonia for a yellow mongrel you never saw before, but you grumble your head off about helping a little cat that's practically your own flesh and blood."

"Practically," snapped Killian McBean. He went down in the cellar and carried the long ladder up, panting and swearing. The yellow dog followed at his heels. Smoky was pacing up and down the topmost branch, peering with what seemed to the uninitiated to be anxiety.

"Now, Smoky," said Killian McBean without much hope. "Come on down!"

Smoky merely wailed piteously. Killian explained in detail the process of climbing down a tree, with gestures. Smoky listened politely, then went on howling. Resignedly, Killian put the ladder against the tree and began to climb it. The yellow mongrel jumped anxiously at the base of it. Killian mounted gingerly and reached for Smoky. She shrank back to nothingness at the furthest end of the branch. There was not a graspable part of her. He reached still further. The branch gave way, and he, Smoky and the ladder came tumbling down with a crash that could be heard for blocks.

"Killian!" The voice was Celia's. "Are you hurt?"

"I wouldn't be surprised," he said with undiluted bitterness, "if I had a broken neck." He reached over and felt the bones of the yellow mongrel, who had been at the bottom of the pile. Smoky, of course, had been on the top. She had landed, in fact, on Killian's stomach. She walked loftily off now, taking a sidewise swipe at the yellow mongrel's nose.

"No, Smoky!" said Killian McBean. "Chase all the other dogs you want, but not this one. He's ours now. He lives here."

Smoky hissed her disapproval, but took no further notice of the yellow dog. She climbed the front steps and sat waiting patiently for Killian to let her in.

"Nothing broken," Killian assured Celia. "But it's damn humiliating!" He sneezed and patted the yellow mongrel. "You'll get used to Smoky. I did." He and Celia and the yellow dog trailed the black cat into the office.

"I thought you were to sleep all day," Killian said to Celia, peeling off his overcoat and starting on the sweaters.

"Killian, you really ought to do something for that cold!"

His head halfway in and halfway out of the second sweater, Killian just groaned. Finally he emerged from all the layers and surveyed Celia critically. She looked very small and white and tired, but better than he had expected. The thing that surprised him most was the expression with which she regarded him. It was unhappy, but the unhappiness was not entirely her own.

"You wanted to see me, kid?"

She nodded, the knot of auburn hair bobbing on her neck. "I was planning on going up to Chicago after—the funeral," she said quite calmly. "Amos Colvin says I can't. He thinks—I killed Denny. He thinks I killed all of them! Killian, you don't think I—you said last night—"

"Do you think I would have left Jean there if I had had the slightest doubt?"

"I didn't tell you the truth, you know. At least, I left enough out so what I said wasn't true."

"You don't have to be in the newspaper business long, kid," Killian said, "to know when a story is phony. I've been in it quite a while."

Celia's chin trembled. "You don't always know when stories are phony. Even you can't always know, Killian."

"I usually find out." He was grim.

Celia's eyes were softer than he had ever seen them. "I suppose so." She continued to regard him unhappily.

"Does it hurt so much, kid?" he asked.

She nodded, quietly. He put a large hand over her small one and for a moment neither of them said anything. It was the girl who broke the silence. "Killian." She stopped. "Amos was telling me what you think about—Rosa Kincaid. Why didn't you tell me?"

"Hardly a pleasant subject for you, was it?"

"But if you had told me, maybe—. Don't you see it was inevitable that she would kill Denny after he didn't get the money? She might have let him live if she could have remarried him and shared his inheritance. But when there was no inheritance and she had a murder to cover and there was always a chance he would recognize her—"

"I should have known it," Killian admitted. "He was killed because the murderer finally thought he had recognized her, through the picture, and would report her identity to the police.

But I wasn't thinking along those lines at the moment. I had conceived the theory that Terrence Gillespie was Rosa's brother. You know, the partner in the knife-throwing act. It was a nice theory, while it lasted. It didn't last long." He explained about the circus.

"Killian," she asked. "Why was Denny here last night?"

"He must have had an employee either listening on the party line for my telegrams or waiting at the post-office or something. Plainly he knew I was expecting a picture of Rosa Kincaid. That was what he was looking for." He explained about the torn and empty envelope.

"Probably he was stopping to look at it under the streetlight when—" He stopped. "Sorry."

Celia shivered, her face white.

"Want to tell me about it now, kid?" he asked gently.

She nodded. "What do you want to know?"

"We might as well start at the beginning. You don't know anything about the man who was found dead under my front porch, of course?"

Celia shook her head. "Amos asked me to look at him. I never saw him before."

"All right. What was Bennet Farr doing out at Indian Mound at five in the morning Wednesday?"

She hesitated. "Denny said his father had an appointment to meet someone. A stranger. Someone that was coming to Cognac, but with whom Father Farr did not want to have any public connection."

"You don't know who it was?"

"Denny said his father never told him the man's name."

"But he was sure it was a man?"

"Yes."

"Bennet Farr had an appointment to meet a strange man

Wednesday morning. The only strange man who has turned up is dead. Probably he was the one Bennet Farr was expecting to meet. But if he was killed on my front porch, it was before Bennet Farr was out at Indian Mound, because the accident Bennet Farr reported was relayed to Amos Colvin while he was here investigating the blood on the front porch. The man's body must have been under the porch then. The question is, had he already seen Bennet Farr or did he ever see him?"

"I don't see how you can find that out now that they're both dead."

"Neither do I," admitted Killian. "But Bennet Farr saw somebody or something that morning that scared him. It may not have been connected with his appointment; it may have been coincidental. Something may have happened while he was waiting for an appointment that was never kept. Whatever happened, we know what he did next. He stopped at his lawyer's house, routed him out of bed, and changed his will, disinheriting Dennis and giving you half his estate."

Celia nodded. "He was going to do that, anyway. Oh, don't worry, Killian; Mrs. Farr told me the whole thing. Father Farr was trying to hurry our wedding plans, but Denny still wanted to wait. Finally, the night before Father Farr was killed, he and Denny quarreled violently about the matter, and Father Farr said he would disinherit Denny and leave his half of the money to me. Naturally Denny was angry at being practically forced to marry me. It wasn't that he didn't want to marry me, but Denny never could stand to be forced to do anything. You understand that he really did want to marry me, don't you, Killian?"

"Sure, kid," said Killian gently. "A guy would have to be crazy not to want to marry you."

Celia smiled faintly. "I wish it had been you, Killian."

"So do I, kid."

"Do you think whatever happened Wednesday morning before Father Farr was killed made him hurry to change his will?"

"It must have. He had an appointment with his lawyer later in the day. Now tell me about what happened when you went to the hotel. Why did you go to the Metropole anyway?"

Celia flushed under her freckles. "Denny—heard that his father had been seen at his lawyer's and he went to the Metropole to see Father Farr. That was pretty early in the morning, I guess; I was still busy looking after Leslie after her accident. They—quarreled pretty violently—Denny and his father. Father Farr refused to change his mind about the money. When Denny was leaving, he told Denny he wanted to see you. That was why Denny and I stopped at your office after breakfast.

"After we left there, Denny and I separated. He didn't say, but I thought he was going back to the hotel to see his father again. Denny was pretty angry. After college, you know, he had other plans; he was interested in geology. He didn't want to come back to Cognac at all, but his father said if he did he would leave him the lumber business and half of everything he owned. Denny had put in four years at work he hated, because of that promise, and he thought his father should keep it. And he said the whole thing wasn't fair to me; now when he married me, everyone, including me, would always wonder if he did it to get the money."

Killian McBean's face was impassive; only his eyes moved. "Go on, kid."

"I was worried," Celia admitted. "Denny was very angry, and both he and his father had terrible tempers. I thought maybe if I told Father Farr I didn't want the money—so I went to the hotel."

"Did you go in the front or back way?"

"The front."

"Aunty Pliny just conveniently forgot to mention your visit to the police or anyone?"

"No," said Celia slowly, "she didn't see me. At least she never said she did, although she rather acted that way. Aunty Pliny wasn't at the desk when I went in."

"She said she didn't leave the desk all morning."

Celia shook her head. "She wasn't there then. She was probably just in the washroom or something, and forgot it, or was too ladylike to mention it to the police. She must have been there shortly afterwards, because she was there when you came, wasn't she?"

"Yes. If I hadn't stopped to talk to her I would probably have run into the murderer myself."

Celia sighed with relief. "I thought you meant you suspected Aunty Pliny!"

"Whoever threw that knife moved a lot faster than Aunty Pliny, Celia. Besides, I think she was talking to me when the murder was being committed. What happened after you went up the stairs?"

"Nothing, at first. I didn't know which way the numbers ran, and I naturally thought Father Farr would have the biggest room, at the back, overlooking where the garden would be in summer. So I went back there and knocked on the door. I didn't notice it was 207. There was no answer, so I tried the door and found the room empty. Then I heard Ethan coming up the back stairs.

"I didn't want him to see me there, so I just shut the door quietly and stayed in the empty room. He was singing pretty loudly and yelling for Father Farr. I—knew how bitter Ethan was about his leg and he'd been drinking quite a lot, and I was worried. So I went downstairs and called Jean to come and get him. I didn't mean to get Jean into anything, Killian, honestly I didn't. I didn't think Father Farr would let Ethan in, and I thought he would make a row in the corridor and get arrested or something, and if Jean came and got him it would save everybody a lot of trouble."

"Where did you call from?"

"The kitchen. There's a phone there."

"Was there anybody else there?"

"Where? In the kitchen? Oh, no. It was quite empty."

Killian McBean shook his head. He sneezed. "Then what happened?"

"I went back upstairs. It didn't take me very long to get Jean, and Ethan was going pretty slowly, falling over things and resting and all. He was still pounding on Father Farr's door when I came up the stairs."

"How did he know which door was Farr's?"

"I don't think he did. I think he had pounded on all the doors, until he came to Father Farr's room at the end."

"And Bennet Farr let him in? Why?"

"I don't know. I think perhaps he thought you were with him, because Ethan yelled *Cognac Courier,* along with a lot of other things. And when Father Farr opened the door he said, 'Oh, it's only you,' in a disgusted tone."

"You heard him say that? You're sure it was Bennet Farr?"

"Yes, I'm sure. I saw him. He almost saw me; I ducked back into the shadow just in time and I don't think he did.

"After Ethan went in, and Father Farr locked the door, I waited in the empty room. I told you most of the rest. After a while Jean came up the back stairs."

"You're sure it was Jean? You saw her?"

Celia nodded. "I opened the door after she passed, because it seemed so short a time since I called. I remember thinking Jean must have run all the way from her house. It's over three blocks, you know."

"Why didn't you leave?"

"I still wanted to see Denny's father."

"All right, Celia," Killian McBean said. "When did Dennis Farr join you in the empty hotel room, 207?"

She hesitated. "It can't matter to Denny now. I couldn't tell you before, because you would have thought he did it; you were just looking for an excuse to think that anyway. Denny came in just after Jean went down the hall."

"Did he come up the back stairs?"

"No," she admitted. "He came the other way."

"From the direction of Bennet Farr's room?"

"Yes."

"Did he say where he'd been?"

"He said he'd been in the broom closet," Celia was evasive. "He said he came in the back way and heard me coming up the front stairs. He didn't know who it was, and he didn't want to meet anybody, so he hid in there."

"I gather from your manner you were slightly sceptical of his story."

Celia was silent.

"Look, kid," Killian pointed out. "Even I don't think Dennis Farr killed his father, at this point. Both killings were obviously done by the same person, and nobody could throw a knife into his own back, including Dennis Farr.

"But if Dennis Farr wasn't in the broom closet, he was somewhere else along the corridor when the murder was committed. I don't think he saw it done, but he knew something about it. He may have seen someone in the corridor who shouldn't have been there, or not have seen someone who should have been there. He probably didn't see the actual murder, but he knew how it was done, and that Ethan didn't do it.

"He might have found a door unlocked and stepped into either Irene Hubbard's or Theodora Meredith's room. That would prove that either or both of them weren't where they were supposed to be. Or—"

"Or," said Celia unsteadily, "he might have been in one of their rooms—with one of them."

Killian cleared his throat. "It would help a lot if we could find out. He must have been practically on the spot when the murder occurred. If he was with either Irene or Theodora, the chances are whoever he was with didn't do it; there wouldn't have been time. If he was alone in either of their rooms, it would prove that person did do it, because she should have been there. What made you doubt Dennis' story?"

Celia explained. "He was surprised to see me; he plainly didn't know I was in the empty room. If he had been in the broom closet he would have heard me go up and down the back stairs to telephone and go back into 207."

"Well," said Killian, "this doesn't get us far. All we know is that you, Dennis, Irene and Theodora were around the scene of the murder and that it occurred after Bennet Farr let Ethan in and before Jean had time to come from home. I don't see how we can make anybody admit Dennis Farr was with her, even if he was. What happened after Dennis came into the empty room where you were?"

"Then Jean and Ethan came down the hall and went down the back stairs. Denny and I left as soon as we were sure they had gone."

"What made you think I'd done it?"

"At the time I didn't know anybody had done anything. I don't think Denny did, either. I can't be sure, of course; he was pretty upset. But the door to the broom closet was open and your cloth raincoat with the blood on it was hanging there. Afterwards we thought it must have been the murderer's."

"How did you know it was mine?"

"I mended the sleeve for you," Celia reminded him. "I could see the mend."

"How did it happen that Dennis Farr and Amos Colvin and Terrence Gillespie never made anything of it?"

"It disappeared so they couldn't identify it. I never told them it was yours."

Killian made no comment. He told her briefly of the events of the last evening, of his finding Dennis Farr in his office, and how his body was found about an hour later by the timid Jones, making his night rounds.

After a moment she said unsteadily, "Denny didn't have to come here to get a picture of Rosa Kincaid, Killian. He had one."

"What?" Killian McBean was excited. "You mean he knew all the time?"

"Not all the time. He got the photograph yesterday afternoon. I saw the postmark when I found it on his desk last night."

"You were the person who went through his things?"

"Yes. I wanted to be sure nothing was found that—shouldn't be."

"All right. Where is it? The photograph, I mean."

Celia watched him carefully. "I didn't bring it."

"Why the hell didn't you?"

"I wasn't going to tell you about it."

"Who is it?"

She shook her auburn hair. "I can't be—absolutely sure. It

was five years ago, you know. That is, I'm sure, but you'd have to say for yourself."

"Well, get it!"

Celia rose. "You're sure you want to see it?"

Killian's eyes met hers. "Certainly I want to see it!"

"I'll get it now," Celia said simply.

"Just a minute," Killian was thinking. "If Dennis Farr got a picture of Rosa Kincaid yesterday afternoon, why did he come here last night to get another?"

Celia's quiet eyes flared suddenly. "He didn't want you to get it, obviously." She slammed the door behind her. Killian sat at his desk and sneezed and thought. Smoky sat on the edge of it and glared at the yellow dog. The tired mongrel simply slept on, oblivious of her wrath and scorn.

Killian McBean heard someone opening the doors of his garage. Instantly he was on his feet, pulling a coat on and running out the front door and down the driveway. Someone was getting into his car and starting the motor. In a minute the little car shot backwards out of the garage with a jerk of tremendous power.

"Stop!" yelled Killian McBean. "Stop or I'll shoot!"

There was a great grinding of gears and brakes simultaneously. Finally the engine coughed and died abruptly. "Well, *gee whiz,* Mr. McBean," said Willie's patient, surprised voice. He put his homely face out the car window. "What d'ya want to shoot *me* for?"

Killian grinned reluctantly. "To tell the truth, Willie, I thought you were our murderer trying to escape. It's about time for her to pull up stakes, I think. She can't hope to stall detection off much longer." He remembered to be stern. "And just what *are* you doing with my car?"

"Didn't you tell Miss Hubbard to call me up?"

"You mean Miss Hubbard, the librarian? No. Did she?"

"She *said* you told her to call me up," protested Willie aggrievedly.

"How do you know it was Miss Hubbard?"

"Well, gee *whiz*, Mr. McBean. She *said* it was Miss Hubbard."

Killian regarded Willie with a peculiar gleam in his eye. "Did it sound like Miss Hubbard?"

"I guess so. I never paid any particular attention to what Miss Hubbard sounds like," Willie floundered helpfully. "All skirts sound alike. What would any other skirt call up and say she was Miss Hubbard for?"

The newspaper editor sighed. "What did she say, Willie?"

"She said you wanted me to bring your car to the Hotel Metropole right away."

Killian did not ask where Willie had gotten the keys; he knew. The honesty of Cognac was such that nobody ever took them out of the locks. His had been in since he bought the used car several years before.

"All right, Willie," he said. "Leave the car in the driveway and if you get any more messages, just tell me."

"You aren't mad or anything, are you, Mr. McBean?" Willie asked anxiously.

Killian sighed. "No, Willie. I'm not mad."

He went back into the newspaper office and cranked the phone. "Hello, Betsy." His voice was very tired. "Get me Amos Colvin, please. That you, fat stuff? McBean speaking. I want you to round up your pal the People's Friend Terrence Gillespie and his fiance Miss Irene Hubbard. Then stop at the hotel and pick up Leslie Landis and Theodora Meredith. Bring 'em all down here. Celia's coming. And I guarantee Rosa Kincaid will be here."

CHAPTER TWENTY-ONE

"Sit down," said Killian McBean out of the corner of his mouth. "I'm telephoning."

The yellow dog Killian had put upstairs, but Smoky was in Leslie's chair. She opened one eye and regarded the visitors suspiciously. Terrence Gillespie scooped her up and gallantly held the chair for Irene Hubbard. The assistant librarian accepted it graciously, as her due, casting a covert look at the other women to see how they were taking her conquest.

They took it most unsatisfactorily; neither of them noticed. They sat in straight chairs beside her. The blond Leslie Landis was looking at Killian McBean, and Theodora Meredith sat nervously twisting the ring on her finger, not looking up. Amos Colvin plopped his fat form into the easy chair, without a glance at any of the women. Terrence Gillespie sat down on a straight one, his eyes on Irene. Smoky pushed violently against his chest and escaped his grasp.

"Tobacco," explained Killian McBean. "Smoky doesn't like it. You smell of it." He went on telephoning. Someone was reading to him; he made shorthand notes on the back of an envelope, nodding violently but saying little. Finally he hung up.

"Well," said Terrence Gillespie irritably. "Stop this omniscient act." The young state's attorney glared at Killian. "Either you know something or you don't. If you do, tell it. If you don't, I'm going home."

"I'll tell it," said Killian, "in my own way and my own time. And if I were you I wouldn't go anywhere. You might regret it."

Terry growled angrily, but stayed.

Killian grinned at his guests. "Perfectly comfortable?" he asked solicitously. "Coffee, anyone?" He leaned back in his chair and lit his pipe. Smoky, who was on his desk, moved to the furthest corner and sat regarding him with fixed disapproval.

There was a pause, nervous for Theodora and Terrence Gillespie, but not apparently bothering the others. Irene smiled at her new fiancé; Leslie Landis smiled at everybody; Amos Colvin had some coffee.

"To begin with," said Killian, "before I start explaining it, we might as well get straight what happened at the hotel the morning Bennet Farr was killed. First, Bennet Farr called in and reported seeing a wrecked car with a girl in it out at Indian Mound. Then he stopped at his lawyer's and changed his will, disinheriting his son Dennis. Dennis subsequently went to the hotel and had a quarrel with his father, but left before seven, without harming him. Irene had a disagreement with Bennet Farr after breakfast, before she and Theodora went out for a walk."

"That's a lie!" said Terrence Gillespie hotly.

Irene calculated for the space of about thirty seconds. "No, dear," she said sweetly. "It's perfectly true. But Mr. Farr was quite alive when we left. Ask Theodora. And ask her what was in the note she put under his door, while you're at it."

Theodora flushed and twisted in her chair, but made no reply.

"Don't be cats, darlings," said Leslie Landis placidly.

"Irene and Theodora went out for a walk," Killian continued as if he had not heard any of them. "Meantime, Celia entered the hotel by the front door and went up the front stairs to the second floor. She heard Ethan coming, and hid in the empty room at the back of the hall." Killian did not mention her trip to the kitchen.

"Bennet Farr, very much alive, let Ethan in. Pretty soon Dennis Farr came down the hall and joined Celia. A moment later, Ethan left Bennet Farr's room." Killian carefully avoided mentioning Jean. "At the time he left Bennet Farr was dead. The crucial time, therefore, is the few minutes after Ethan entered the room and before he left. During that time, nobody came up the back stairs; Celia would have heard them. But the hall carpet is so thick she would not have heard anybody going along the hall. Therefore the murderer who entered Bennet Farr's room was already upstairs in the hotel when Celia arrived, or came up the front stairs subsequently.

"This leaves only four people admittedly on the second floor of the hotel: Celia, Theodora, Dennis Farr and Irene Hubbard."

"You can't pin this on me!" said Irene, now thoroughly alarmed.

"No? What makes you think so? I know you told an untrue story giving me a perfect alibi. Since we were only casual acquaintances, there was no reason for you to do it, and I couldn't understand it. Until I realized one thing: it placed you in your room with a witness at the time the murder was supposedly taking place. It also gave you a perfect alibi, in providing one for me."

"Irene," said Terrence Gillespie in a tone proper to a disapproving state's attorney and fiancé. "That story you told wasn't true?"

"Of course it was true," she said sullenly.

Killian shrugged. "It's your word against mine, city girl. But if it were true, what purpose would I have in denying it? I only make myself a suspect in a murder case, without gaining a thing."

"Irene," began Terrence Gillespie doubtfully, "if you—"

"Oh, all right!" snapped Irene. "So it wasn't true. But it wasn't my idea, either. You can't pin this on me. I didn't do it. I wasn't even alone at the time!"

Killian McBean nodded in a satisfied way. "I figured you weren't."

"What do you mean, you weren't alone?" demanded Terrence Gillespie angrily.

Irene had the grace not to look at him. "Dennis Farr was with me."

The young state's attorney looked shocked and hurt. Only Killian McBean watched him; the others turned their eyes away. Killian did not miss an expression.

"You needn't look like that!" said Irene Hubbard. "It wasn't anything. He was going to see his father, and heard voices in the room and knew somebody was with him. So he just stopped to talk with me a minute. That was all we did, talk. Don't you believe me?"

"No," said Terrence Gillespie, unexpectedly.

"It's true! Anyway, you can't pin this on me. We heard whoever it was open the door. That must have been when she threw the knife in. Only we didn't know it at the time, of course."

"You and Dennis Farr were in your room," said Killian, "when Ethan went into Bennet Farr's room?"

She hesitated. "Yes."

"Then who," demanded Terrence Gillespie hotly, "was in Bennet Farr's room talking to him? You said Dennis only stopped to see you because he heard voices!"

Irene lowered her eyes again. "I don't know." Then she added defiantly, "Dennis Farr was already in my room when I came up, if you must know."

"Did you hear anybody leave Bennet Farr's room before Ethan went in?"

"No," she admitted. "But I was the second door away, of course."

"Tell the truth, Irene," prompted Killian coldly. "You've already manufactured enough stories. Dennis Farr didn't say anything about anybody being in his father's room. He just came to see you. Isn't that it?"

"Yes," she said sullenly. "But we were just talking!"

"I'm sorry, Irene," Terrence Gillespie was unhappy, but firm. "I have my professional standing to consider. I shall have to ask you to return my ring and consider our engagement at an end."

"Oh, all right," she said wearily. "Here. But we were just talking!"

"You were talking when Ethan came along the hall?" Killian pursued the subject ruthlessly.

"Yes. He banged on all the doors and finally Mr. Farr let him in. Mr. Farr was alive then, because he said, 'Oh, it's only you,' to him. Then he locked the door behind him. We were talking, and then there was a thud. Like something heavy falling."

"Bennet Farr's body," Killian McBean pointed out to Amos Colvin.

"I get it. I get it." The fat chief of police grunted. "Then what did you hear?"

Irene Hubbard hesitated. "A door shut and some one ran up the stairs to the third floor."

"A woman?"

"Yes. I'm sure it was a woman's step."

"Then what did you do?"

"We didn't know what was wrong, of course, but we thought something was up. Dennis decided he'd better leave. So he went down the hall toward the back stairs. I thought he left."

"Irene," said Terrence Gillespie, "I feel it my duty to point out to you that you have only your unsupported word for your statements. The only person who could possibly have confirmed them is dead. If you will accept my legal advice, you will retain an attorney and do no further talking without his counsel."

"You don't believe me?"

"Calm down, Irene," said Killian McBean. "I believe you. At least I believe you've told the truth about where you were and with whom and what you heard. What happened then?"

Irene gave Terry a defiant glance. "Jean came and got her father. I knew it was Jean because I heard her afterwards in the hall. They went down the hall just after Dennis Farr. He apparently had time to get out of sight, though, because neither of them ever said they saw him. Then Theodora came out in the hall from her room. She kind of gasped at the door of Mr. Farr's room, and then she went in and shut the door."

"I did not!" said Theodora Meredith unconvincingly.

"It's all right, Theodora," Killian's tone was a shade gentler. "Or at least it will be if you tell the truth. You saw that Bennet Farr was dead and you went in and got the note you put under his door earlier that day, isn't that right?"

"Yes. You see, he'd found out about—who I was, some way. He was going to tell the school board. The note I wrote him—I didn't mean it to be, but if anyone had found it, they might have thought it was—threatening. I didn't mean to do anything wrong. But when I saw him lying there dead, I thought that if I could find the note, no one would know—about me, I mean. So I went in and closed the door and looked for it." Theodora shuddered. "It was right on the desk. I took it and left. I didn't touch anything else."

"You heard her go into her own room afterwards?" Killian asked Irene Hubbard, who nodded.

"Sister, *you'd* better get a lawyer," exclaimed Amos Colvin.

"I don't think so," said Killian coldly. "I think this ties up all the loose ends, and clears both Irene and Theodora."

"Killian!" said Leslie Landis in a shocked tone. "You don't mean, you can't mean, that Celia did it?"

"Celia?"

"You said yourself she was the only other person there. Dennis Farr and Irene and Celia, you said."

"I said the only *known* persons were Dennis and Irene and Celia. How could Celia have gone up the stairs to the third floor as Irene said the murderer did and been in the back hotel room on the second floor when Dennis Farr got there?"

"You have only Celia's word that she was there," Terrence Gillespie pointed out sourly. "That may be enough for you, but not for me. I think she did it. And I think she found out about Dennis Farr's philandering and killed him too. I'm going to arrest Celia Austen for the murders of Bennet and Dennis Farr!"

Killian studied him contemptuously. "I believe you would, at that."

The door opened and Celia came in. Her face went even whiter than it had been, and she took a tight grip on the edge of the desk.

"I brought you the picture, Killian," was what she said.

"Thanks, kid." Killian took the envelope carelessly and dropped it on his desk without opening it.

Celia took a step toward the door and then suddenly whirled, firing a gun. The shot went wild, striking the wall above the heads of Irene, Leslie and Theodora. Before she could fire a second shot, Killian had seized Celia's hand and forced the gun from it. It dropped on the floor. She struggled madly, then suddenly went limp against Killian.

"I couldn't help it, Killian!" she sobbed. "I had to kill her!"

"Now, kid," said Killian. "You didn't even come close enough to give her a good scare."

"I m-missed her?"

"Completely," he assured her. Celia fainted.

"Now who says she isn't the murderer?" Terrence Gillespie snarled triumphantly.

"I do." Killian snarled back at him.

Theodora Meredith began to get over the shock of the near proximity of the bullet and became slightly hysterical. "She tried to kill me!"

Killian put Celia carefully down on the floor, full length. He turned to grin at Theodora. "Not you, Theodora. Rosa Kincaid."

"I'm not Rosa Kincaid!"

"Neither am I!" said Irene Hubbard.

"That leaves you, darling," said Killian McBean to Leslie Landis.

She smiled at him. "The others may not know you're joking, darling."

"I'm not joking."

Leslie Landis laughed merrily.

"Let me read you a description I just got over the telephone," said Killian McBean. "Height, five feet eight. Blue eyes, brown hair. Weight, one hundred seventy pounds. Large mole on right cheek near nose. Scars show on neck from mastoid operation."

"That's the guy who was under your porch!" roared Amos Colvin.

"Yes. It's also a description," said Killian McBean, "of a California newspaper man named Leslie Landis."

"Leslie Landis?" The blonde young woman known by that name stared at him. "Then whom am I?"

"You, darling," said Killian McBean, "are Rosa Kincaid."

"I don't understand," she said in bewildered fashion. "You were the ones who told me I was Leslie Landis. That driver's license description fits me. I told you I didn't remember who I was. I still don't. If you're sure that isn't my name—"

"I'm sure."

"It still doesn't prove I'm Rosa Kincaid. Why, you think she's the murderer, don't you? Killian, you can't mean you think I—"

"I always knew you were good," Killian stated coldly, "but right now you're surpassing yourself."

"Killian, you kissed me! You said you loved me!"

"I also told you not to try to play me for a sucker. I warned you the first night what would happen if you did."

"I don't get it," said Amos Colvin. "How do you know she's Rosa Kincaid?"

"Leslie Landis," Killian explained, "was a reputable newspaper man who had a yen to own a small town paper. Somehow Bennet Farr got hold of him and sold him on the *Cognac Courier*. Farr told him that the mortgage was going to be foreclosed, probably, but he didn't tell him he was expected to be a Bennet Farr stooge while running it. Landis's record is too good for that; he wouldn't have touched the deal.

"Anyhow, Bennet Farr made the mortgage on the paper over

to Leslie Landis and arranged for him to come to Cognac and take over. Bennet Farr didn't want to have any official connection with Landis, so he made an appointment with him outside the town at Indian Mount Wednesday morning. Farr had to be sure nothing slipped; it was pretty important to him to control public opinion in Cognac and he'd been trying to get hold of the *Courier* for a long time."

"Did he keep the appointment?" Terrence Gillespie was showing interest in spite of himself.

"I don't think so," said Killian. "Poor Landis was dead and under my porch by that time. Rosa Kincaid meant to keep it for him and kill Farr. But Rosa herself had a pretty nasty bump on her head. That wasn't faked. Old Doc says that. Only a person with a fierce hatred and tremendous will power could have moved around at all, let alone thrown knives. She apparently collapsed after getting back to the car. She was genuinely unconscious when we found her. Bennet Farr must have seen her there and recognized her.

"Steve, my detective, knew from checking on the car ownership that Landis was a man, but assumed we knew it. When I asked him for descriptions and genders this morning, he told me.

"I did check to see if the driver's license was genuine, and it was. That is, the description fitted Rosa here, and the name had not been altered. I didn't want to mention names in my telegram, so it didn't occur to me to check further. The license, you see, was torn. It was genuine, even to the name, except that one word was torn off. It was MRS. The license was issued to *Mrs.* Leslie Landis. Rosa used Landis's first name instead of her own on purpose, to further hide her identity. Apparently Rosa here got the license by posing as Landis's wife while actually his mistress.

Maybe she actually married him, but I doubt it. If she did, Steve hasn't been able to check the record of it."

"I'm confused," Amos Colvin stated. "Start at the beginning. Where did this—Rosa Kincaid, if that's who she is—pick up this guy Landis?"

Killian shook his head. "Maybe we'll never know that, unless she tells us. Somehow she got wind of the paper deal and made it her business to meet and captivate Landis. Solely, of course, because it gave her a way of entering Cognac without attracting attention to her true identity.

"They drove down to Cognac from Chicago in Landis's car. He could get the gas because he was moving, changing his place of business. Somewhere along the way, without Landis' knowing it, Rosa disposed of his luggage and dog. She must have, because the luggage hasn't turned up around here, and the woods were searched. The dog wasn't at the scene of the accident. He must have followed his master here from wherever Rosa hit him on the head and dumped him. I don't know how dogs do these things, but they do.

"Of course the mortgage wasn't due for nearly two months, but both Landis and Farr were smart enough to realize he would need time to look the land over, get to know the community and people. Maybe Bennet Farr figured I would look up Landis' record and seeing nothing phony in the deal, hand things over to him in friendly fashion."

"He didn't know you!" grunted Amos Colvin.

"Anyhow, Rosa shot Landis in his own car, out by Indian Mound, causing the accident. It was a completely cold-blooded killing, to get him out of the way. Only in the resulting crash she was knocked out. Landis came to first and badly wounded as he was, managed to stagger here through the rain. I doubt if he knew it was the *Courier* office; probably to him it was just the first house he came to. He fainted on the front porch and Rosa caught up with him there and finished him off with a knife."

"This dame done that?" Amos asked.

Killian sneezed. "That's right. She must have planned in advance to kill him, too. The lack of luggage and disposing of the dog prove that. Anyhow, she killed him."

Amos Colvin regarded the blonde girl with awe. "She did! Then what did she do?"

"Smoky must have come right after Landis was killed; she walked over his body on the porch while the blood was still fresh. Maybe the cat frightened Rosa here, or maybe she heard me getting up or maybe she just panicked because it was her first murder. It was your first murder, wasn't it, darling?"

"Killian, I don't see how you can say these awful things!"

Killian laughed. "Anyhow, a little time elapsed, while I was asleep. Then she decided she had better not leave the body there; she didn't want it discovered until after she had murdered Bennet Farr. So she came back and dragged it under the porch. She didn't think about the bloodstains, because it was dark and she couldn't see them, but fortunately the rain took care of that for her. She left Landis there and went back and got in the wrecked car again, maybe to keep the appointment with Bennet Farr."

"I refuse to listen to any more of such ridiculous fabrications," said the blonde girl. "When you come to your senses and wish to apologize, Killian, you will find me at my hotel."

"Sit down!" bellowed Amos Colvin.

She looked at him in polite bewilderment. "Surely you can't believe that I—"

"Sister, at this point I can believe anything. Sit down!" said Amos Colvin.

Leslie Landis laughed merrily. "All right." She sat down, took out her mirror, and put on more lipstick with an absolutely steady hand. Even Killian watched her with awe.

"She'd have to have steady hands, to throw knives with such accuracy," he pointed out. "Especially after that bump on the head."

"Why didn't she disguise herself?" Irene Hubbard decided to take an interest in the questioning.

"She had no reason to think anyone could recognize her. Dennis Farr didn't remember what she looked like, and everybody changes in five years. Even Bennet Farr was not absolutely sure; he only saw her once. That was why he wanted the clipping with her picture."

Celia Austen had come to now, and was sitting up, leaning against the wall, her eyes fixed on Killian's face. Now and then they slid to the place on the floor where her gun had dropped.

"Rosa, here, is an opportunist. She came here without any very definite plan, except a determination to kill Bennet Farr. She provided herself with two outs in event of emergency; the driver's license with her description and Leslie Landis' car. Probably she originally got the license for her own convenience in driving and only later decided to use it another way. If his true sex had been established, finding Landis' car by Bennet Farr's body would naturally have caused him to be suspected, especially when he had disappeared. By the time his body was found, Rosa Kincaid would have been miles away. Or, if she was caught, as she was, at the scene of the murder, she could still fake amnesia and claim ignorance of the whole affair. Naturally she leaped at the chance to assume Landis' identity, and let the driver's license be found, conveniently torn.

"She planned to kill Farr at the original appointment, of

course. After she lost that opportunity, however, she only had to wait. Another chance to kill Bennet Farr was sure to present itself. It did, at the hotel. But there were two unfortunate developments. Bennet Farr recognized her before she had a chance to kill him, and started an investigation that eventually led us to Rosa Kincaid. Otherwise Rosa would have been perfectly safe in her assumption that no one would ever think of connecting the brief five year old marriage with Bennet Farr's death. Even with the clipping, nobody was sure. The second unfortunate development was Steve, my detective's, happening on Rosa Kincaid's knife-throwing experience. After all, she had used another name and covered her trail pretty well. Without that knowledge, nothing could have been definitely pinned on her, even if her true identity had been established.

"She was lucky in that there happened to be two other strange young women in Cognac who also might have been Rosa Kincaid. There was nothing out of the way in this, of course; there might have been six. Most small towns have young schoolteachers or librarians or something who are strangers. Nevertheless it was a piece of good luck for Rosa that Theodora and Irene were here. It enabled her to accept the fake identity thrust on her as Leslie Landis, use it as an alibi and sit calmly back and watch us investigate Irene and Theodora.

"If Irene and Theodora hadn't turned up, however, Rosa could still have used her other emergency outlet; she could have recovered her memory and remembered seeing Leslie Landis murder Bennet Farr. While we put on a manhunt for the supposed murderer, Landis, Rosa would have slipped mysteriously out of sight."

Celia's hand slid gently along the floor toward the gun as Killian talked. It was slow progress, inch by inch. Nobody was watching her—nobody but the statuesque blonde now accused of being Rosa Kincaid.

"After Celia accidentally let slip Bennet Farr's whereabouts at the scene of the accident," explained Killian, "it was child's play, except that Rosa must have had a terrific headache. She found the hotel by its sign. She hid somewhere on the third floor for a while and waited until after Ethan had gone into Bennet Farr's room. Then things settled down for a couple of minutes, and that was all she needed. She opened the door with a pass key she had apparently provided herself with in advance or stolen from the desk while Aunty Pliny was away from it. She threw the knife she had picked up in the hall where Ethan dropped it, and that was the end of Bennet Farr. No doubt she had the other knife, the one that subsequently killed Dennis Farr, with her, but decided to use the strange knife instead, because it could not possibly be traced to her."

"Then what did she do?" Theodora's eyes behind her glasses were wide with astonishment.

"She hid on the third floor awhile. Then she probably just walked down the back stairs and out the door."

"Pretty risky," objected Terrence Gillespie.

"Not particularly. Not unless she was actually caught with the knife in her hand while she was throwing it. Otherwise she would just have said she was following somebody that looked familiar, or something of the sort. She was badly hurt, and a stranger. There would be no reason to suspect her of murdering Bennet Farr. If it hadn't been for the clipping in his wallet, maybe we would never have connected Rosa Kincaid with the murder at all. Certainly there was nothing to connect this girl with Rosa Kincaid."

"She's trying to get that gun again!" the girl accused of being Rosa Kincaid shouted. Killian kicked the gun beyond Celia's reach. "Not nervous, darling?" he asked the blonde solicitously.

"I have nothing to be nervous about, and you know it!" But her poise was shaken and everyone there was aware of the fact.

Killian did not change his expression.

"If I threw the knife at Mr. Farr," said the girl heretofore known as Leslie Landis, "who threw the knife at me here in the office and threatened my life?"

"You wrote the notes yourself right here on the office typewriter. And you threw the knife at your own chair. Only it wasn't aimed at you; it was aimed at Smoky, who was in the chair when the lights went out."

"I never heard such nonsense. Why should I threaten my own life?"

"To throw us off the trail, principally; to give you another reason for staying, too. But you weren't very smart about it. If I had been functioning reasonably at the time I would have known you did it. Nobody else could have."

"Why?"

"Because there were no rocks in the room, or whatever was supposed to have been thrown in to break the windows. And most of the glass was on the outside, not the inside. Of course Terry and Amos knocked some of the jagged pieces in when they climbed in the broken windows, but most of it went out with whatever you threw to break the windows. Besides, if someone else had been trying to kill you, they would have tried again, not dropped the matter with one very clumsy attempt."

Killian kicked the gun once more from Celia's reaching fingers. "Cut it out, kid. She isn't worth it."

"Dennis Farr sent for a picture of the girl he had married but did not remember. When he got it, he decided to say nothing, at least temporarily. He came here to get a duplicate picture which he had found out was being sent to me. He wanted to destroy it, to protect Rosa Kincaid. But she did not know this; she thought he was discovering her identity. So she killed him to keep him from notifying the police."

Celia drew a long painful breath that was almost a cry.

"And Jean?" Theodora Meredith asked the question.

Killian shook his head. "I was pretty dumb about that. Jean told me she found something by my porch the morning the real Leslie Landis's body was there. Later she told me it was in her purse. And I looked there, saw it and never recognized its significance."

"What was it?"

"A bright red lipstick. Rosa is the only woman in town who would dare use that outrageous shade. It's her own special color, as unmistakably hers as a calling card. Jean's one experiment at paint was Orange Flare. That lipstick in Jean's purse belonged to Leslie. Jean picked it up by my porch Wednesday morning.

"Maybe the murderer didn't actually know what Jean found that morning, but she apparently heard us discussing it and knew she had dropped something dangerous to her and that she could not let Jean show it to me. So she followed Jean along the river until she was alone, threw a rock and stunned her, and pushed her in the river near the rapids. If we hadn't come just then—" Killian's face was dark with anger.

"It's a very pretty theory," said Terrence Gillespie doubtfully. "But I can't see you have much proof."

"I'm glad somebody has a little faith in me, Terry," the girl Killian called Rosa Kincaid said to him.

"I'll get you some proof." Killian opened the door, sneezing, and whistled up the stairs. Presently the lop-eared yellow mongrel padded sleepily down them. He came into the room blinking his eyes and watching Smoky warily. Suddenly he stiffened. He bristled. A furious growl formed in his throat. He bared his teeth and leaped at the blonde girl.

As she screamed, Killian caught the dog's collar and pulled him back. Smoky watched with interest from the corner of the desk, from which she had not moved. "The dog was hit on the head and left for dead by Rosa here, but later came to and traced his master here and stayed in the cold to guard his body. Look." He pointed.

The fat chief of police waddled forward to look at the dog's collar. "Property of Leslie Landis," he read in an awed tone. He straightened up to fix the accused girl with his beady ratlike eyes. "If you were Leslie Landis, the dog would have known you. He hasn't got amnesia."

"Dogs don't like me. No animals do. But I didn't kill anybody!"

"If you need further proof," said Killian McBean. "That's a picture of Rosa Kincaid Celia just brought. And the Chicago police have picked up her so-called brother: the other half of the knife-throwing act. He claims she walked out on him with all their receipts. He also says she was very skillful at throwing knives, and very bitter about Bennet Farr and often threatened to kill him. I imagine he'll identify her fast enough."

The girl had Celia's gun in her hand, pointed at the group of them as she backed toward the door. "Don't move, any of you!"

"Careless," murmured Killian. He sneezed.

"McBean," roared Amos Colvin, "you gave her that gun on purpose to get away!"

"I didn't give it to her. It was on the floor. You could have picked it up if you wanted to," Killian pointed out calmly. "I suppose you're not going on denying you're Rosa Kincaid?"

"No," she said. "You'll know it when you see the picture anyway. All right. I killed them, all of them. I wasn't going to kill Leslie. I was just going to pose as his wife but he found out why I wanted to and was going to tell Bennet Farr. I had to stop him. I'm not sorry I killed either of the Farrs, though. They deserved to die. I hated them, both of them, for what they did to me!"

"I had it figured out about right?"

"Just about," she admitted. "And they never would have found out if you hadn't been nosing around! You—telling a girl you love her and scheming behind her back to get her hung!"

"Leslie Landis was a newspaper man," he said. "So am I. Ethan is almost a father to me; he was accused of murder. Jean—" Killian's jaw became even tighter.

"If you loved me, I would have come first! I loved you. I could have married Dennis Farr and been perfectly safe. Even if Dennis and I didn't get all the money, we would have gotten some of it. More than you could ever give me, from his mother alone. Or I could have left Cognac and been perfectly safe. I just stayed to be with you. And this is the thanks I get!"

Killian McBean actually grinned at her. "If you go to trial," he said coldly, "be sure to get a jury. You'll probably end up marrying the foreman."

"That's a slander on the courts!" screamed Terrence Gillespie.

Rosa Kincaid stood in the doorway now. "If any of you try to follow me," she warned, "you won't live long."

"I think they're aware of that, darling," said Killian McBean. "Me, I am not going to move."

Rosa Kincaid shifted the gun to her left hand. "Don't try anything; I'm a dead shot with either hand." Her right hand went into her pocket and then darted out and back with speed and sureness. "Nobody makes a sucker of me either, Killian McBean!" she cried.

Killian flung himself flat on his face without pride or hesitation, but the knife just missed the top of his head. It stuck firmly in the wall behind him, at precisely the height of his heart a few seconds before.

Rosa Kincaid was out the door and in Killian's car, which was in the driveway, and off down the street at top speed by the time the badly shaken newspaper editor had managed to get to his feet. For a moment nobody said anything. Then Amos Colvin and Terrence Gillespie were cranking the phone, giving a description of Rosa Kincaid and the car and ordering all roads blocked.

"She can't get away!" boomed Amos Colvin.

Killian shook his head, still slightly green. "Don't underestimate her. I did."

He sat down at his desk, almost mechanically. Smoky, who still had not moved, came over and rubbed against his shoulder. Killian put a sheet of paper into the typewriter slowly. Lackadaisically he picked out a few words, tore the sheet out, put in another. He sneezed. Willie came in and stood at his side.

"That skirt was *dangerous*," he said solemnly. "Want me to take that knife out of the wall, Mr. McBean?"

The newspaper editor shook his head. "No," he said. "I want to look at it." He straightened up. "Bring that picture over here. I want to look at it, too."

Killian went to the wall safe and took out the mortgage. "Property of Leslie Landis." He tore it into little bits and put it in the stove. "My fee for finding your murderer," he said to no one in particular. "No relatives, anyway."

He propped the picture of Rosa Kincaid in front of him, next to the knife in the wall. He looked at them both carefully. Finally he opened his watch and placed the woman's picture it contained on the desk in front of him, too. Sneezing several times, he began to type. The grim look gradually faded. He typed faster and faster. Presently he looked up, his eyes far away but shining with genuine enthusiasm.

"Whatta story!" he said. "Whatta story!"

THE END

DISCUSSION QUESTIONS

- Did any aspects of the plot date the story? If so, which?

- Would the story be different if it were set in the present day? If so, how?

- Did the social context of the time play a role in the narrative? If so, how?

- If you were one of the main characters, would you have acted differently at any point in the story?

- Did you identify with any of the characters? If so, which?

- Did this book remind you of any present day authors? If so, which?

OTTO PENZLER PRESENTS
AMERICAN MYSTERY CLASSICS

All titles are available in hardcover and in trade paperback.

Order from your favorite bookstore or from
The Mysterious Bookshop, 58 Warren Street, New York, N.Y. 10007
(www.mysteriousbookshop.com).

Charlotte Armstrong, *The Chocolate Cobweb*. When Amanda Garth was born, a mix-up caused the hospital to briefly hand her over to the prestigious Garrison family instead of to her birth parents. The error was quickly fixed, Amanda was never told, and the secret was forgotten for twenty-three years . . . until her aunt revealed it in casual conversation. But what if the initial switch never actually occurred? **Introduction by A. J. Finn.**

Charlotte Armstrong, *The Unsuspected*. First published in 1946, this suspenseful novel opens with a young woman who has ostensibly hanged herself, leaving a suicide note. Her friend doesn't believe it and begins an investigation that puts her own life in jeopardy. It was filmed in 1947 by Warner Brothers, starring Claude Rains and Joan Caulfield. **Introduction by Otto Penzler.**

Anthony Boucher, *The Case of the Baker Street Irregulars*. When a studio announces a new hard-boiled Sherlock Holmes film, the Baker Street Irregulars begin a campaign to discredit it. Attempting to mollify them, the producers invite members to the set, where threats are received, each referring to one of the original Holmes tales, followed by murder. Fortunately, the amateur sleuths use Holmesian lessons to solve the crime. **Introduction by Otto Penzler.**

Anthony Boucher, *Rocket to the Morgue*. Hilary Foulkes has made so many enemies that it is difficult to speculate who was responsible for stabbing him nearly to death in a room with only one door through which no one was seen entering or leaving. This classic locked room mystery is populated by such thinly disguised science fiction legends as Robert Heinlein, L. Ron Hubbard, and John W. Campbell. **Introduction by F. Paul Wilson.**

Fredric Brown, *The Fabulous Clipjoint*. Brown's outstanding mystery won an Edgar as the best first novel of the year (1947). When Wallace Hunter is found dead in an alley after a long night of drinking, the police don't really care. But his teenage son Ed and his uncle Am, the carnival worker, are convinced that some things don't add up and the crime isn't what it seems to be. **Introduction by Lawrence Block.**

John Dickson Carr, *The Crooked Hinge*. Selected by a group of mystery experts as one of the 15 best impossible crime novels ever written, this is one of Gideon Fell's greatest challenges. Estranged from his family for 25 years, Sir John Farnleigh returns to England from America to claim his inheritance but another person turns up claiming that he can prove he is the real Sir John. Inevitably, one of them is murdered. **Introduction by Charles Todd.**

John Dickson Carr, *The Eight of Swords*. When Gideon Fell arrives at a crime scene, it appears to be straightforward enough. A man has been shot to death in an unlocked room and the likely perpetrator was a recent visitor. But Fell discovers inconsistencies and his investigations are complicated by an apparent poltergeist, some American gangsters, and two meddling amateur sleuths. **Introduction by Otto Penzler.**

John Dickson Carr, *The Mad Hatter Mystery*. A prankster has been stealing top hats all around London. Gideon Fell suspects that the same person may be responsible for the theft of a manuscript of a long-lost story by Edgar Allan Poe. The hats reappear in unexpected but conspicuous places. But when one is found on the head of a corpse by the Tower of London, it is evident that the thefts are more than pranks. **Introduction by Otto Penzler.**

John Dickson Carr, *The Plague Court Murders*. When murder occurs in a locked hut on Plague Court, an estate haunted by the ghost of a hangman's assistant who died a victim of the black death, Sir Henry Merrivale seeks a logical solution to a ghostly crime. A spiritual medium employed to rid the house of his spirit is found stabbed to death in a locked stone hut on the grounds, surrounded by an untouched circle of mud. **Introduction by Michael Dirda.**

John Dickson Carr, *The Problem of the Wire Cage*. Death and tennis collide in one of this impossible crime master's most memorable cases. After a storm, a man lies strangled on a clay tennis court with no footprints on the damp ground other than his own. This puzzle requires ace amateur sleuth Dr. Gideon Fell to serve up a dazzling stroke of genius to outplay the culprit. **Introduction by Rian Johnson.**

John Dickson Carr, *The Red Widow Murders*. In a "haunted" mansion, the room known as the Red Widow's Chamber proves lethal to all who spend the night. Eight people investigate and the one who draws the ace of spades must sleep in the cursed bedroom. The room is locked from the inside and watched all night by the others. When the door is unlocked, the victim has been poisoned. Enter Sir Henry Merrivale to solve the crime. **Introduction by Tom Mead.**

John Dickson Carr, *The Three Coffins*. Called *The Hollow Man* in the UK, this tale was voted the best locked room mystery of all time by a 1981 survey of mystery experts. Dr. Gideon Fell sets out to solve two impossible murders: A professor is found dead in his study just moments after his housekeeper watched him greet a mysterious visitor and an illusionist is shot in the snow with no footprints nearby but his own. **Introduction by Otto Penzler.**

Frances Crane, *The Turquoise Shop*. In an arty little New Mexico town, Mona Brandon has arrived from the East and becomes the subject of gossip about her money, her influence, and the corpse in the nearby desert who may be her husband. Pat Holly, who runs the local gift shop, is as interested as anyone in the goings on—but even more in Pat Abbott, the detective investigating the possible murder. **Introduction by Anne Hillerman.**

Todd Downing, *Vultures in the Sky*. There is no end to the series of terrifying events that befall a luxury train bound for Mexico. First, a man dies when the train passes through a dark tunnel. Then the train comes to an abrupt stop in the middle of the desert. More deaths occur when night falls and the passengers panic as they realize they are trapped with a murderer on the loose. **Introduction by James Sallis.**

Mignon G. Eberhart, *Murder by an Aristocrat*. Nurse Keate is called to help a man who has been "accidentally" shot in the shoulder. When he is murdered while convalescing, it is clear that there was no accident. Although a killer is loose in the mansion, the family seems more concerned that news of the murder will leave their circle. *The New Yorker* wrote than "Eberhart can weave an almost flawless mystery." **Introduction by Nancy Pickard.**

Erle Stanley Gardner, *The Case of the Baited Hook*. Perry Mason gets a phone call in the middle of the night and his potential client says it's urgent, that he has two one-thousand-dollar bills that he will give him as a retainer, with an additional ten-thousand whenever he is called on to represent him. When Mason takes the case, it is not for the caller but for a beautiful woman whose identity is hidden behind a mask. **Introduction by Otto Penzler.**

Erle Stanley Gardner, *The Case of the Borrowed Brunette*. A mysterious man named Mr. Hines has advertised a job for a woman who has to fulfill very specific physical requirements. Eva Martell, pretty but struggling in her career as a model, takes the job but her aunt smells a rat and hires Perry Mason to investigate. Her fears are realized when Hines turns up in the apartment with a bullet hole in his head. **Introduction by Otto Penzler.**

Erle Stanley Gardner, *The Case of the Careless Kitten*. Helen Kendal receives a mysterious phone call from her vanished uncle Franklin, long presumed dead, who urges her to contact Perry Mason. Soon, she finds herself the main suspect in the murder of an unfamiliar man. Her kitten has just survived a poisoning attempt—as has her aunt Matilda. What is the connection between Franklin's return and the attempted murders? **Introduction by Otto Penzler.**

Erle Stanley Gardner, *The Case of the Rolling Bones*. One of Gardner's most successful Perry Mason novels opens with a clear case of blackmail, though the person being blackmailed claims he isn't. It is not long before the police are searching for someone wanted for killing the same man in two different states—thirty-three years apart. The confounding puzzle of what happened to the dead man's toes is a challenge. **Introduction by Otko Penzler.**

Erle Stanley Gardner, *The Case of the Shoplifter's Shoe*. Most cases for Perry Mason involve murder but here he is hired because a young woman fears her aunt is a kleptomaniac. Sarah may not have been precisely the best guardian for a collection of valuable diamonds and, sure enough, they go missing. When the jeweler is found shot dead, Sarah is spotted leaving the murder scene with a bundle of gems stuffed in her purse. **Introduction by Otto Penzler.**

Erle Stanley Gardner, *The Bigger They Come*. Gardner's first novel using the pseudonym A.A. Fair begins a series featuring the large and loud Bertha Cool and her employee, the small and meek Donald Lam. Given the job of delivering divorce papers to an evident crook, Lam can't find him—but neither can the police. The *Los Angeles Times* called this book "breathlessly dramatic . . . an original." **Introduction by Otto Penzler.**

Frances Noyes Hart, *The Bellamy Trial*. Inspired by the real-life Hall-Mills case, the most sensational trial of its day, this is the story of Stephen Bellamy and Susan Ives, accused of murdering Bellamy's wife Madeleine. Eight days of dynamic testimony, some true, some not, make headlines for an enthralled public. Rex Stout called this historic courtroom thriller one of the ten best mysteries of all time. **Introduction by Hank Phillippi Ryan.**

H.F. Heard, *A Taste for Honey*. The elderly Mr. Mycroft quietly keeps bees in Sussex, where he is approached by the reclusive and somewhat misanthropic Mr. Silchester, whose honey supplier was found dead, stung to death by her bees. Mycroft, who shares many traits with Sherlock Holmes, sets out to find the vicious killer. Rex Stout described it as "sinister . . . a tale well and truly told." **Introduction by Otto Penzler.**

Dolores Hitchens, *The Alarm of the Black Cat*. Detective fiction aficionado Rachel Murdock has a peculiar meeting with a little girl and a dead toad, sparking her curiosity about a love triangle that has sparked anger. When the girl's great grandmother is found dead, Rachel and her cat Samantha work with a friend in the Los Angeles Police Department to get to the bottom of things. **Introduction by David Handler.**

Dolores Hitchens, *The Cat Saw Murder*. Miss Rachel Murdock, the highly intelligent 70-year-old amateur sleuth, is not entirely heartbroken when her slovenly, unattractive, bridge-cheating niece is murdered. Miss Rachel is happy to help the socially maladroit and somewhat bumbling Detective Lieutenant Stephen Mayhew, retaining her composure when a second brutal murder occurs. **Introduction by Joyce Carol Oates.**

Dolores Hitchens, *The Cat Wears a Noose*. Walking home, Jennifer Murdock sees a drunk man shot dead on his doorstep. A young girl from that house on Chestnut Street then seeks the help of Jennifer's sister Rachel, a vigorous senior sleuth, after a series of nasty pranks culminate in her pet bird's death. Neither her prim and proper sister nor Det. Lt. Mayhew can stop Rachel from finding out what is going on. **Introduction by Rhys Bowen.**

Dorothy B. Hughes, *Dread Journey*. A bigshot Hollywood producer has worked on his magnum opus for years, hiring and firing one beautiful starlet after another. But Kitten Agnew's contract won't allow her to be fired, so she fears she might be terminated more permanently. Together with the producer on a train journey from Hollywood to Chicago, Kitten becomes more terrified with each passing mile. **Introduction by Sarah Weinman.**

Dorothy B. Hughes, *The Fallen Sparrow*. When Kit McKittrick learns that his friend Louie has taken a long dive out of a high window, he refuses to believe it was a suicide and sets out on a quest for vengeance that leads him to wrestle with past demons from his time spent in a Spanish prison. It was adapted into a now-classic film noir starring John Garfield and Maureen O'Hara. **Introduction by Otto Penzler.**

Dorothy B. Hughes, *Ride the Pink Horse*. When Sailor met Willis Douglass, he was just a poor kid who Douglass groomed to work as a confidential secretary. As the senator became increasingly corrupt, he knew he could count on Sailor to clean up his messes. No longer a senator, Douglass flees Chicago for Santa Fe, leaving behind a murder rap and Sailor as the prime suspect. Seeking vengeance, Sailor follows. **Introduction by Sara Paretsky.**

Dorothy B. Hughes, *The So Blue Marble*. Set in the glamorous world of New York high society, this novel became a suspense classic as twins from Europe try to steal a rare and beautiful gem owned by an aristocrat whose sister is an even more menacing presence. *The New Yorker* called it "extraordinary . . . [Hughes'] brilliant descriptive powers make and unmake reality." **Introduction by Otto Penzler.**

W. Bolingbroke Johnson, *The Widening Stain*. After a cocktail party, the attractive Lucie Coindreau, a "black-eyed, black-haired Frenchwoman" visits the rare books wing of the library and apparently takes a headfirst fall from an upper gallery. Dismissed as a horrible accident, it seems dubious when Professor Hyett is strangled while reading a priceless 12th-century manuscript, which has gone missing. **Introduction by Nicholas A. Basbanes.**

Baynard Kendrick, *Blind Man's Bluff*. Blinded in World War II, Duncan Maclain forms a successful private detective agency, aided by his two dogs. Here, he is called on to solve the case of a blind man who plummets from the top of an eight-story building, apparently with no one present except his dead-drunk son. **Introduction by Otto Penzler.**

Baynard Kendrick, *The Odor of Violets*. Duncan Maclain, a blind former intelligence officer, is asked to investigate the murder of an actor in his Greenwich Village apartment. This would cause a stir at any time but, when the actor possesses secret government plans that then go missing, it's enough to interest the local police as well as the American government and Maclain, who suspects a German spy plot. **Introduction by Otto Penzler.**

C. Daly King, *Obelists at Sea*. On a cruise ship traveling from New York to Paris, the lights of the smoking room briefly go out, a gunshot crashes through the night, and a man is dead. Two detectives are on board but so are four psychiatrists who believe their professional knowledge can solve the case by understanding the psyche of the killer—each with a different theory. **Introduction by Martin Edwards.**

Jonathan Latimer, *Headed for a Hearse*. Featuring Bill Crane, the booze-soaked Chicago private detective, this humorous hard-boiled novel was filmed as *The Westland Case* in 1937 starring Preston Foster. Robert Westland has been framed for the grisly murder of his wife in a room with doors and windows locked from the inside. As the day of his execution nears, he relies on Crane to find the real murderer. **Introduction by Max Allan Collins.**

Lange Lewis, *The Birthday Murder*. Victoria is a successful novelist and screenwriter and her husband is a movie director, so their marriage seems almost too good to be true. Then, on her birthday, her happy new life comes crashing down when her husband is murdered using a method of poisoning that was described in one of her books. She quickly becomes the leading suspect. **Introduction by Randal S. Brandt.**

Frances and Richard Lockridge, *Death on the Aisle*. In one of the most beloved books to feature Mr. and Mrs. North, the body of a wealthy backer of a play is found dead in a seat of the 45th Street Theater. Pam is thrilled to engage in her favorite pastime—playing amateur sleuth—much to the annoyance of Jerry, her publisher husband. The Norths inspired a stage play, a film, and long-running radio and TV series. **Introduction by Otto Penzler.**

John P. Marquand, *Your Turn, Mr. Moto*. The first novel about Mr. Moto, originally titled *No Hero*, is the story of a World War I hero pilot who finds himself jobless during the Depression. In Tokyo for a big opportunity that falls apart, he meets a Japanese agent and his Russian colleague, and the pilot suddenly finds himself caught in a web of intrigue. Peter Lorre played Mr. Moto in a series of popular films. **Introduction by Lawrence Block.**

Nancy Barr Mavity, *The Tule Marsh Murder*. In this mystery inspired by a real case that captivated the San Francisco Bay Area in the 1920s, newspaper reporter Peter Piper teams up with psychologist Dr. Cavanaugh to investigate a woman's body found burnt beyond recognition. The cutting-edge forensics in the story were based on the pioneering work of criminalist Edward Oscar Heinrich who became known as "America's Sherlock Holmes." **Introduction by Randall Brandt.**

Stuart Palmer, *The Penguin Pool Murder*. The first adventure of schoolteacher and dedicated amateur sleuth Hildegarde Withers occurs at the New York Aquarium when she and her young students notice a corpse in one of the tanks. It was published in 1931 and filmed the next year, starring Edna May Oliver as the American Miss Marple—though much funnier than her English counterpart. **Introduction by Otto Penzler.**

Stuart Palmer, *The Puzzle of the Happy Hooligan*. New York City schoolteacher Hildegarde Withers cannot resist "assisting" homicide detective Oliver Piper. In this novel, she is on vacation in Hollywood and on the set of a movie about Lizzie Borden when the screenwriter is found dead. Six comic films about Withers appeared in the 1930s, most successfully starring Edna May Oliver. **Introduction by Otto Penzler.**

Q. Patrick, *S.S. Murder*. Cub reporter Mary Llewellyn's pleasant sea cruise sours when a wealthy businessman dies from drinking strychnine in his cocktail, and another passenger is shoved overboard in a connected murder. Mary takes it upon herself to snoop above and below deck to get to the truth and halt this seafaring slayer's onslaught. **Introduction by Curtis Evans.**

Otto Penzler, ed., *Golden Age Bibliomysteries*. Stories of murder, theft, and suspense occur with alarming regularity in the unlikely world of books and bibliophiles, including bookshops, libraries, and private rare book collections, written by such giants of the mystery genre as Ellery Queen, Cornell Woolrich, Lawrence G. Blochman, Vincent Starrett, and Anthony Boucher. **Introduction by Otto Penzler.**

Otto Penzler, ed., *Golden Age Detective Stories*. The history of American mystery fiction has its pantheon of authors who have influenced and entertained readers for nearly a century, reaching its peak during the Golden Age, and this collection pays homage to the work of the most acclaimed: Cornell Woolrich, Erle Stanley Gardner, Craig Rice, Ellery Queen, Dorothy B. Hughes, Mary Roberts Rinehart, and more. **Introduction by Otto Penzler.**

Otto Penzler, ed., *Golden Age Locked Room Mysteries*. The so-called impossible crime category reached its zenith during the 1920s, 1930s, and 1940s, and this volume includes the greatest of the great authors who mastered the form: John Dickson Carr, Ellery Queen, C. Daly King, Clayton Rawson, and Erle Stanley Gardner. Like great magicians, these literary conjurors will baffle and delight readers. **Introduction by Otto Penzler.**

Otto Penzler, ed., *Golden Age Whodunits*. This collection of fifteen puzzling tales is a cross-section from an era when the whodunit flourished. These short mysteries were published far and wide by a variety of authors, such as the masters of the genre featured in this volume: F. Scott Fitzgerald, Ellery Queen, Mary Roberts Rinehart, Ring Lardner, Melville Davisson Post, Helen Reilly, and more. **Introduction by Otto Penzler.**

Ellery Queen, *The Adventures of Ellery Queen*. These stories are the earliest short works to feature Queen as a detective and are among the best of the author's fair-play mysteries. So many of the elements that comprise the gestalt of Queen may be found in these tales: alternate solutions, the dying clue, a bizarre crime, and the author's ability to find fresh variations of works by other authors. **Introduction by Otto Penzler.**

Ellery Queen, *The American Gun Mystery*. A rodeo comes to New York City at the Colosseum. The headliner is Buck Horne, the once popular film cowboy who opens the show leading a charge of forty whooping cowboys until they pull out their guns and fire into the air. Buck falls to the ground, shot dead. The police instantly lock the doors to search everyone but the offending weapon has completely vanished. **Introduction by Otto Penzler.**

Ellery Queen, *Cat of Many Tails*. In the summertime, a serial killer called the Cat preys on New Yorkers seemingly at random, strangles them, and miraculously escapes without a trace. It is now the 1940s, and Ellery Queen, the brilliant amateur sleuth, is retired, but he pounces on a chance to crack the case when he discovers a clue that could hold the secret to untangling the puzzling crimes. **Introduction by Richard Dannay.**

Ellery Queen, *The Chinese Orange Mystery*. The offices of publisher Donald Kirk have seen strange events but nothing like this. A strange man is found dead with two long spears alongside his back. And, though no one was seen entering or leaving the room, everything has been turned backwards or upside down: pictures face the wall, the victim's clothes are worn backwards, the rug upside down. Why in the world? **Introduction by Otto Penzler.**

Ellery Queen, *The Dutch Shoe Mystery*. Millionaire philanthropist Abagail Doorn falls into a coma and she is rushed to the hospital she funds for an emergency operation by one of the leading surgeons on the East Coast. When she is wheeled into the operating theater, the sheet covering her body is pulled back to reveal her garroted corpse—the first of a series of murders. **Introduction by Otto Penzler.**

Ellery Queen, *The Egyptian Cross Mystery*. A small-town schoolteacher is found dead, beheaded, and tied to a T-shaped cross on December 25th, inspiring such sensational headlines as "Crucifixion on Christmas Day." Amateur sleuth Ellery Queen is so intrigued he travels to Virginia but fails to solve the crime. Then a similar murder takes place on New York's Long Island—and then another. **Introduction by Otto Penzler.**

Ellery Queen, *The Siamese Twin Mystery*. When Ellery and his father encounter a raging forest fire on a mountain, their only hope is to drive up to an isolated hillside manor owned by a secretive surgeon and his strange guests. While playing solitaire in the middle of the night, the doctor is shot. The only clue is a torn playing card. Suspects include a society beauty, a valet, and conjoined twins. **Introduction by Otto Penzler.**

Ellery Queen, *The Spanish Cape Mystery*. Amateur detective Ellery Queen arrives in the resort town of Spanish Cape soon after a young woman and her uncle are abducted by a gun-toting, one-eyed giant. The next day, the woman's somewhat dicey boyfriend is found murdered—totally naked under a black fedora and opera cloak. **Introduction by Otto Penzler.**

Patrick Quentin, *A Puzzle for Fools*. Broadway producer Peter Duluth takes to the bottle when his wife dies but enters a sanitarium to dry out. Malevolent events plague the hospital, including when Peter hears his own voice intone, "There will be murder." And there is. He investigates, aided by a young woman who is also a patient. This is the first of nine mysteries featuring Peter and Iris Duluth. **Introduction by Otto Penzler.**

Clayton Rawson, *Death from a Top Hat*. When the New York City Police Department is baffled by an apparently impossible crime, they call on The Great Merlini, a retired stage magician who now runs a Times Square magic shop. In his first case, two occultists have been murdered in a room locked from the inside, their bodies positioned to form a pentagram. **Introduction by Otto Penzler.**

Helen Reilly, *McKee of Centre Street*. In one of the first-ever police procedurals written by a woman, a famous dancer is murdered in a New York speakeasy. Everyone in the crowd is an eligible suspect for Inspector McKee of the NYPD, who examines the witness statements and pieces together a rich and confounding story of blackmail and stolen emeralds. **Introduction by Otto Penzler.**

Craig Rice, *Eight Faces at Three*. Gin-soaked John J. Malone, defender of the guilty, is notorious for getting his culpable clients off. It's the innocent ones who are problems. Like Holly Inglehart, accused of piercing the black heart of her well-heeled Aunt Alexandria with a lovely Florentine paper cutter. No one who knew the old battle-ax liked her, but Holly's prints were found on the murder weapon. **Introduction by Lisa Lutz.**

Craig Rice, *Home Sweet Homicide*. Known as the Dorothy Parker of mystery fiction for her memorable wit, Craig Rice was the first detective writer to appear on the cover of *Time* magazine. This comic mystery features two kids who are trying to find a husband for their widowed mother while she's engaged in sleuthing. Filmed with the same title in 1946 with Peggy Ann Garner and Randolph Scott. **Introduction by Otto Penzler.**

Mary Roberts Rinehart, *The Album*. Crescent Place is a quiet enclave of wealthy people in which nothing ever happens—until a bedridden old woman is attacked by an intruder with an ax. *The New York Times* stated: "All

Mary Roberts Rinehart mystery stories are good, but this one is better." **Introduction by Otto Penzler.**

Mary Roberts Rinehart, *The Door*. Elizabeth Bell runs a quiet household but the old woman's life is upended when a young cousin comes to visit and the nurse vanishes while taking the dogs for a walk. Then the nurse is found murdered and police insist that the killer must be one of the household. More deaths are quick to follow in this atmospheric whodunit bursting with family secrets and period details. **Introduction by Otto Penzler.**

Mary Roberts Rinehart, *The Great Mistake*. Maud Wainwright rules in her elaborate house known as the Cloisters, but recent attacks on her estate and a shocking murder threaten her power. Thankfully, her right-hand woman, Pat Abbott, is determined to unmask Maud's enemy hiding among her crowd of high-society friends. Pat also endeavors to protect Maud's married son, whom she secretly adores. **Introduction by Otto Penzler.**

Mary Roberts Rinehart, *The Haunted Lady*. The arsenic in her sugar bowl was wealthy widow Eliza Fairbanks' first clue that somebody wanted her dead. Nightly visits of bats, birds, and rats, obviously aimed at scaring the dowager to death, was the second. Eliza calls the police, who send nurse Hilda Adams, the amateur sleuth they refer to as "Miss Pinkerton," to work undercover to discover the culprit. **Introduction by Otto Penzler.**

Mary Roberts Rinehart, *Miss Pinkerton*. Hilda Adams is a nurse, not a detective, but she is observant and smart and so it is common for Inspector Patton to call on her for help. Her success results in his calling her "Miss Pinkerton." *The New Republic* wrote: "From thousands of hearts and homes the cry will go up: Thank God for Mary Roberts Rinehart." **Introduction by Carolyn Hart.**

Mary Roberts Rinehart, *The Red Lamp*. Professor William Porter refuses to believe that the seaside manor he's just inherited is haunted, but he has to convince his wife to move in. However, he soon sees evidence of the occult phenomena of which the townspeople speak. Whether it is a spirit or a human being, Porter accepts that there is a connection to the rash of murders that have terrorized the countryside. **Introduction by Otto Penzler.**

Mary Roberts Rinehart, *The Wall*. For two decades, Mary Roberts Rinehart was the second-best-selling author in America (only Sinclair Lewis outsold her) and was beloved for her tales of suspense. In one of her most popular cozy mysteries, set in a magnificent mansion, the ex-wife of one of the owners turns up making demands and is found dead the next day. And there are more dark secrets lying behind the walls of the estate. **Introduction by Otto Penzler.**

Hake Talbot, *Rim of the Pit*. A family conducts a seance at a snow-bound lodge to ask their dead father if they can sell his treasured pine grove, and then one of them ends up dead in a locked room. This impossible murder with an inexplicable trail of footprints and a gun hung high out of reach defies logic and suggests a supernatural presence in this creepy Golden Age cult classic. **Introduction by Rupert Holmes.**

Joel Townsley Rogers, *The Red Right Hand*. This extraordinary whodunit that is as puzzling as it is terrifying was identified by crime fiction scholar Jack Adrian as "one of the dozen or so finest mystery novels of the 20th century."

A deranged killer sends a doctor on a quest for the truth—deep into the recesses of his own mind—when he and his bride-to-be elope but pick up a terrifying sharp-toothed hitchhiker. **Introduction by Joe R. Lansdale.**

Roger Scarlett, *Cat's Paw*. The family of the wealthy old bachelor Martin Greenough cares far more about his money than they do about him. For his birthday, he invites all his potential heirs to his mansion to tell them what they hope to hear. Before he can disburse funds, however, he is murdered, and the Boston Police Department's big problem is that there are too many suspects. **Introduction by Curtis Evans.**

Vincent Starrett, *Dead Man Inside*. 1930s Chicago is a tough town but some crimes are more bizarre than others. Customers arrive at a haberdasher to find a corpse in the window and a sign on the door: *Dead Man Inside! I am Dead. The store will not open today.* This is just one of a series of odd murders that terrorizes the city. Reluctant detective Walter Ghost leaps into action to learn what is behind the plague. **Introduction by Otto Penzler.**

Vincent Starrett, *The Great Hotel Murder*. Theater critic and amateur sleuth Riley Blackwood investigates a murder in a Chicago hotel where the dead man had changed rooms with a stranger who had registered under a fake name. *The New York Times* described it as "an ingenious plot with enough complications to keep the reader guessing." **Introduction by Lyndsay Faye.**

Vincent Starrett, *Murder on "B" Deck*. Walter Ghost, a psychologist, scientist, explorer, and former intelligence officer, is on a cruise ship. His friend, novelist Dunsten Mollock, a Nigel Bruce-like Watson whose role is to offer occasional comic relief, accommodates when he fails to leave the ship before it takes off. Although they make mistakes along the way, the amateur sleuths solve the shipboard murders. **Introduction by Ray Betzner.**

Phoebe Atwood Taylor, *The Cape Cod Mystery*. Vacationers have flocked to Cape Cod to avoid the heat wave that hit the Northeast and find their holiday unpleasant when the area is flooded with police trying to find the murderer of a muckraking journalist who took a cottage for the season. Finding a solution falls to Asey Mayo, "the Cape Cod Sherlock," known for his worldly wisdom, folksy humor, and common sense. **Introduction by Otto Penzler.**

S. S. Van Dine, *The Benson Murder Case*. The first of 12 novels to feature Philo Vance, the most popular and influential detective character of the early part of the 20th century. When wealthy stockbroker Alvin Benson is found shot to death in a locked room in his mansion, the police are baffled until the erudite flaneur and art collector arrives on the scene. Paramount filmed it in 1930 with William Powell as Vance. **Introduction by Ragnar Jónasson.**

S.S. Van Dine, *The Greene Murder Case*. The heirs in the illustrious Greene family die one after the other as an elusive killer stalks their New York City mansion and fires shots at them. Part-time supersleuth Philo Vance consults detailed floor plans, fairly clued testimonies, and the obscure texts in the family's secret criminology library to provide his brilliant solution to this third mystery in his detective saga. **Introduction by Otto Penzler.**

Cornell Woolrich, *The Bride Wore Black*. The first suspense novel by one of the greatest of all noir authors opens with a bride and her new husband walking out of the church. A car speeds by, shots ring out, and he falls dead at her feet. Determined to avenge his death, she tracks down everyone in the car, concluding with a shocking surprise. It was filmed by Francois Truffaut in 1968, starring Jeanne Moreau. **Introduction by Eddie Muller.**

Cornell Woolrich, *Deadline at Dawn*. Quinn is overcome with guilt about having robbed a stranger's home. He meets Bricky, a dime-a-dance girl, and they fall for each other. When they return to the crime scene, they discover a dead body. Knowing Quinn will be accused of the crime, they race to find the true killer before he's arrested. A 1946 film starring Susan Hayward was loosely based on the plot. **Introduction by David Gordon.**

Cornell Woolrich, *Waltz into Darkness*. A New Orleans businessman successfully courts a woman through the mail but he is shocked to find when she arrives that she is not the plain brunette whose picture he'd received but a radiant blond beauty. She soon absconds with his fortune. Wracked with disappointment and loneliness, he vows to track her down. When he finds her, the real nightmare begins. **Introduction by Wallace Stroby.**